# THE HUSTLE

## BY

## FRAZIER BOY

Published by DC Bookdiva Publications
Copyright © 2011 by Frazier Boy

ISBN-10: 0-9846110-4-5
ISBN-13: 978-0-9846110-4-1
Library of Congress Control Number: 2010942639

**Publisher's Note**

*This is a work of fiction. Any names historical events, real people, living and dead, or the locales are intended only to give the fiction a setting in historic reality. Other names, characters, places, businesses and incidents are either the product of the author's imagination or are used fictiously, and their resemblance, if any, to real life counterparts is entirely coincidental.*

**DC Bookdiva Publications**
#245 4401-A Connecticut Ave
NW, Washington, DC 20008
www.dcbookdiva.com
www.twitter.com/dcbookdiva
www.facebook.com/thedcbookdiva

# THE HUSTLE

NOVEL BY
**FRAZIER BOY**

# Chapter One

It had been 3,650 days, to be exact, since Sean Martin had last walked the streets of his old stomping grounds. The memories of being involved in the dope game had haunted him his entire stay behind prison walls. He recalled the stench of trash, weed, crack, and pollution that infested his neighborhood air, heavy like overly exposed, cheap cologne. No matter how long Sean had been away, he still couldn't seem to get that distinct odor out of his head.

Year after year during his incarceration, he continued to think about all of the things that he could've done differently, the things that he wished he'd done, and the things he'd planned to do upon his release. But, none of that shoulda, woulda, coulda mattered anymore. Today, he was being released from the Hell Hole of Madness.

Sean started his journey in the Missouri department of corrections when he was young and wild. Back then, he didn't care about anything except his family, his baby's mother, Cynthia, and his only child, Lil' Sean. At the tender age of 19, he entered the prison gates on charges ranging from weapons to drug offenses. However, by the grace of God, he was now leaving as a man with integrity, sanity, and a new sense of direction in life.

As he sat quietly on the Greyhound bus, Sean began to reminisce about everything that transpired throughout his stay in the pen. He was truly elated to be heading home after finishing what most guys in the 'hood called a vacation.

It was nothing like a vacation. Nor was it anything like the movies portrayed it to be. When Sean was popped off 10 years ago, he had the dope game on smash, so his money was long. In the 'hood, having money was having power and with that power, a street nigga could make shit happen. However, while going to trial, he soon found out that, regardless of how much money a person had, if the DA wanted your ass, there was nothing money could do to save it.

To Sean Martin, his stay at the Walls in Missouri's capital, Jefferson City, was far from any vacation he'd ever dreamed of taking. He thought about how dudes in the 'hood often bragged on their people that were doing bids upstate and in the feds. To him, there wasn't shit cool about being locked up and having your rights literally stripped from you.

Most of the dudes he dealt with in the joint on a day-to-day basis would have never gotten close to him on the bricks. Since his dealings with those individuals were more of a force play, he made it his business to limit his association except with those whom he really clicked with. The individuals that he kicked it with were mainly old-heads. He noticed that the old-heads were more settled in their ways. They were much more laid back and not on bullshit like the guys in his age bracket.

"Fuck that shit!" He suddenly thought aloud, talking to no one in particular. He had paid his debt in full. Ten long, hard years and now, he was a free man. He was free to pick up his life and start all over again, which was exactly what he planned to do.

Sean was fortunate enough to learn the art of freeing his mind three years into his bid. Now that his flesh was finally free, things seemed surreal. He leaned back in his oversized seat and closed his eyes, instantly dozing off into a comfortable nod, which was something he hadn't been able to do in years due to the constant noises of the other men around him. His primary focus was on his future that consisted of making music. Rap music to be exact. He was labeled as one of the most gifted rappers in the department of corrections after winning every talent show he'd ever entered. Most inmates often asked him what the hell he was doing in a place like that with all his talent. The only answer he could come up with was the honest one, he'd gotten caught up in the game.

Looking around at all of the occupants of the bus, Sean wondered what each individual's circumstance was and if any of them had faced the same obstacles in life that he had. When the bus driver made his first pit stop, a McDonald's sign seized Sean's attention. He thought about how long it had been since he'd tasted his favorite burger, the Big Mac. Thinking about that burger and how good it used to taste made him immediately hop off the bus and run into the restaurant.

Although he decided to become a vegetarian five years ago, he felt as if he just had to indulge in just one burger for old time's sake. Since it had been five years of no red meat, he figured one burger wouldn't hurt. As he entered the restaurant, Sean felt as if he was on foreign grounds. Being inside seemed like déjà vu. Sean made it his business to keep to his strict diet and besides eating right, he also kept a steady exercise routine. Occasionally, he would indulge in sweets, but not often. That regimen provided him with the chiseled physique he now possessed. "Bitches are going to love putting their hands all over a body like this," he would often say to himself whenever he looked into a mirror. It made him think about his ex, who left him stranded eight years ago. He knew as soon as Cynthia saw him, she would be all over his dick again.

Cynthia was once the love of Sean's life. There was nothing in the world that he wouldn't have done for her. To him, everything about her was beautiful from her head to her toes. Standing at 5'10, her skin color was lightly toasted brown with big, beautiful, dark brown eyes and a figure as curvy as the letter S. Her race was a mixture of Italian and African American heritage. She possessed a very curvaceous body, courtesy of her mother. She also inherited most of her mother's African American features. Her presence demanded any man's attention. The only thing she actually inherited from her father was his height.  She was stunning. Her mother and father relocated to St. Louis from New York when she was only six years old. Being that her father was affiliated with the mob and its underworld, he decided to move to the Midwest in search of a different life for his wife and daughter. Now, at age 29, St. Louis was the only place Cynthia acknowledged as home.

She vaguely remembered her childhood memories of growing up in Spanish Harlem, New York. Her life and world revolved around her son and his father. That was, until the unforgivable day in the courtroom when she heard the judge's gavel slam down on his oak wood desk, sentencing Sean to 10 long years in the department of corrections. She broke down into a river of tears, wondering how in the world she and her newborn baby would survive without their better half for the next 10 years. When the court adjourned, the judge was nice enough to let her talk to Sean for a minute to say their goodbyes. With Sean Jr. being only six months old, he had no idea that his family was being torn apart and would never be the same again.

She could definitely be considered a 10. With her beauty and brains, Cynthia could've had any man she desired. But, she chose Sean. When Sean was sentenced, he tried to tell her to push on with her life and find someone she'd be happy with, but she wasn't trying to hear any of that. Since he saw that she was planning to be stubborn, Sean told her he only had two requests. One, that if she did decide to get involved with someone she'd never give her heart away and, two, the most important one of all, that she would always use protection.

It wasn't that Sean didn't care if she gave her body to another man, because he did. He was just a realist about the entire situation. He approached the issue as if he was in her shoes, so he knew she would end up having sex one day. Since he didn't want her to feel fucked up about cheating, he figured he'd just give her the okay. As long as she didn't end up pregnant with some other nigga's child and didn't flaunt the relationship in his family's face, he was cool. Cynthia always insisted that he was talking nonsense. She constantly told him she wasn't going anywhere. For the first two years of Sean's bid, she kept her word by staying faithful and being by his side to the fullest. But, by the third year, everything began to slow down as far as mail and visits. However, she stayed on point with the money situation.

Then, all of a sudden, all communication came to a complete halt. He could no longer even get in touch with her or his son, Lil' Sean. That began to puncture Sean's spirit to the point where he was almost at the brink of going insane. That was just how much he loved this woman. Facing the possibility of losing a lifelong companion left him with a different outlook on love and life in general. What really hurt was the lack of seeing or talking to his son. Sean knew, with time, he would eventually get over the fact that Cynthia moved on. However, his main concern was Lil' Sean.

The whole ordeal was crazy because he explained to her numerous times how incarcerations usually broke up happy homes. He told her that he feared being too attached to her while being locked up, and then somewhere down the line during the course of his bid, she may meet someone new and reconsider. Not only did the ultimate heartbreak happen, he later found out from Muggs, a cat from his 'hood, that the mother of his child was now fucking his close friend, Tez.

Tez was what most people would call a cut-throat nigga that was strictly for self and self only. If it came down to it, he would fuck over his own mother to get what he wanted. He figured since he had the pretty boy thing going on, he could get any girl he wanted, which was somewhat true. Tez knew he was way out of bounds when he stepped to Cynthia, but he didn't care. He felt that since Sean had 10 years to do and Cynthia would soon be fucking someone else, it might as well be him.

He was determined to get the pussy before it got all beat up. That was when he started popping up unannounced at her house, playing the concerned friend role, and acting as if he was only checking up on her to see if she or the baby needed anything. Since he and Sean were somewhat tight before he was locked up, Tez knew Sean was straight financially. He knew Sean was holding some serious paper for a cat coming up out of the ghetto. Knowing that Sean was the type of guy that took care of home, Tez figured that Cynthia, more than likely, had access to everything that Sean owned. To put things cut and dry, he wanted a piece of both pies. He was well aware of the fact that she was at her most vulnerable state, so he played on that to the fullest, working his mojo. Until this day, it all remained a mystery to Cynthia how she ended up getting herself involved with Sean's close friend.

To her, it felt as if it happened overnight. Even though Tez was cute, she never really found herself attracted to his type. She was so hurt about the fact that she deceived Sean, betraying his trust, that she didn't even have the courage to face him. That was the reason why she decided to stop all communication. She knew she had made a huge mistake that was unforgivable in his eyes. She remembered how Tez used to claim he was just stopping by to check on Sean at first. Then, he switched to checking on her and the baby.

After about five or six visits, Sean was the furthest person on Tez's mind; it was all about Cynthia. How to get close to her was his mission. He went as far as having flowers sent to her once a week and constantly asking her to dinner and a movie. He claimed the date would strictly be platonic. At the time, she had no problems declining his offer. She would explain to Tez how deeply in love she was with Sean and how she would never do anything to jeopardize their relationship. That only lasted so long. Tez spotted the loneliness in her, seeing that she was getting weak and would soon give in to his affection.

Cynthia had everything she desired and wanted, except Sean. Since Tez was persistent, she unconsciously began to let down her defense down.

One weekend, while Cynthia was enjoying a girl's night out , she happened to run into Tez. Intoxication, mixed with distorted thinking, led to her and Tez becoming intimate that night. That night happened to be the first night she'd been out to a club since Sean's incarceration from the streets, by the time she awoke from her drunkenness the next morning...it was to late. She had given into Tez.

Cynthia knew that there was a strong possibility that Sean would have nothing to do with her once he found out that she had a relationship with Tez and had his child. Little did she know, the streets talked, so it was nothing for news to travel inside those prison walls.

The only thing she was sure he'd be happy about was the fact that he still had some money to come home to. When Sean went to prison, he left Cynthia with a 300,000-dollar house, three cars, one SUV, and a little over $800,000 in cash. Every month, for the past 10 years, she sent him $250 faithfully. She made sure he didn't want for anything and his bid was as comfortable as possible. That, along with the side hustles he had going on, had Sean straight. He had everything a convict desired. In addition, there was always someone paying him for something.

Whether it was his sports tickets or weed that he sometimes hustled, he was good. Since someone was always in his pocket, he hardly ever shopped at the prison's canteen. Whenever he needed something, he would simply pass out store lists to those who were in debt to him. After six months of running tickets, he began to run his own little jail house store that he ran out of his cell. With all of the hustles he had going on, he soon became, what most prison inmates would call, penitentiary rich. From the money he had coming in and his inside hustle, he managed to save a decent amount to put towards his goals. Each month, he would send a substantial amount home to his mother for her to put in the account she'd opened for him.

Once upon a time, Cynthia and Sean's mother, Ms. Martin, used to be very close. That was, until she pulled that low down stunt by going out with one of her son's supposed friends. After that, Ms. Martin wanted nothing else to do with her. What drove the nail in the coffin was when Cynthia acted as if she wasn't home when Ms. Martin went to pick up her grandson, attempting to take him to see his father. All week before the visit, Sean had been expressing how excited he was about seeing his son. She was hurt when she saw the disappointment in her son's eyes.

What Ms. Martin didn't know was that Cynthia was actually paranoid about letting her son leave with his grandmother. She thought that if she was to let Lil' Sean go with his grandma, she would never see him again. Tez was mostly to blame because he always corrupted her with those negative thoughts. Not only that, he would constantly try to talk Cynthia into giving him Sean's money, claiming that he just wanted to work it. She would always tell Tez that he was tripping and that Sean didn't leave any money with her. She knew if she were to fork over the money she had stashed, there was a strong possibility that she would never see it again.

Cynthia knew she had already fucked up royally with Sean by messing with one of his friends, so she at least she wanted to show him that she still had a little loyalty. She knew Sean probably thought that she'd long ago jacked off all the money he left her with. Truth be told, that was the reason why he hustled as hard as he did inside the joint.

# Chapter Two

Once the bus was finally back in motion, Sean put his headphones on and vibed out to the sounds of some new cat in the industry name Drake. Even though it was a bootleg copy he'd just scored at the last stop the bus driver made, he was impressed with the quality of the mixtape. The dude was nice. As he sat there enjoying his ride, he was glad that he decided to tell his mother not to worry about picking him up. He felt that he really needed the time to himself in order to collect his thoughts before he entered back into *society*.

He also used the time to think about one of the most important issues he knew he was about to face, approaching Cynthia and his son. He remembered how, on countless occasions, he would often rehearse in the mirror the things he'd say to Cynthia whenever the time and opportunity came that would bring them face to face. Now that he was less than hours away from seeing Cynthia and his son, his mind drew nothing but a blank. He was completely at a loss for words. Thoughts of the near encounter had him nervous as hell, leaving his palms sweaty. As he desperately tried to calm himself through the music he was listening to, he began to bob his head to th*e music.*

Suddenly, the feeling of being watched became overwhelming. When he looked to his left, he locked eyes with a beautiful, golden brown-skinned honey. For the second that their eyes met, Sean felt as if they somehow shared a complete conversation. All of sudden, she looked away. The chemistry was so strong between the two of them that he knew she was staring again. It was as if they had somehow connected with each other without using words. Her smile was beautiful and breathtaking; he couldn't help but to return her gesture. It was amazing how she possessed a smile that brightened the mood of the ride. Her presence made it hard for Sean not to approach her.

"How you doing, baby? My name is Sean. Do you mind if I sit down?"

"Well, Sean, my name is Meloney, not baby, and to answer your second question, it all depends on what your motive is."

"Well, Meloney, to be honest with you, I have no motive. It's just that heartwarming smile you gave me encouraged me to come over and say something to you."

After thinking for a second, Meloney began to speak. Sean figured she was probably feeling him out, trying to detect if he was genuine or not.

"I can respect that. I like honesty in a man. Sit down." she said, after gathering her carry-on bag she had sitting next to her.

"Shit! Honesty is my middle name and truth is my last," Sean said, as he sat down. Meloney cracked a smile. "Excuse me if I sound a little corny or outdated, but you are drop dead gorgeous."

"Yeah, that was a little corny, but flattery is good. It'll get you very far with most women."

"Well, damn! Did I tell you how beautiful your hazel eyes are?"

"Whoa! When I said flattery would get you far with most women, I wasn't talking about me. So, slow down. What are you trying to do, anyway, charm me up out of my panties or something? Wait a minute; did you just get out of prison or something?"

"Damn. Is it that obvious?"

"Yeah, by the way you're talking. Plus, you kinda have that same 'just came home' glow that my brother had after serving five years."

"Man. I wish I only had to do five years. Then, maybe my life would still have some sort of order to it and my relationship with my son would be different," he announced, in a low, saddened tone.

"Damn, Sean, how much time did you serve?" she curiously asked.

"Well, when I first went to prison, I had 10 years for guns and drug trafficking . Since it was my first time going to prison, I was supposed to only do three and a half, at the most."

"So, what happened?" She was now giving Sean her undivided attention.

"With me being fresh in the system, somehow the word got out that I was this major factor on the streets. So, to make a long story short, six months into my bid, I caught a first degree assault for stabbing someone really bad."

"You mean to tell me that they gave you more time for defending yourself? That's fucked up!"

"Yeah, tell me about it. Anyway, they gave me eight

years for the charge, which I had to do eighty-five percent of. But, get this, that time didn't start until I got paroled from the first sentence."

"So, you did three and a half and got paroled, then had to do another six and a half more years?"

"Damn. You're kinda good with that math shit, huh? I might have to hire you as my accountant when I start my record label," Sean said, while smiling at her.

She instantly began to blush. That was what usually happened whenever she was around someone she was attracted to.

"Okay! So, now you're considering me for a job, huh? First of all, whether or not I take the job depends on what my starting salary is," she said, giving him that irresistible smile again. "So, tell me, how does it feel to finally be a free man after all that time?"

Meloney was now staring directly into his eyes. That alone earned her a few extra brownie points in Sean's book. He actually loved when a woman kept total eye contact. It told a lot about the individual.

"I still can't believe I'm finally out. Shit seems so surreal! A decade is hella time for a person to waste out of his life; you feel me?"

*Shit! You have no idea how much I would love to feel you*, Meloney thought, while watching his lips move.

"Meloney, are you okay? You still with me, right?"

"Yeah. Oh, I'm sorry. I was just thinking about how rough it may have been for all the guys who tried to start some shit with you. I know I wouldn't be as quick to start trouble with you with all those gunz you got." Her compliment caused Sean to blush, something else he hadn't done in years. *Damn, this fine ass nigga just don't know how wet he got me right now,* she thought.

"I wasn't always like this, baby. This body right

here," he said, raising his shirt so that, his abs were visible, "Comes from years of dedication, hard work, and discipline. I used to be a slim lil' nigga, so I made it my business to get my weight up. Umph, its fuckin' gorillas in there, ma. But, enough about my sob stories; tell me some'n about you."

"What exactly do you want to know about me?"

"Everything! Well, for starters, where are you from? Because I know wherever it is, it has to be a place of nothing but beauty."

"Look at you. You just don't quit, do you?"

"Nah. So, tell me, where are you from? Where are you on your way to; do you have a man; what are your interests?"

"Whoa! Slow down, playa. Let's try to answer one question at a time. First of all, I'm from Kansas City, where I was born and raised. But, right now, I'm currently attending school at St. Louis University College, majoring in accounting."

"So, you telling me you're staying in the Lou while you're going to school, huh? Damn, that's where I'm from. So, I should be able to see you again. That is, if you'd like to see me again."

"I don't know. It seems to me like you have a lot of catching up to do. Do you think you'll have time for something like that?"

"I'm sure I'll manage to find time to hang out with a beautiful woman like yourself."

"What about your woman? With you being fresh out, I seriously doubt if she'll just let you out of her sight like that," she said, making it sound like a statement and a question at the same time.

"Unfortunately, I don't have anyone special waiting for me at home. As far as my son's mother, two years into my bid," she decided she couldn't stick it out. So, she opted to fuck with one of my supposed to be friends. I can honestly say that I'm as single as a slice of cheese. What about you?"

"Well, I was involved in a relationship about six months ago. That is, until I came home to surprise him on one of my holiday breaks. To make a long story short, I caught him in the bed fucking my best friend."

"Damn! That sounds like some Jerry Springer shit."

"That's what I thought, too. It took a while, but I'm over it now. So, my main focus is getting my degree. I have one more year left. Anyway, all that time you had on your hands, I just know you put together a master plan for your future, right? One of my brother's famous quotes is, "A person who fails to plan, plans to fail."

"Yeah, baby. That's all I been doing is planning. Matter of fact, I have a plan with a backup plan that has a backup plan." They both laughed.

Sean thought about how good it felt to share a laugh with someone other than an inmate or a prison staff member. "But, seriously, though, my first plan consists of getting to know my 10-year old son, who I haven't seen since he was two. Then, I'm going to get me a job and, on my days off, jump in the studio and get this rap shit going." Meloney could hear the excitement in his voice as he spoke about going to the studio.

"So you rap?"

"Yeah, I can do a little some'n" he boast.

"Let me hear you flow." she insisted.

"Ummm, ummm, simple conversations with you got me lusting yo' body. Thick thighs, dreamy eyes, you's a natural born hottie. Though I try to relax, play cool, and keep it calm. Entertaining thoughts of you sexing me on and on. Is it love I'm feeling or just infatuation, 'cause whenever we're apart, I'm like anticipating. Should I let you in my heart, that's what I'm contemplating, now I'm knocking at your door, so please don't keep me waiting." After Sean finished rapping his few bars, he left Meloney speechless and in a daze. He knew he had her. "So what you think?"

"Damn! I wanna hear some more!" she replied, anxiously.

"Next time we get together, I'll kick some more for you."

"Wait a minute; what makes you so sure that there will be a next time?" She inquired, with a sly smile on her face. "Because it's destined for you and I to see each other again. I don't know about you, but I believe everything that happens on earth happens for a reason. See, it's a reason you are on this particular bus, at this particular time, sitting right across from me; it's all in God's design."

"You're right; there is a reason why I'm on this bus at this particular time. Because I happen to be on my way back to school! With yo' slick talking ass!"

They both laughed. "Okay, okay, you got me. But, can we at least exchange numbers so that maybe we can keep in contact with each other?"

"I don't know, boy. For all I know, you could be a serial killer or some'n!" she joked.

"Take a good look at me and tell me if you really think this is the face of a serial killer? I've kilt hella bars of cereal in my life, but serial killer? Nah, I'll admit I've done some wrong in my past, but I'm no longer that person. Girl, you know you's sexy as a motherfucker! I'd drink yo' bath water."

Meloney looked over her shoulder and smiled, showing her perfect pearly whites. "Sean, you just ain't goin' quit, are you?" she said, and then turned back around to hide the fact that she was blushing. "You're not too bad yourself. And, you say it's been 10 years, huh? I don't know if I should call you. You might do some serious damage."

They both shared another laugh. The two were so busy talking; they ended up being the last two to exit the bus. As Meloney walked ahead of him, Sean couldn't help but to admire her shapely ass and how phat it looked in her blue True Religion jeans with the white stitching. He had to admit, the girl was looking rather fly.

With his smooth, mocha-colored skin, dark brown eyes, and freshly cut Caesar with deep waves and goatee trimmed to perfection, he felt as if he was on point as well. While he stood on the side of the bus waiting to receive the box that held his personal belongings, he handed her his number.

"You take care of yourself, Sean," Meloney said, as she headed in the direction in which her friend's car was parked. When she got into the car, she thought to herself, *damn, that nigga is too fine! He got my juices flowing just by talking to me.*

"Damn, Mel! Who's that fine ass nigga that just waved at you?"

"Un-un, bitch! Don't even think about it! He's already taken," she said, in a playfully serious way.

"You better snatch his ass up before somebody else do, bitch!" Rachel replied, as she pulled out of the parking lot.

After finally getting his belongings from the grey haired bus driver, Sean copped a squat on a bench inside the bus station. He was waiting on his friend, Derrick, to pick him up. Derrick was the only one left out of his five-man crew who he still considered a true friend. When

# The Hustle

Sean was popped off, Derrick was already in prison on drug related charges, which he ended up doing four years on. The dope that Derrick was knocked for was really Sean's, but he took the charge anyway. For that, and the fact that he didn't snitch, Sean had hella love and respect for his man. He made sure that Derrick was taken care of to the fullest. Before Sean turned himself in to do his time, he had his mom put 50,000 in a safe deposit box for Derrick. He also told his connects that Derrick would be calling them very soon.

With the financial backing he had and being fresh out of prison, Derrick felt as if he had the world in the palms of his hands. So, of course, he went for broke. Two years after his release, he was labeled as the man that everybody who was really trying to come up needed to fuck with. The streets were his, in every sense of the word. Because of his dark skin and his long dreads, most people thought he was Jamaican.

Standing six feet in height with a slender build and an itchy trigger finger, although he didn't physically look it, he was a very dangerous man. Sean was very thankful to have a friend such as Derrick. In the game that he was in, he knew he needed a ride or die type of dude like him on the team. Sean was far from a coward. If the time came, he, too, would put in work. However, Derrick wasn't someone he'd want to go to war with because it would bring entirely too much heat. Moreover, he knew that static and money never mixed.

He'd much rather have Derrick on his team than against him. Derrick was the type that took pride in getting in niggas' asses. Putting in work was like a pastime to him. When he found out about the stunt that Tez pulled, he told Sean he would gladly take care of that situation for him, but Sean declined his offer because that was something personal he felt that he had to handle himself. Being that he felt where Sean was coming from, Derrick left it alone. However, whenever he would run into Tez, whether it be on the block or out in traffic, he would remind him of how fucked up he was about how he played Sean. In reality, he was hoping and praying that Tez would pop slick out the mouth so he could be the one to close it for him permanently.

As Sean waited patiently for his friend, his thoughts drifted to Cynthia and how much he used to love her. He and Cynthia once had the perfect, fairytale relationship, the kind that every young woman dreamed of having. He thought back to the first day he laid eyes on her. That was back at Central Middle School in Wellston, Missouri. For him, it was love at first sight, but Cynthia wasn't exactly seeing things as he was. To put it plain and clear, she couldn't stand Sean. At least, that was what her actions said.

They argued so much any stranger would have thought the two hated each other. That was, until one fateful evening in 1990 at their school's sock-hop dance. That was when the romance began. It all started with a lie. Since Sean was the shy type, one of his friends lied, telling Cynthia that Sean wanted to dance with her, thinking it would bring a good laugh. With nothing but a good practical joke on his mind, Sean's friend, Ronald, pulled the same process with Sean, not knowing that Cynthia had been secretly crushing on Sean for the longest time.

Once they shared their first dance together, it seemed as if that dance lasted for the next eight years, until he went to prison. Now, she was dancing to someone else's music and, in return, leaving Sean heartbroken. He loved Cynthia with everything a man could love a woman with until she pulled an unforgivable stunt, getting pregnant with another man's child. That straw broke the camel's back. He remembered how he would constantly stress to her that was the only thing that would sever their bond. Sean figured since he'd already given her everything a woman could possibly want materialistically, there would be no reason for her to cling to another man. She had an expensive home, plenty of cars, clothes, and more than enough money to hold her down. He never took the time to realize that, out of all those things, she was still missing the most important thing in the world to her- him and his presence.

"Damn, playa. So what, you just gon' sit there and daydream all day, or you trying to roll with yo' peeps?" Derrick asked, interrupting Sean's thoughts.

"What up, my nigga? I thought you forgot about yo' boy!" Sean excitedly stated, as he embraced his close friend.

"Shiit, nigga, I haven't left you hanging all these years, have I? So, what makes you think that I would start now?" Derrick responded, after breaking the brotherly embrace. "Yo' moms told me you turned down her offer to come pick you up at the joint; what was up with that?"

"I don't know; I just wanted to take in the scenery and savor the moment of becoming a free man once again. Plus, I needed to get my mind right. Shiiit, you know how a nigga be feeling a few weeks before it's time to bounce! Thoughts be straight racing and shit. So many of my old head partnas have been constantly trying to explain to me how wonderful it feels to just zone out on the long ass bus ride."

"Yeah, I know exactly what you're talking about. That's a therapeutic ass feeling," Derrick replied, while smiling, flashing his gold fronts. The first thing Sean thought about was how much things had changed in the past 10 years. Derrick was truly looking like a boss player.

"Well, nigga, let's roll! I'm trying to see my son sometime before he gets grown!" As soon as Sean mentioned his son, he instantly noticed a sudden change in Derrick's demeanor. He also felt heaviness on his heart, as if something was wrong. "Damn, D, you okay? Did I say some'n wrong when I mentioned my lil' man?"

"C'mon, homie, let's dip," was all he said, as he led Sean over to a dark blue Yukon that was sitting on 26" blades.

As soon as Sean hopped into the passenger seat, he immediately began to question Derrick. "D, what the fuck is up, dirty? Is some'n wrong with my son, man?" His voice was filled with desperation.

"Man...I... I don't know how to tell you this, but I got some fucked up news early this morning." He couldn't even look his friend in the eyes. All he could do was lower his head and shake it from side to side.

"What the fuck do you mean you got some fucked up news this morning? What Cynthia do, take my kid off to New York or some'n?"

"Nah dirty, it's worse than that, homie. I was watching the news this morning and I heard them mention her name along with that nigga, Tez. They say some stick up dudes ran up in her spot and murked everybody in the house."

"D, what the fuck is you talking 'bout, nigga? You scaring me with this shit, man! Are you trying to tell me that my son is dead?" he declared, as he stared at Derrick, hoping that it was some type of practical joke. Derrick's facial expression never changed. That let Sean know that it was real. He suddenly felt his heart getting heavier by the second, as if it was slowly sinking into his stomach. The news had changed everything. He thought of all the years he spent daydreaming about this moment and all the things he planned to say and do with his son. With Lil' Sean gone, none of those thoughts or dreams would ever become reality. As he stared out of the window, tears began to fall freely from his eyes.

"I couldn't believe it myself, so I called your moms and she confirmed it, homie. She told me not to say anything to you about it because she wanted to be the one to break the news to you. I'm sorry cuz, but Lil' Sean, Cynthia, her daughter, and Tez got killed."

So many emotions flooded Sean all at once. The thought of never seeing his son alive again was very discouraging to him. No matter how hard he tried, it seemed as if he just couldn't stop the tears from flowing. The only thing that kept him going inside of that concrete jungle was the fact that he had two very special people waiting on his return, his son and his mother. Now, all he was left with was the pictures of his son he'd received over the years. That was one thing good he could say about Cynthia. Although she stopped writing and visiting, she still made sure Sean knew his son through photos. He never once heard his voice, so he had no clue as to what he sounded like. There were times when Sean longed to hear his son call out to him. He just wanted to hear him say the word Daddy one time. Although he didn't know him physically, Sean still loved his son unconditionally. He was made of his own flesh and blood. However, without that father/son relationship that really bonded a father and his son, Sean wasn't sure how to grieve for him. True enough, he was upset with Cynthia, but he never wanted to see anything bad happen to the mother of his only child.

Over the years, he tried to convince himself that he didn't love her anymore, but he knew that was a lie. Deep in his heart, he would always love Cynthia. Cupping his face with his palms, he slowly wiped his weeping eyes. Now, he would never get answers to any of the questions he desperately wanted to ask her. As for Tez, he didn't feel a pinch of sympathy. Whoever was responsible for his death did him a favor by putting that snake out of his misery. However, Cynthia, Lil' Sean, and his little sister didn't deserve to die a cruel death.

He didn't know who was responsible for their death, but he promised himself if he was to ever find out who they were, he'd make every one of them pay with their lives. The rest of the ride home was mostly in silence. From time to time, Derrick would try to spark up a conversation in order to ease his friend's mind of his son's untimely death. Although he knew that was virtually impossible, he still tried. He could tell Sean really didn't want to talk because he'd reply with a one-word answer to every question.

Derrick understood where his friend was coming from, so he decided to cease the small talk for now. As he exited off I-70 expressway making a right turn onto Jennings Station Road, heading toward Sean's mother's house, Sean finally broke his silent treatment. "So, what else is new, D?"

"Man, same ol' shit, homie. A nigga just been grinding heavy. Look here, I don't know what your plans are, but if you thinking 'bout getting back into the game, you know I got you, right?"

"Yeah, I know, but fo' real, I'm on some other shit now, homie. I wanna get into a studio."

"Oh, okay. Damn, I didn't know you were still rapping."

# The Hustle

"Hip hop is my first love, I thought you knew?"

"Well, you know I'm here for you, but my ends ain't all the way right, right this minute. I'm still trying to recover from that drought that hit six months ago."

"Damn, I overheard some new niggas talking 'bout that shit in the joint. They said mafuckas was getting hit hard by some Dominican niggas out of New York. Don't tell me them niggas got you, too?"

"If I said they didn't, I'd be lying. Them niggas got me for a buck 20. Eight fuckin' bricks, homie!" he stressed, as he slammed his bare fist on the steering wheel.

"Damn, dirty, how'd that shit happen? I left you with a raw connect."

"I know, but ol' boy got caught up in this big conspiracy case about a couple years after you got knocked. I was lucky enough to dodge the bullet. I thought you knew."

"Nah, this the first time I've heard about some'n like that," Sean said, with disappointment in his voice.

"Yeah, man. That's why I started fucking with dem New York cats. I been fucking with 'em every since Will got jammed up. Which is the reason why I couldn't understand how they could fuck me out of that chump change. I know for a fact, since I've been seeing them dudes I've took them well over two mill."

"Shiiit, it seems to me that one of them fools may have caught a case and before they skipped town, they decided to gather up as much money as they could to bounce with."

"Damn! I've never thought of that, dirty."

"That's because you out here in the mix. See, a nigga that's locked up has nothing but time on his hands, so he tends to think a lot. I know if I wasn't trying to go to jail and I was on some out of town hustle type shit, I'd do the same thing."

"You gotta be right because I heard rumors about this other cat that got shook for 200 stacks. But, you know me; I was taught by the best," he said, smiling. "I'll never put all of my eggs in one basket."

"So, what you working with now?"

"A couple hundred stacks, but majority of that is tied up in work right now. Only if Cynthia was st... Oh, my bad, fam."

"It's cool, D. Don't even trip. Anyway, she wouldn't have been no help because she been jacked off my lil' change a long time ago. Especially fucking with that nigga, Tez."

"No, she didn't, cuz! I ran into her and one of her girlfriends out at Mills Mall and she told me she know you probably think that she fucked yo' money off, but she didn't. "She said the only money she ever spent was to take care of you and your son. She also said she knew you hated her for what she did to you and she couldn't blame you. She just wished you could understand she was in a really fucked up place at that time. She said she was lonely, vulnerable, and confused. Then, Tez started showing up at the house constantly. She also said that Tez seen the state she was in and took advantage of her weakness. She told me to tell you when I talked to you that she'll always love you regardless of what happens between the two of you when you come home. Homie, she was going to surprise you with the rest of your loot and give you custody of Lil' Sean so you wouldn't miss out on anymore of his life." All of that news caught Sean by surprise. Everything he was hearing was exactly what he was hoping and praying would happen. However, it was too late.

"Nigga, you bullshitting! She told you all of that, dirty?" he asked with bright, hopeful eyes.

"Now you know I wouldn't game you like that, especially at a time like this."

"Damn!" he mumbled, and then silence fell over him. As he thought about it, that sounded exactly how Cynthia would think and react. She was always trying to right her wrongs. "So," he said, changing the subject, "How yo' people doing? You still with Tasha?" Sean was speaking about Derrick's baby's mother.

"Naw! That's been over for quite some time now. That bitch skipped town and took my seed with her. I ain't seen Lil' D in hella long! I don't even know where they at, cuz. But, my moms just hired a private detective to find her ass, so I should know some'n soon," he continued, as he pulled in Sean's mother's driveway, the house that Sean and his sister grew up. When his mother and father decided to split, his father kept the house in Wellston while his mother chose to move back to Vinita Park. All of Sean's childhood memories of living in the house were still fresh in his mind as if it were yesterday. He and his sister had plenty of fun times. He was the older of his mother's two children. His sister, Rhonda, was 21 and in her last year at LSU in Louisiana. He was very proud of his little sister and the decision she made to further her education. There was a time when she was talking about quitting high school; now she was about to be a college graduate.

As he and Derrick exited the car, he briefly thought about Tina, his first girlfriend, and their first kiss, which happened on the front porch of her house. He couldn't believe her parents still lived in the same house, two houses down from his mother and were still together after all that time. Thinking about Tina, he thought back to the first time he'd laid eyes on her 20 years ago.

Coming from a friend's house, Sean spotted a moving van on his street. He remembered how excited he got thinking that he'd finally have some new friends on his block to play with. The first thing he did was ride his black Huffy down to the empty house to investigate the scene. He was hoping he'd see a bunch of boys that were around his age. When he made eye contact with a tall, slender man, later identified as Tina's dad, Mr. Drakes, he gave him a warm smile.

After taking the liberty to introduce himself, Sean began to ask question after question as any curious nine year old would do. He was very disappointed when he found out that Mr. Drakes only had daughters. At that time, he had no interest in girls whatsoever. To him, girls were the enemy. That was until he met Tina. Immediately, Sean felt different about her for some particular reason. As they later got to know each other, they became closer than any of his male friends. Tina was a tomboy at heart, so he felt as if he was actually hanging with one of the fellas.

One evening, as the two of them were playing over at Tina's house, they suddenly became curious about one another's body parts. Tina happened to be the one that initiated the kiss. Now, as Sean thought back, he figured that she must have seen someone kissing on television and wanted to imitate it just to see how it felt. Since she and Sean were close, she must have decided she'd try her technique on him. That was the day their first kiss took place. At that time, he was about 11 and she was 10. After that kiss, they considered each other boyfriend and girlfriend. Three years later, his parents were moving to a strange place he'd never heard of, Wellston.

The fact that he had to up and leave his friends and

girlfriend devastated Sean. If you were to ask him today, he'd say that the move was what actually tore his family apart because his parents soon divorced after they made that move to Wellston. Sean stayed with his father, only because his mother suggested that he do so. However, if it were his choice, he would have chosen to continue to live with his mother with whom he felt much closer to.

Sean's father was a hustler as well. But, he was different from the average street hustler. Being that he kept a nine to five, one would actually have never guessed that he lived a double lifestyle. That was just how well he kept it hidden. Even his own son didn't know what his father was up to. He didn't put it altogether until he was around 17-years old. It was during that time when he found out that his father's numerous lady friends and their secret relationships were what really caused his parent's divorce. Hearing his mother's sweet voice snapped Sean back to reality.

"Ahhh, look at my baby!" she said, interrupting her son's trip down memory lane. "Boy, you went and got all swoll' up on yo' momma! It's gone be hard trying to keep them fast ass girls away from here now."

"Ma, why you always talk to me like I'm still a baby?"

"Because you are still my baby! You my baby boy. Now, come over here and give yo' momma some sugar. Or, as you young folks now say, show me some love, playa!" Both Sean and Derrick laughed at her attempt to sound young and hip. As she embraced her only son, it took all the inner strength she had in her to hold back the tears that were forming in her eyes. She had been crying all morning about her grandson, so she knew she had to be strong for Sean, especially when she gave him the heartbreaking news.

"Ma, you looking good. What you do, drop a few pounds or some'n?" he asked, stroking his mother's ego because he knew she spent most of her free time in the gym.

"Yeah, I knocked off a lil' some'n some'n." The boys laughed. "Just because I'm a mother, it doesn't mean I have to look like one."

"Derrick, so you're too grown to speak now, huh? Don't make me pull out my belt on yo' ass. Y'all c'mon inside."

"I'm sorry, Ms. Martin. I was just thrown from how young, beautiful, and vibrant you're looking. If Sean wasn't my best friend, I'd be all over you," he stated, in a playful manner. Sean caught Derrick off guard with an elbow to the rib cage. Even though he knew Derrick was only playing, it struck a nerve to hear a friend talk about his mother in such a lustful way. "Nawl, but seriously, though, I was just letting you greet your son first, but anyway, how are you doing, Ms. Martin?" he replied, as they all took a seat in the living room.

"I'm doing fine. So, how's your mother doing? I haven't seen her at the boat in the last three weeks. She must got herself a new man. You know how funny her ass acts whenever she meets someone new." She and Derrick's mother were avid gamblers at the boat.

"I don't know, Ms. Martin. Why don't you call her up and see what's up."

"Baby, Momma got some bad news." Ms. Martin started taking a seat next to her son. She figured she might as well break the dreadful news to him and get it over with. As soon as she said that, she noticed a shift in Sean's demeanor. "Derrick has already opened up his big mouth, hasn't he?" she said, looking over at Derrick and giving him a no nonsense look.

"Yeah, I know," he replied, with his head hung low. "It isn't his fault, Ma. I kinda made him tell me." She immediately burst into tears.

"Baby, I'm so, so sorry. Those bastards killed my grandson and I was just beginning to get to know him!" she exclaimed, as she wiped her eyes.

"Ma, what are you talking 'bout? Was Cynthia bringing my son over here to see you?" She shamefully shook her head in an up and down manner. "Ma, why didn't you tell me this?"

"Baby, please, don't be mad at me because I didn't tell you. She wouldn't let him stay the night. She would only pop up unexpectedly when she knew I was off of work and sit over for awhile."

Derrick and Sean looked at each other. "How long has this been going on, Ma?"

"The first time she brought him over was about two months ago. You can't be mad 'cause you told me not to write anymore since you'd be coming home in a couple months. Plus, you know you don't call home that often, so how was I supposed to tell you, anyway?"

"Yeah, you're right, Ma, but do you always have to do as I ask?"

"Yes, son. It was a decision you made and I respected your wishes. Anyway, Derrick and I were going to surprise you at the bus station with your son. Until thi..." She then began to cry again.

"Ma, please, don't cry. We have to be strong for him," he said, as he embraced his mother.

"I'm sorry, baby...You're right. We have to get through this together, and we will. That boy was so much like you, Sean."

Seeing that the conversation desperately needed to be changed, Derrick took the initiative to do so by asking

Ms. Martin several questions. As they engaged in conversation, Sean began to day dream about the first time he made love to Cynthia. ."Damn, girl, why you gotta act all scared? Everybody else is doing it! You said you love me, right?" he inquired.

"Sean, you know I love you, I just don't want to end up pregnant."

"I promise you, I'll take it out when I feel myself cumming. I know what I'm doing."

"Alright, Sean. But, you better pull it out. I don't want to be pregnant at thirteen like Wanda, okay!"

She finally gave in and agreed to give him some, Sean remembered how scared he truly was. Despite all the lies, he told her about him being experienced, this was his first time as well. The only experience he had with sex was sneaking and watching his father's porno movies. He figured after watching enough of them, he had a general idea about what to do. The more clothing she took off, the more nervous Sean got.

"Boy, are you even paying your mother any attention? Derrick and I have been talking to you for the last three minutes." Ms Martin stated, breaking into his thoughts like a burglar.

"My bad, moma. What was y'all saying? I was just thinking about when I was younger and how you use to tell me and Rhonda to stay off this old chair. By the way why do you still have that old thing sitting in here with all your new furniture? Sean replied. He hated that he just lied to his mother but he didn't want to tell her that he was thinking about his son and get her to crying all over again. As painful as it was he was hoping to began the healing process as quickly as possible. Little Sean will never be forgotten, but thinking about his death right now was a little too much to bear.

"Because it has sentimental value to me, that's why I still have it. Why, do you have a problem with my chair?"

"No, Mother," he replied submissively.

"Good! Now, maybe later sometime I can explain the history of that chair. Hey, your sister called this morning. She told me to tell you that she loves you and she'll be down for spring break. She also said for you to call her once you get settled in. Well, baby, I have to go get ready for work, but your house and car keys are on the key rack in the kitchen," she said, kissing him on the cheek while turning around to leave.

"Hold up, Ma! What do you mean car keys? I thought you told me Cynthia got rid of all my cars."

"She did. But you need to talk to Derrick about that fancy little thing that's sitting in my garage." When Sean looked over at Derrick, all he could do is smile.

"What you waiting on, nigga?" said Sean. "Let's see what you got ya boy rolling in. Bet not be no bullshit!"

"Sean Allen Martin! Watch your damn mouth, boy!" yelled Ms. Martin from the other room.

"My bad, Ma," he yelled back, apologizing.

"Now, you should already know I'm not gone put my dude in nothing that I wouldn't floss myself! This here is family, nigga. What, you ain't know?" Sean was in awe after the garage door lifted up, revealing a brand new 7-series black BMW.

"Now, that's what the fuck I'm talking about, homie!" he yelled as he showed his gratitude to his friend with a brotherly embrace.

"Damn, nigga, you trying to cut my oxygen off or some'n?" Derrick spoke in a muffled tone as if he was being suffocated.

"My bad, dirty. I guess got a little excited."

"Well, fool, don't kill me the midst of all yo

excitement! So, what you gone do 'bout that house that Cynthia was living in?"

"I don't know, dirty. It was in her name, so I might not have no say so about it. I might just let her shitty ass family have it 'cause I know I can't live up in that bitch after what happened in it."

"Yeah, I can see your point. So, what's up for the night? There's no need to hang around this bitch sad and shit. I know you're itching to get yo nuts out of the pawnshop; it's been hella long, fool! You probably forgot how to use yo joint," he joked.

"So, you got jokes, huh? Shiiit, I ain't gone have no problem using this big mafucka here! It's gone be hell to tell the captain for somebody's daughter!" They both laughed.

"Peep game, though, I got some business to handle. Here goes five Gs, go do some shopping and call me around nine tonight, then we'll hook back up, a'ight? And ahh, I left a burnout in the glove compartment. It's got some numbers programmed in there just in case you're trying to hit some'n before we hit the club tonight."

"A'ight my, nigga, and good look on the change."

"C'mon now! You don't owe me no thanks. This here is family. So, I'm only doing what I know my family would do for me."

Sean and Derrick made their exits at the same time. While Derrick went to handle his business, Sean headed toward North County Mall to do a little shopping for women and a wardrobe. Ten years ago, that mall was the spot to meet them fine county women, but so many things had changed since then. He was truly hoping that the women the mall attracted hadn't change.

Knowing how to save and budget money was Sean's specialty, so whenever he shopped, he made sure to get his money's worth. From Famous & Barnes, to Dillard's, then to Harold Pener's, Sean did his thing catching up on the latest fashions. Finally, before making his exit he stopped at Foot Locker, his favorite shoe store, to fulfill his tennis shoe fetish. Most of the things he purchased would only suit him temporarily. His desire for expensive fashion ran much deeper than Famous & Barr, Dillard's or any store the average hustler shopped. He was on grown man time, which called for expensive, grown man's attire. However, he was planning to make due with what he had to work with. Rest assured, when his money got right his gear would be tight.

Two hours later, with the remainder of eight hundred dollars, Sean was finally about to exit the mall. It wasn't nearly as flooded with women as he thought it would be, but it still didn't stop him from flirting with the few that he found attractive. It felt good to be able to have a casual conversation with a woman without the worry of crossing a boundary. Walking to his car, all Sean could think about was going home and soaking in his mother's Jacuzzi. Ever since she'd installed it, she'd been bragging to Sean about how soothing it truly was. He was about to see for himself.

Pulling up at the house, Sean still couldn't believe he was really out of prison. As he got out of the car, he looked up toward the sky and silently thanked God for delivering him from the belly of the beast. At the moment he vowed never to indulge in anything that could possibly jeopardize his freedom. "Damn, it feels good to be able to unlock a door again," he mumbled to himself as he stuck his key in.

As he turned the key, he suddenly thought back to what Derrick said about the phone he left in his glove compartment. "Let me see what this fool got on the line."

He headed back to his car to retrieve the phone. As he walked back to the house, he thoroughly examined it. The phone was nothing like the ones he frequently used before he went to prison. The thing was much smaller and it looked like a mini computer. He had no idea how to work the modern technology. After experimenting with the many buttons, the phone came to life and a beautiful face appeared on the screen, along with her name and number.

Another touch of a button that had an arrow that pointed downward brought about another lovely face on the screen. Browsing through the phone's memory, an attractive chick named Maxeen seized his attention. Something about her really stood out from all the rest. That was what made him call her up. After pushing the send button and waiting for the call to transfer through, he suddenly realized why she caught his attention. She favored Cynthia tremendously.

"Hello," answered a female. Her tone was very relaxing and it caught Sean by surprise.

"How you doing, Maxeen, this..."

"Sean, right?" she questioned, completing his sentence. "Derrick programed your number in so your name automatically showed on the screen when you called. That's how I knew it was you. Anyway, he told me all about you. Just in case you're thinking it, no, he and I never fucked around. He kicks it with my girl, Asia."

"Damn. What makes you think I was thinking some'n like that?"

"Because Derrick already explained to me that, that would be your first thoughts. He said you'd think that he and I had been involved. He also said that you were very outspoken, and that you'd probably ask that question again later on."

# The Hustle

"So, Derrick does know me, huh? Damn, I didn't think I was that predictable. But anyway, what's really good, ma, where you at right now?"

"Right now I'm over one of my girlfriend's house out in Pinelawn. Why, you trying to see me or something?"

"Shit, if it's possible. I mean, if you're not too busy."

"Love, if I was busy, trust me, I wouldn't have answered the phone. So, are you going to give me the address or what?"

"Whoaaa. The address is 4212 Madison, right off of North and South Rd. Are you familiar with that?"

"Yeah. Give me twenty minutes and I'll be out front."

"Hey, just come inside, the door'll be open. You'll see a black BMW in front of the house."

After hanging up the phone, Sean immediately hopped into the Jacuzzi bathtub to wash away the years of frustration, pain, and resentment he held for not only Cynthia, but also life in general. As he soaked inside the massive tub, he began to drift into a relaxing, sleep like state. Although his eyes were fully open, his mind and body were getting it's much needed rest. Listening to Trey Songz singing his heart out about his woman making faces had Sean ready to fuck . He totally forgot about Maxeen and that she was on her way. What he didn't know was that she had arrived and let herself in and was sitting in the living room waiting patiently for him.

After a mere five more minutes. Maxeen's patience began to grow thin.

She knocked. "Uhn, Sean, are you okay in there?"

"Come in," he yelled through the door.

"Do you know I've been in your living room for the last 15 minutes?"

37

"Damn. I'm sorry. A nigga just got caught up in the moment. I haven't been in a tub in like ten years. This is like heaven on earth right now," he said smiling.

"I know it must be, baby. Ten years is a long time without a bath."

"Don't get it twisted. I've showered every day in the last 10 years; I just haven't had the luxury of a bath."

"Boy, I know. I'm not that green to the penal system," she declared as her eyes examined every part of his flesh that was visible. Maxeen wasn't the shy type, either. If she saw something she desired, most likely she'd go after it. Right then, she very much desired Sean. "So, being that you haven't taken a bath in years, I'm guessing that you might need a little help getting your back. Looks like you're having a hard time." With all those damned muscles, umm, umm, umm, it should be against the law for a man to be this fine, she thought as she began to sensually wash his back. That was how forward she was, she didn't even wait for him to give her an answer.

"Damn, that feels so good. What, you a masseuse or some'n?"

"Naw, baby, I'm just a registered nurse with some good healing hands, that's it." It was taking a tremendous amount of will power for Maxeen to keep her composure. *I know damn well I shouldn't be in here with this strange man like this*, she thought. If I keep touching him like this, I might fuck around and give him a taste of the coochie, she continued in thought. As she caressed his back, Maxeen fell deeply into a lustful trance.

"You okay back there?" Sean questioned, breaking the awkward silence.

"Yeah, I'm okay. I was just back here thinking."

"And, may I ask about what?"

## The Hustle

"I was just thinking that since my job here is done, I'm going to step out and let you finish bathing." Beads of sweat had taken its form on her brow and between her decent sized breasts. She was getting heated, and it wasn't because of the temperature of the room. She knew she was feeling Sean in a major way. He had her pussy muscles throbbing vigorously. Without saying another word, she left the bathroom and copped her seat on the sofa in the living room.

Upon taking a seat, she picked up a Better Homes and Gardens magazine, and instantly began to fan herself. She was hoping she could cool her body back down to its normal temperature. While fanning herself, Maxeen took notice of how beautiful and spacious the living room was. From the high ceilings to the vintage and new furniture, it all flowed well together. The color scheme of white and coconut gave the room a comfortable, all year round summer feel.

"This is how I want my shit to look when I buy my first house," she stated as she walked around viewing Sean's domain.

Sneaking up behind her, Sean whispered softly in her ear, "So, do you like what you see?"

"Yeah, this place is beautiful," she mustered, slightly trembling from the heat of his voice and closeness of his body. Once she gathered the nerve to turn to face him, she found herself dangerously close, causing her to become speechless.

Without hesitation, Sean took the cue and went in for the kiss. First, he gently pecked her lips just to see if he detected any resistance. Noticing that there was none, he went in for another, but that time made it a little more passionate. He even slid a little tongue in the mix. As his tongue danced inside of her mouth, he began to caress her thigh. With it being the first time in ten years having any intimate contact with a woman, it was obvious that he was a little nervous. While embracing in a long, passionate kiss, Maxeen slowly started to back away from Sean, heading in the direction of his mother's favorite love seat. With no objection, Sean followed her lead, falling on top of her as she stumbled onto the sofa.

While still entangled in the steamy kiss, Sean unbuttoned the last of the buttons on her shirt, the ones that he hadn't broke, exposing her white lace bra that held her voluptuous 34Ds captive. Once he removed her bra, her perky mounds of flesh stood firm and erect. Sean admired them, thinking how on countless occasions he'd masturbated to pictures of women with breast just as lovely as Maxeen's. Before going to prison, Sean was strictly an ass and hips man. However, as time passed he learned to appreciate every part of a woman's body from her head to her toes, he was willing to give her entire body his undivided attention.

With both hands, he caressed her breasts while running his fingers across her nipples, causing them to stand up. Then, he began to breast feed himself as if he was a newborn baby clinging to its mother's tit. Maxeen's moans got louder and louder with the more pleasure she received. He unbuttoned her jeans and slid his hand down her pants toward her sacred spot. With each touch to her clit, Sean sent shock waves of pleasure throughout her body, causing it to shake and tremble. From the angle her body was in, it was hard for Sean's finger to penetrate Maxeen's golden tunnel.

Lifting her backside up off the sofa, she made it easier for him to pull down her pants. When he got her jeans past her thighs, she sat back down and lifted her legs in the air, allowing Sean to completely free them from the fabric. With nothing but her panties on, she spread her legs eagle, giving him a formal invite. Sean got down on his knees and seductively removed her lace panties, revealing a perfectly manicured pussy. He then used his two index fingers to split her pussy lips open. Maxeen's clit popped out like a Jack-In-Box. That gave him full access to please her every which way possible. Simultaneously, his tongue and middle finger went to work. While he licked on her clit, he fingered her dripping wet snatch.

"Ooooh! Ooooh, oooh, Sean, damn! It feels so goood! Suck this pussy, boy, oh, suck it! I'm 'bout to cum, daddy! Oooh, here I cum... I'm cumming! I'm ...cum...in... ooh shit! Unh-unh, you gots to give me some of that dick right now," she said as she pushed Sean's head away from her vagina. Without saying another word, she turned around and assumed the doggy style position, placing her knees on the sofa's cushion. Looking at all that ass from behind had Sean's dick throbbing. He couldn't wait to get inside of her.

No matter how good it looked, Sean wasn't about to enter her bare back. He reached into his pants that were around his ankles and pulled out one of the condoms that Derrick had stashed inside of the glove compartment. Being that he was very knowledgeable about the HIV epidemic and how widely it spread throughout his city over the past five years, Sean wasn't about to take that chance. There was no way he was coming home to a death sentence by sexual intercourse, especially after surviving ten years of hell!

It was mesmerizing to Sean how perfectly shaped her ass was. After placing the extra sensitive condom on, he was ready. He eased up behind her, solid hunk of meat in hand, and slid in between her pouty pussy lips. Since her juices were already flowing, he didn't have a problem entering her. Matter-of-fact, she was so wet that within his first few strokes, his manhood slid right out of her. Just to make sure that it wouldn't happen again, Sean gripped her ass cheeks tightly with both hands to make sure his aim was accurate. At first, he started stroking her slowly, but as he got more into the groove, he increased his speed a couple notches. Before long, he was humping as fast as a jackrabbit. All throughout the living room, the sound of flesh slapping against flesh, intense moaning, and dirty talking could be heard clearly. The dirtier Maxeen talked, the faster Sean stroked. He hadn't been turned on like that in ages.

"Damn, what's up? Did you come already, Sean?" she asked, fighting to catch her breath. Although he was a little embarrassed, he still owned up to the truth.

"Yeah. Some'n like that. But, don't go doggin' a nigga, tho. It's been 10 years, feel me?" he replied, as his dick went soft while still inside of her.

"You good, baby! I mean, like literally, you are good!" she said, putting emphasis on her words. "Seriously though, I ain't got shit bad to say about your performance. I've had a nigga to fuck me for three hours straight and it wasn't near as good as this. See, I'm cool because I know it's going down whenever round two start up. I just hope you don't think any less of me because I fucked you on the first day we met. But, I just couldn't resist your fine ass," she said, smiling while looking into his eyes.

"Nah, baby, I'm not judgmental like that. I'm not going to think nothing less of you because we got down. To be honest, I respect you even more for being a woman that knows what she wants and not afraid to go after it. I like a woman that's spontaneous."

"Can I use the bathroom to clean myself up?" she asked.

"Of course. You know where it is." She then gathered up her things and headed toward the bathroom. "I wouldn't mind going another round, but I'm supposed to meet up with D at 8 o'clock. But, you can best believe I'll be calling later. That's if you want me to?" he yelled loud enough for Maxeen to hear.

Once she closed the door again, Sean quickly found his cell phone and called Derrick.

"What up, player? You over there fucking with Maxeen's crazy ass, huh?"

"Damn! Nigga, how'd you know she was over here?"

"Asia called and told me she was on her way to come see you. So, what's really good?"

Aww, man! Baby girl ain't shit nice! I mean damn! Look, I'll fill you in when we meet up tonight. Anyway, where you at right now?"

"Dirty, I'm in Baden right now fucking with a few people I see on the regular, you feel me?"

"Fo' sho! So, where we meeting up at tonight?"

"You remember that house that my granny used to stay in on Grand, right off of I-70 right by the Tower?"

"Yeah."

"Meet me there in forty five minutes."

"What we meeting there for? Yo' granny don't live there anymore," Sean inquisitively replied.

"I know, but we still own it. That's my city spot now. I got my other baby mother in there holding shit down."

"A'ight, fool! In a minute."

"One, my nigga." Maxeen walked in looking extra sexy.

So, when will I get to see you again? And, not just on no sex tip, either, I'm trying to vibe with you."

"That right there is all up to you, sweetheart. You got my number, right?"

"Fo' sho. Well, can a nigga get a hug before you leave?" he stood up extending his arms .With no hesitation, she embraced Sean, hugging him tightly.

Then, she whispered into his ear, "Sean, I'll be here if you're looking to start a solid relationship. Although we got down today, don't mistake me for the type of chick that fucks every nigga she meets. I'm looking for something more stable. One thing you should know is, there are too many STDs going around to be having multiple sex partners. You understand where I'm coming from?"

"You right, baby. How about I call tomorrow and we talk about whatever?"

"Okay," she said, and then gently kissed him on the lips. "And, Sean, welcome home!"

# Chapter Three

Forty-five minutes later, Sean found himself pulling up in front of old familiar grounds to be greeted by a beautiful young woman he'd never seen before. Her name was Asia, and she was Derrick's baby mother.

"Sean, Derrick told me to tell you he'd be here in ten minutes and for you to come on inside," she said, leaning into the passenger's window that Sean had just let down. He glanced at the gold and diamond Movado that Derrick had also left in the car for him to find.

He didn't really feel comfortable entering Derrick's domain without him present, so he decided to wait in the car until his friend showed up. Before the whole prison incident, Derrick was the one that was usually running late when the time came to meet up. Sean figured that things were probably the same since he was late picking him up at the bus station. While waiting in the car, he began to reflect back on all the love, loyalty, and respect Derrick had shown him throughout his stay in prison, and especially coming home. He was very proud of his

45

friend and the accomplishments he had made over the past 10 years.. There were plenty of guys that called themselves hustlers, but never actually made any progress in the game.

Even though he'd made up his mind about not hustling again, it still felt good to know that Derrick had his back if he decided to change his mind. Throughout all of the daydreaming, Sean was instantly brought back to reality when a bluish, purple 430 SC convertible Lexus pulled directly behind him. Looking down at his watch, he noticed that 10 minutes had come and gone like a summer breeze. Maybe Derrick moves on time now, he thought, as he looked back up, expecting to see his friend hop out of the vehicle. Derrick was sharp as a tack stepping out of his ride. He had on a quarter length, Blue Fox mink, a pair of tan Gucci slacks, and a pair of Gucci loafers the exact same color of his fur. In that attire, Derrick looked like a very different person. Nothing like the person Sean knew ten years ago.

It was weird for Sean. There was a time when Derrick wouldn't be caught dead in formal dress wear. For him, it was all about jeans, sweat suits, and sneakers. Things have really changed over the past ten years, thought Sean.

"Damn, fool, why you still sitting in the car? Didn't Asia tell you I said wait for me inside the crib?"

"Yeah, she did. But, I figured I'd just wait out here until you showed up."

"C'mon, big homie, don't ever do that shit no more. Niggas out here hatin' at an all time high! I just got you back; I definitely ain't trying to lose you to no bullshit. Besides, you already know, mi casa es tu casa. Remember that, cousin."

Sean got out of his car and followed Derrick inside.

# The Hustle

As Sean entered the place, his eyes danced around the living room, taking in the scenery. Asia had the place looking spotless and feeling cozy. The entire spot looked as if it had been newly renovated. It looked nothing like it did ten years ago when Grandma Davis was living there. From the soft brown, cashmere sofa set to the 60-inch flat screen plasma television, the décor released a youthful, yet, adult vibe. The color scheme for the living room was based on soft brown and egg shell white, and the carpet was a custom made swirl brown and egg shell white, matching perfectly.

"Sean, this is Asia, my daughter's mother," Derrick introduced.

"So, this is the man Maxeen's been running off at the mouth about, huh? What you do to my girl? You got her nose wide open," Asia said, smiling.

"You should be asking yo' girl what she did to me. She tried to get a nigga sprung." Just the sound of Maxeen's name sent chills through his body. He knew just by their first encounter if he were to see her on a regular basis, he'd quickly catch feelings for her. That was something he felt he wasn't quite ready for. He needed time to focus on his career.

"Sean, you cool? You want a beer or some'n?"

"Yeah, give me a beer, dirty."

"Asia baby, grab two beers out of the fridge and bring them down in the basement, a'ight?" Derrick asked right before walking off toward the basement stairs.

"Damn, boy! Asia's a bad mafucka!" Sean complimented his friend.

"Yeah, I know. And, if anything ever happen to me, nigga, you better take care of her, but don't take care of her. You feel me?"

"Nigga, what the hell is you talking 'bout? Ain't

47

nothing going to happen to you."

"I know that, fool, but I'm just saying, just in case, make sure she straight. But, don't cross that line that Tez did. I'm just bullshitting, fool," he said, laughing it off.

"Boy, you's a fool, fo' real." Sean knew Derrick was serious about what he'd just said.

"Damn, D," he said, obviously impressed by what he was looking at. "You got yo own lil' game room down in this bitch! I'm loving this shit, dirty," he continued to speak as he walked over to the Donkey Kong game.

"Just trying to keep my homies entertained whenever they decide to come through. But, check this, I got some'n fo' you. C'mere, dirty, that game ain't going nowhere." Sean walked behind the bar where Derrick was standing and watched him flip the light switch that was located on the wall, remove a painting that was directly above the bar, and revealed a built in, fire proof safe. Once he opened it, Sean was in awe looking at the stacks of money and jewelry that was staring back at him. He figured that Derrick was doing well for himself, but he had no idea that his lil' homie had moved into the major league status.

"That money looks good, don't it, fool? I know it looks like a meal ticket but, trust me, it's far from that. Believe it or not, it's only about 50 thou'. You know you welcome to it if you need it, but right now I got this for you." He pulled out a platinum chain with a letter S emblem encrusted in diamonds. Welcome home, my nigga!" he said, placing the chain over his head and hugging his partner. He then gave Sean ten thousand dollars for pocket change.

"I would've given you more, but this is all the loot I have besides the ten bricks I got in just last night. Man, I wish you would reconsider and get back down with yo boy. I need you, fo' real, my nigga. Just say the word and five of them thangs is yours right now!"

"Nah, man. I'm good right now. I tell you what; let me see how this studio shit pans out first. A'ight, dirty?" After hearing Asia's footsteps coming down the stairs, it forced him to cut the discussion short. That was just an old habit he picked up when he was grinding. He never talked any business around women that he didn't do business with.

Catching the cue, Derrick grabbed the beers out of Asia's hands and dismissed her. "Thank you, baby. And, ummh, if Sean ever comes by here, I don't care if I'm not here, make sure that door is wide open. Don't let him tell you that he'll wait in the car. If he says that again, drag his ass up out of it." Everybody laughed. "Look here, baby, I got a couple runs to make, then I'm gone hit the club with Sean, so don't wait up for me, a'ight?"

"Okay. I'm probably gone stay over my mother's house since I have to pick up our daughter, anyway."

"A'ight, baby."

"Wait a minute nigga! I know you happy and shit about yo partna coming home, but don't get fucked up in front of yo family! You better give me a kiss," she said, grabbing on to her man. Sean couldn't help but to watch as Derrick passionately kissed his woman while grabbing a hand full of ass.

"Don't start nothing you can't finish!" Asia stated sarcastically.

"A homie, do me a favor and wait up in the living room for a minute." Without saying another word, Sean waltzed up the stairs.

Fifteen minutes and one orgasm later, Derrick was in the driver's seat of his rental while Sean rode shotgun. The first stop Derrick made was to his safe spot where he kept his dope stashed, which wasn't too far from the place he and Asia shared. Riding with his friend knowing that he was on the verge of doing something illegal had Sean on paranoid status. He was constantly checking his surroundings and watching his rearview mirror, making sure Derrick wasn't a wide-open target. Old street habits are hard to break, Sean thought as Derrick bent another corner.

The neighborhood that Sean once thought was fairly decent at one point now looked a complete wreck. Garbage had been thrown on the streets freely as if folks hadn't yet learned of the trashcan. Dope fiends walked the streets looking like zombies, searching for their next fix. What really struck a chord was when Sean realized that there was practically a liquor store on every other corner they passed. No wonder so many innocent people fell victim to the streets. At that very moment, Sean promised himself that he would never again be the cause of his people's destruction.

Making sure to arrive at the safe spot without carelessly leading any unwanted guests, Derrick zigzagged through the neighborhood before ducking off into an alley. While driving, he explained to Sean that it was the normal routine he displayed whenever he came to the safe house. Pulling up to a garage, Derrick grabbed the remote garage opener that was clipped onto his visor. When the door raised just enough for the car to enter, it slowly pulled into the black hole.

Being that the garage was connected to the single story home, it enabled Derrick to enter and leave without attracting attention. That particular house was nothing like the one Derrick shared with Asia. Sean could tell he specifically designed the spot into his own little getaway bachelor's pad, and his baby mother knew nothing about it. It had everything a single man could possibly want and need. Moreover, it was decorated very tastefully.

From the solid black L-wall sectional to the vintage African wood and glass middle and end tables, the living room had a masculine feel to it. With the walls painted a crème color, it only enhanced the furniture pieces. He also had a digital state of the art entertainment system with complete surround sound that ran throughout the house.

"C'mon, fam, let me show you this hella tight stash I had custom built. It's in the basement." As they entered the basement, Sean noticed that it was designed exactly like the house he and Asia shared, minus the arcade games. "Here, help me get these balls off this pool table," requested Derrick.

When the balls were free from the table, Derrick pulled downward on the rail that was the width of the table. A couple seconds later as if it was remotely controlled, the surface of the table raised to about two feet, revealing the ultimate, air proof stash spot that even canines couldn't smell through. In the guts of the pool table, there was a compartment that was big enough to house a human body.

In it, were 10 neatly stacked kilos of the best cocaine on that side of the Mississippi that money could buy.

"Damnnn! Them bricks, nigga?"

"Shiiit, those aren't only bricks, fool! That right there is houses, boats, cars, and any other fancy shit money could buy. See, that shit right there, each one of them joints could be stretched to two, maybe three. But, I'm not in this shit for the greed. I'm serving that shit as is, homie. The connect I got now is out of this world."

"Who built this stash? That shit is tight!" Sean

expressed with excitement.

"Ah, man, my Mexican patna name Carlos hooked it up for me. That mafucka could build a stash spot in practically anything! That nigga's the truth!" Derrick stated, giving Sean dap. "Don't nobody know about this hideaway spot but me and you, dirty, that's just how much love and trust I got for you." He then reached deep into the pool table and pulled out one of the tightly saran and duct tape wrapped packages, and then pushed the top of the table back down until he heard a click sound, which indicated that the lock had been attached. After that, he snapped the rail back in its rightful place and put the balls back on it.

Sean studied the table carefully as if he was looking at it under a microscope to see if he could tell exactly where it had been altered. He couldn't. "D, this shit is on point! I can't even tell that it's been fucked with. The green still looks like it's a full cover."

"That's how it's supposed to look, ain't it? C'mon, let's ride out. I have to go meet this dude that wanna snatch this bird, then we off to the club."

"D, what niggas paying for birds nowadays?" Sean questioned, trying to see if the prices had changed as well.

"Shiiit, for this butta, I be taxing niggas 28! Mafuckas telling me ounces is jumping back like 30 grams. That's without putting the whip on it. And, it's fire! This that heat fo' real!"

"Damnnn! It's like that, huh? Sounds like you got that 1987 blow."

"And, the shit is poppin' like back in 1987, too. The dude I'm hooked up with is a Spanish cat that owns this nightclub called Club Liquid right next to Union Station. You'll meet him tonight."

# The Hustle

"Fool, you know I already told you I'm not trying to get down! I'm serious, D!"

"I know, I know. That's why I'm gone spot you that buck fifty so you don't have to get down. I want to see you do yo thang. It's a lot of bullshit rap that's out right now. You what the game been missing," he complimented.

"Shiit, tell me about it! I gotta put the Lou on the map. That nigga Nelly blew the fuck up! I'm trying to get where he at!

"And, you will! Especially when you got a real nigga like me who you can depend on. But, on some real shit, though, if I was doing bad and I knew you were on your way home, I would have probably ran up in one of those banks or some'n. There was no way I could've faced you knowing that I jacked off the fifty K you gave me and not have shit to show for it."

When they pulled on Popeye's Chicken parking lot on Grand and Natural bridge Road, Derrick told Sean to sit in the back seat for a second so his hook-up could get in the front to handle business. Sean was impressed to see that Derrick still remembered what he told him about trusting someone in the back seat, while doing business. That was a complete no-no! He also expressed to Sean how he liked to arrive at the designated meeting spot a few minutes early just to check out the scenery, and when he was forced to ride by himself he usually handled business inside the restaurant, leaving the dope in various hiding spots within the area. That way, if it were ever a set-up, the suspect, whether it is Fed or jacker, would get nothing. Handling business that way was one of the many reasons why he was still standing on the streets. A few minutes later, a blue Olds Cutlass pulled up on the lot.

"Here this nigga is. The money is usually on point

with him, so we ain't gone worry about counting that shit." All the while Derrick was talking, Sean kept a watchful eye on the stocky young cat that exited his car and headed toward their direction. He figured the dude to be in his late twenties. As a glare from another customer's headlights hit the strange man's face, Sean instantly noticed a distinctive mole right above the left side of his upper lip.

"Tony, what up, fool? You know a nigga don't like to be sitting here looking all suspect with this shit on me, dirty. You fifteen minutes late," Derrick stated, looking down at his watch. "I was giving yo ass a few minutes more, then I was ghost. You would've just had to catch up with me tomorrow."

"C'mon, my nigga, you knew I was coming. I had to get gas. My bitch left the hooptie on empty."

"Yeah, yeah, whatever, sucker fo' love ass nigga! You got that change counted up, right?"

"C'mon now, D. You acting all brand new on a nigga! You know I comes correct, playa!"

"Okay! Let's do this shit then. Me and my homie trying to hit the club sometime tonight if you hurry yo slow ass up," Derrick said in a joking manner. He and Tony always kidded with each other like that, but they also knew when it was time to do business as well.

After the transaction was complete, Derrick navigated the rental through traffic heading downtown to Club Liquid for the surprise welcome home party he'd put together for his best friend. He had been waiting on this day for the longest time. Now that his big homie was out, he was sure that a lot of things on the street was about to change. He figured the nonsense Sean was talking as far as not getting back in the game would soon wear off. He just had to get a taste of the lifestyle he'd been missing for the last 10 years. Regardless of what he was talking about, Derrick knew in his heart that the call of the game would soon be much too loud for Sean to ignore. It was all he knew.

When they finally pulled up on the club's parking lot, Derrick turned, looked at his friend, and said, "Damn I'm glad you home, man!"

"That makes two of us, homie," Sean replied. He was about to get out of the car but was stopped short by his friend.

"Hey. Here go the keys to the hideout. I know you gone need a spot to take that fly bitch you leave the club with tonight."

"Good lookin', cousin, 'cause you know how I feel about hotels. Especially if I don't know the bitch fo' real," he replied, grabbing the keys out of Derrick's hand.

"Speaking of bitches, what's up with Maxeen?"

"Ahhh, mannn! Baby girl, ain't shit nice, fool! She got that fire, ya' heard!" They both laughed.

"I knew she was off the chain! I knew it! That's why I locked her info in yo phone."

"The crazy thing about her is how much she favor Cynthia. That shit is scary man."

"She do, don't she?" Derrick agreed.

"That was a really good look, though. But, tell me, is ole girl a stone freak or what?"

"Nah, fam. She's actually a stable broad. But, from the way that Asia talks about her, she's the type of chick that'll go all out for her dude, you feel me?"

"Yeah. I did get a strong vibe when I was with her. Like a nigga could really do some things with her."

"Aw shit! This nigga catching feelings already," Derrick said, laughing.

"C'mon now, you know it ain't like that with me.

Shiiit, I been gone for ten flat years, I got a lot of catching up to do. I just wish my son was still here," he said, lowering his head.

"I know, dawg. I wish he was, too. That's fucked up."

"I can't do no funerals, dirty, not right now. So, I'm gone hit the wake and pay my last respects to my son and his mother," he continued in a low tone. Derrick knew that his boy was hurting deeply, so he was determined to make sure he helped his friend through his hard grieving process.

"A'ight! Enough of that talk! Let's go in here and celebrate your release like real boss players supposed to," Derrick spoke, breaking the sad mood. Before getting out of the car, he took the paper bag that contained the money he'd just received and stuffed it under the driver's seat. Sean couldn't believe what he was seeing.

"Damn, D, you sho' it's safe to leave that in the car like that?"

"It's good. I just got the rental today. Don't nobody know I'm driving this joint. But, on the real, I gotta give you a little history about this club. It's bi-racial, so you're destined to see the baddest Black, White, Asian, Latin, or mixed bitch in the city up in this spot tonight. So, don't be so quick to sell yourself short by choosing the first chick you see. And, the last but most important advice I can give you is to remember to strap up."

"Shiiit, ain't that much changed about yo' boy! I still strap up, dirty! Sean's confidence level was so high, his walk turned into a ditty-bop. With his baggy fit, Paper Denim jeans, an old school navy and white stripe Rugby Polo shirt, topped off with some six-inch wheat colored Timberland boots, he was fresh dressed and feeling real hood. Derrick decided to change clothes at the safe spot, after observing Sean's attire. He settled in a blue, True

# The Hustle

Religion jean suit with a pair of ash grey colored Timbs. His dreads were braided to the back, cascading over his shoulders. Sean took one look at the long line and was instantly reminded of the noontime meal line in prison he hated so much.

"What you think you doing?" Derrick questioned as he saw Sean walk toward the end of the line.

"I'm getting ready to get in line. What you think!"

"Man, I don't do lines no more. Shit has changed, big homie!"

He was speaking the truth. With the pull Derrick had, they didn't have to wait in line at all. He simply walked right up to the front of the line as if it didn't exist. As soon as a bald headed, three hundred pound bouncer spotted Derrick, he nodded, indicating that he was aware of who he was. He came right over, shook hands with him, and immediately granted him access to go in.

Squeezing through the club, the sounds of voices could be heard clearly by both male and female. The women were desperately trying to get their attention, hoping that they could get them in the club as well. As far as the guys that were waiting in line, most of them had to have been drinking hater-aid that night because they began to mouth off. Derrick wasn't really tripping off it because he was used to haters hating, but one cat just wouldn't shut the fuck up.

"Why y'all bitches hawking these fake ass hustlers! Them niggas ain't shit!" His remark stopped Derrick dead in his tracks.

"Who the fuck you talking 'bout, nigga?" he growled.

"I'm talking about you two bitches! Why, you got a problem with what I said?" the guy shot back.

"C'mon, D! Leave them clown ass niggas outside where they belong! Them bitch ass niggas ain't on our level, homie!" Sean replied, tugging on his partner's jacket. Although Derrick didn't say another word, Sean knew he was heated as fuck.

Once they entered the club, it was as if they stepped into another dimension. Sean was completely in awe. He hadn't seen anything like it in a long time, except every Saturday night on Soul Train. Even that didn't come close to what he witnessed at the moment. Women were parading around in practically nothing. Thighs, cleavage, and ass cheeks were sprinkled all throughout the club. This is truly the place to be, thought Sean. He was confident that he'd leave the club with something exotic.

The deep bass from the club's system was truly a force to be reckoned with. Bumping through the speakers was the sounds of St. Louis' very own icon, Nelly. As the music vibrated throughout Derrick's body, he quickly forgot about the incident that had just taken place less than five minutes ago, not Sean who had just left a place where a simple argument such as that could have easily escalated into something else.

As Derrick continued to navigate his way through the crowd, Sean followed, observing everyone that was in seeing eye distance. The relatively dim lighting made it somewhat hard to see past 20 feet. The one thing that shocked him most was the fact that it looked as if everyone he passed had a blunt or joint in his or her hand, smoking as if it was legal.

"I got a surprise fo' you, S!" Derrick said as he looked back in Sean's direction.

"What?" Sean yelled, attempting to out talk the music. It was so loud that he couldn't hear a word Derrick had just said.

"I SAID I GOT A SURPRISE FOR YOU!" replied Derrick. "FOLLOW ME!"

# The Hustle

A few seconds later, they were walking into an off limit, exclusive part of the club that was set up especially for them. The VIP section. The section was a nice sized room that had the biggest view window ever. Inside, Sean could look out its window and see practically the entire club. In the VIP room, the volume on the music was set at a moderate tone so that conversations could easily be heard without yelling. Now that he was finally able to hear, Derrick began to talk at a normal tone.

"You know I had to welcome you home the right way," he said, referring to the bottles of champagne along with the huge sign that read, Welcome Home, Sean!

Another bouncer, similar looking to the one that controlled the club's entrance, re-hooked the velvet rope that was connected to two knee-hi gold posts that sat in front of the VIP's doorway as soon as Derrick and Sean entered. The VIP area was set up like a plush living room that was extremely cozy. There was a huge flat screen television mounted on the wall that played the most graphic soft porn and uncut videos, and there were fine honies that lounged on the sofas sipping on every drink Club Liquid had to offer, courtesy of Derrick.

Scoping out all the beautiful women that mingled in the room, Sean had a hard time choosing where he wanted to cop a seat until he found a few that seized his attention.

"Where we sitting at?" Derrick questioned.

"What about right there?" he replied.

"That's what's up then! It's your night, big homie!" With each step, he took toward the two fine, olive honeys sitting in a booth seat, Sean took notice to how his feet literally sunk into the dark green, thick cushioned carpet. He loved the fact that there were mirrors all around the walls because it made it easier to watch his surroundings.

As soon as he took a seat, one female immediately began to pour him a glass of Ciroc.

"What's up, Derrick. So, this is the brother you've been bragging about all this time, huh? Damn, you forgot to mention he was this fine!"

"Sean, this is Stacy. Stacy, this is Sean." He was mesmerized at how beautiful she truly was. On the outer surface, she appeared to be perfect. Her skin complexion was the color of caramel honey. Sean imagined that she probably tasted as sweet as honey, too. Her perfect sized titties looked so soft, firm, and succulent. There was no doubt about it; they were 100 percent real. Sean thought to himself how he would definitely add Ms. Stacy to his women-to-fuck list because that night he was trying to fuck a few of her boss' customers, not the help.

"What can I get y'all?" she asked with her hand on her hip.

"Where's Felix at, Stacy?" Derrick asked.

"Oh, he hasn't made it in yet. But, I'll be sure to send him over as soon as he gets in. Now, what do you want, Derrick? And, for the last time, pussy isn't on the menu."

"Damn! What makes you think I was about to ask you for some?"

"Well, the fact that you do every time your ass is up in here may have something to do with me thinking thoughts such as that," she stated sarcastically. "You know damn well that shit isn't happening, so let's move on already!"

"Stacy, why you always acting so mean? I know somebody that'll put a smile on that pretty little face of yours," he said, looking over at Sean. "But for now, bring us a couple more bottles of Ciroc and some Henny. Also, send some more of those bad ass bitches back here, it's a celebration!"

"I'll see what I can do, boy," she replied while staring at Sean the entire time. Something about him looked very inviting to her. When she walked away, she put an extra lil' some'n some'n in her walk. The girls at the table turned their noses up at her.

"Damn, nigga! Stacy is hawking yo ass like crazy! I been trying to hit that ever since I met her ass. She just won't fuck with a nigga like me for some reason."

"Baby, you don't have to worry about that bitch not wanting to fuck with you because there's a gang of other fine bitches, like myself, in line waiting to get her turn." A cocoa complexioned honey boldly stated before pouring Derrick and herself another glass of Ciroc.

He wasn't really feeling her, so he didn't reply to her statement. In his eyes, she had an average look about her. The type of look that came a dime a dozen. Therefore, she would be his last alternative. The only reason he didn't run her off was because she was easy on the eyes, and, it was a celebration in which everybody was invited.

"Man, I have to tell you, Ms. Stacy's about that work. I'm talking major figures, dirty!"

"Aw yeah! Well, I'll just have to catch up with her later. But, right now, I'm trying to hit some'n exotic tonight!" he said, eying the two females that had just entered the VIP section.

"A'ight, ladies, beat it!" Derrick stated in a playful like manner. The women that were seated at the table obviously thought he was playing because they didn't move. "Didn't y'all regular bitches hear what the fuck I just said? My man said he's trying to hit some'n exotic tonight, and being that y'all some regular looking bitches, that excludes y'all so beat it! Let them exotic bitches have that seat!" he said, flagging the two broads over that just came in. Behind them, in came two more bad, exotic looking broads. "Sean, these exotic bitches must travel in pairs, huh?" he said, waving over the other two.

As each of the females took their seats, they introduced themselves consecutively. There was Na-Na and Tasha, who sat on the same side as Derrick. Then, there was Adrian and Monae, who sat next to Sean. Each of the women were equally beautiful and openly flirtatious amongst themselves and the men as well. At that time, the only thing in Sean's mind was how he could persuade the two women to go home with him. Sean wasn't hip to the fact that some women were down for things like that without having to be convinced or tricked into a ménage.

Sean was instantly attracted to Monae's looks because she looked a bit more exotic. She looked like she'd been born and raised on one of those beautiful islands with long, silky, jet black hair that came slightly past her shoulders, skin golden brown, looking as if it had been kissed by the sun with eyes almost the color of her skin. She stood five feet, four inches tall, weighing about a hundred and twenty five pounds. For such a small frame, Monae's body was extremely curvaceous and she had strong, model like features.

As far as Adrian, it was obvious that she was half-black, but what he wasn't sure of is what else she was mixed with. Her ass was much bigger than Monae's, which gained her a few extra points with Sean because he was truly an ass man. She was a yellow-bone chick with chinky eyes and smooth, baby like skin. Sean could tell she was hairy because of the amount of hair that was on her arms. He loved hairy women! The DJ put on one of Sean's favorite songs It's *Going Down Tonight* Celly Cell. He looked over at Derrick immediately after the song began to play. Derrick nodded.

# The Hustle

After the first few shots of Henny and the couple of glasses of Ciroc, Sean slowly began to loosen up and flirted back with the women. From time to time, he would catch Derrick peering over at him, checking out how he worked his mojo with the ladies. The two women Derrick had under his arms turned out to be super freaks, especially after the liquor took kicked in.

It didn't take long for Sean to figure out that the two women were bi-sexual.

Between the music, the videos, the liquor, and the women, the entire scene had become very hypnotizing to Sean. By that time, the VIP room had become profusely packed with more women who also showed interest in the contest that was going on. Everything that was going on in the club seemed so surreal to Sean. Other players in the game were also being recognized as they entered the private party. By the time mafuckas were smoking Dro, popping X, drinking, and freaking like there was no tomorrow, Felix walked in showing love to every important person in the VIP room, starting with Derrick.

After the two embraced, Derrick introduced Sean as his brother, speaking very highly of him. Felix shook his hand and then gave him one of his business cards, telling him if he ever needed anything not to hesitate to call. Any brother of Derrick's was like a brother of his. Then, he began to talk to Derrick about Sean as if he wasn't sitting right there.

"Derrick, I like our brother. I look at him, and instantly, I see he good man. Maybe someday we can do business together, like you and I," he continued, looking Derrick in his eyes. "Welcome home, me brother, drinks are on de house!" he said in a heavy Spanish accent.

Three hours later, everyone in the VIP section was pissy drunk and high as a test pilot. Derrick knew Sean was ready to shake the spot with the two ladies that were hanging on each of his arms, so he gave him the okay to take the rental on to the hideout. He, himself, had plans of lying up in a nice four-star hotel with, both Na-Na and Tasha.

# Chapter Four

As the morning sunlight played a game of peeping Tom through the sheer curtains, it caused Sean to wake from a blissful, eventful dream. The dream consisted of him having his way with two very beautiful women. Looking to the left and right side of him, he realized that it wasn't a dream. What he experienced was real. The throbbing headache he was experiencing had him struggling to remember. He struggled with the questions of whose bed he was in, how'd he get there, and where was Derrick? For the life of him, he could not remember anything that transpired after he left the club.

"Damn! That fuckin' Ciroc and Henny mixed ain't shit to be fucked with," he spoke aloud to no one in particular as he got up to use the bathroom. He picked up his watch to find out the time. While doing so, his leg accidentally grazed up against Monae's leg, which was hanging off the side of the bed. As their flesh touched, he thought about how good it felt just rubbing up against a women's soft, sensual skin. .

The time on his watch read 9:17 a.m. Sean grabbed his phone to find out that he had several missed calls. The frequent moving of the bed instantly grabbed Monae's attention, which caused her to reach out and touch Sean's thigh. Feeling her hand on his thigh gave him an erection. He thought about how, just two days ago, he was sleeping alone in prison on a thin ass mattress, fantasizing about being with a woman again. Adrian was out like a light, and none of the motion on the bed affected her whatsoever.

"Sup, boo? You know yo' phone was ringing like crazy last night," Monae stated as she opened her eyes.

"Man, I don't even remember. Was I that fucked up?" asked Sean.

"Yeah, you was. Me and Adrian thought you died or some shit because you wasn't responding to anything we was doing to yo' ass.

"The last thing I remember is pulling up in the garage. After that, everything else is a blank."

"Shiiit! We practically had to rape you and take that dick," she declared.

"Is that so? Looks to me like you all succeeded at whatever y'all was trying to do," he replied, while looking over at the three empty condom wrappers.

"You lucky that we were feeling you and that you have a big dick, 'cause we would've been ghost on yo' ass."

"Damn! I can't believe that I was in the middle of all this action and I don't even remember shit," Sean said, pulling the covers off her, exposing her beautiful breast. "We might have to do a replay so I can see what you working with," he continued.

 . "Boy! Stop playing, it's cold!" she barked, snatching the covers out of his hands. Next thing you knew, they began to kiss while Monae's hand found its way to Sean's rock hard manhood.

"You sure you wanna do that right now? What about yo' girl, she still sleeping?" he whispered through kisses.

"Don't worry about her, she good. Besides, I took really good care of her last night," she stated matter-of-factly as she continued to stroke Sean's shaft.

"Man. Now I'm really mad at myself for getting that drunk. I can't believe I missed out on that," he said, leaning back on the bed, she gently started to stroke his dick.

"Either I was hella high and tripping, 'cause it seemed like your dick just wouldn't stop growing!" she giggled. " I almost choked trying to deep throat this mafucka last night."

"Well I'm awake and sober now. So, let's see how far you can get 'em down right now!" With no hesitation, Monae's head ducked between Sean's legs as if she was bobbing for apples.

"Ooooh shit! Damn, yo' head game is tight, ma. That's right, suck this dick, baby." It seemed the dirtier Sean talked, the more aggressive she got with his dick. She possessed one hell of a technique. She used a massive amount of saliva, a lot of tongue, neck, and head, jacking and free styling without missing a beat. Sean wasn't used to jaws so ferocious. When he left the streets, chicks weren't taking pride in sucking a dick. All he could think about is how happy he was to finally be home.

When Monae felt Sean's body tense up, she knew he was about to come. That was when she began to suck with much more force. Her intention was to drain all of the juice from Sean's pipeline. For some reason, she was really feeling him despite the fact that she'd only known him for a few hours. To her, he seemed much different from all the other simple-minded ass dudes she'd fucked with in the past. She promised herself if he was to call her after that day, she'd really take the time to get to know him without focusing on what she could possibly get from him. Nevertheless, she knew in order for him to take her seriously, she may have to place him on pussy punishment. Anyway it went, Monae felt if for some reason he didn't call and she never saw him again, she'd be okay with the decision she made to sleep with him because that time she used a man for her own selfish desires instead of letting a man use her.

At the moment, all of that was irrelevant to her. The only thing she was concerned with was climbing on top of Sean's throbbing hunk of meat and riding the shit out of it. Getting him back hard was no problem at all. All she had to do was guide his hand down to her love nest, let him slide a finger or two inside of her so he could see for himself just how wet and hot she was for him. Realizing that they were going to need much more room than the bed possessed, Sean suggested that they take their party to the floor. He didn't want to disturb Adrian. Besides, the thick beige carpet was just as comfortable as the bed. When she stood up, Sean admired every visible part of her naked body as the sunlight danced off her skin. That got him even more excited. Her breasts were round and full, just the way he liked them.

"I want you to hit this pussy from the back," she announced, and then got on her hands and knees in a doggy style position, revealing nothing but pussy and ass. Reaching on top of the nightstand, Sean grabbed a fresh condom and carefully unrolled it. He loved the way her pussy muscles contracted as it closed in on his dick, gripping it tightly.

At first, Monae's moans started at somewhat of a

whisper. However, with each stroke he took, she got louder and louder. "Oooh, fuck me, daddy! Yes! Fuck me! Fuck me!"

"Ah, so y'all just gone fuck without me, huh?" stated Adrian. She was sitting on the bed with her legs wide open, rubbing her fingers over her clit. Her outburst caught both Sean and Monae off guard. There was no way Sean was going to let her sit there playing with herself when he was gladly willing to do it for her.

"Shiit, you can get it, too, baby. I got more than enough energy for the both of you," he boasted, while he continued to fuck Monae.

Five minutes and two nuts later, Adrian was being slammed from behind while she sucked Monae's pussy. The two women double-teamed Sean as if he was Jordan with the ball in a championship game about to score the winning point. After about three good orgasms, the girls decided that they wanted to take a shower. Of course, they invited the man of the hour. They ended up fucking in the shower as well. The only thing that took Sean's attention away from the girls was the fact that his cell wouldn't stop ringing.

"Hello," he answered, practically out of breath. All he heard was a very distraught woman on the other end of the line that was bawling her eyes out while trying to talk at the same time. "Hello. Wait, wait, wait. Calm down. Take a deep breath, then speak so I can understand you better. Who's this and what's wrong?"

"Shh...Sean. The po...po...police just called.

They said that Derrick was shot la...last night. He's in Barnes Hospital," Asia finally managed to say through tears.

"What! Ahhh, fuck no!" Sean yelled through the receiver. "I'll meet you up there, Asia. And, don't be worrying, he's going to be okay, a'ight?"

"Ooo...okay." Sean hung up without giving her chance to say another word.

As he got ready to leave, he told Monae and Adrian that he had a family emergency so they had to go as well. Being that it was Derrick's safe house, there was no way he could leave the strange women in there alone without his supervision.

Not only was he determined to be there for Derrick, he was also obligated to be there for Asia and their daughter as well. From the short conversation on the phone, it was obvious that she was going to need all the mental support she could get. Driving to the hospital, Sean prayed the entire ride over that Derrick would be okay; he just had to be.

When he finally reached the receptionist desk, he was greeted by a heavy set, middle-aged white woman who had pudgy fingers. "May I help you Sir?" She spoke politely.

"Yes, ma'am. I need some information on a patient. It's my brother. His name is Derrick Brown; I think he came in last night." As he was talking, Ms. Pudgy Fingers was rapidly pecking at the computer keys.

"Un huh. He's in ICU on the second floor," she replied as she looked on her computer screen. Sean took off like a bat out of hell heading toward the ICU.

As soon as he got off the elevator, he immediately spotted Derrick's mother. She looked as if she'd been up all night crying her eyes out. He walked right over to her and gave her a hug. Just by the looks of her mental state, it was obvious that Derrick was probably in there fighting for his life. It was the first time he'd seen Ms. Brown in ten years. It was amazing how she still looked the exact same as she did when he left ten years ago. Father Time had really been good to her. Right as Sean started in with the questions, Asia walked out of the ladies bathroom sniffling and wiping her eyes.

"The doctor said they don't know if he'll pull through. He has a bullet lodged in his heart that they're scared to touch. Sean...somebody shot my baby..." Ms. Brown stated, and then broke down into tears. Her tears caused Asia to break down as well. She disappeared back into the restroom. By that time, Ms. Brown had gotten her emotions under control. She knew she had to be strong for her son. She told Sean that Asia was really taking it harder than she expected her to and how she'd been having crying spells every ten to fifteen minutes.

"The doctor says if Derrick makes it out of his coma, he'll probably be a vegetable. I don't know if I could see him suffer like that, Sean."

Sean reached out and hugged her again. "He'll pull through, Ms. Brown. Derrick's a fighter. Is there anything you'd like me to do, Ms. Brown?"

"Nah, baby. Just being here is enough. I know how much you love Derrick. Just being here says it all, son."

Sean stayed at the hospital for the remainder of the day, just in case his extended family needed him. Unfortunately, around 11 p.m., Derrick's life expired. Sean was devastated about his friend's death, so he took it just as hard as the rest of Derrick's family. As he sat quietly in the driver's seat of the rental that Derrick let him take from the club, Sean began to feel what most would call the survivor's guilt. He felt as if it should have been him since Derrick had so much more to live for. Then, he thought about Lil' Sean, and his mother and sister. It seemed to him as if he was surrounded by death. That had him feeling very low, thinking every possible negative thought a man could imagine.

Once he snapped back to reality, he realized that he actually wasn't the blame, that maybe it was just Derrick's time to leave the face of the earth. He realized that it was all a part of God's plan and there was nothing he, nor anyone else could do about the matter.. After sitting in the car for thirty more minutes, Sean decided that it was time to go. That was when he picked the keys up off his lap and attempted to place it in the ignition. The first key wouldn't fit, so he switched to the second one. In the process of doing so, he dropped the keys in between the driver and passenger's seat. He had to get out of the car in order to reach them.

As he reached his hand under the seat, he touched the bag of money that Derrick had left in the car the night before. Pulling the bag from under the seat, he heard the keys jingle as they came in contact with the bag. Finally, with the correct key in hand, he started the ignition, put the car in gear and slowly pulled out of the parking lot. His destination was Asia's house to park the rental and pickup his car. With twenty eight thousand dollars in hand, house keys to Derrick's secret hideout , and no plan whatsoever, Sean was in deep thought, wondering what his next move would be. The only thing he was sure of was the fact that he wasn't trying to go back to hustling drugs again. For him, that part of his life was over.

# Chapter Five

A few months had passed since the death of Sean's best friend and he still couldn't believe that he was gone. Since leaving prison, he'd attended two different wakes of people that he loved dearly, Derrick and Lil' Sean.

Sean spent his days looking for a job and his nights up in VIP studios in Baden. He was desperately trying to put together a 10-songdemo to shop around. Out of the 28, 000 dollars that was inside of the rental, he only kept 10 grand, and only because Asia insisted that he do so. The rest was divided between her and Ms. Brown. Sean made a promise to himself that when his career took off, he was going to take care of his friend's kids, making sure that they didn't need or want for anything. At the moment, his money was really starting to get low so there wasn't much he could do for them or himself.

He'd already spent more than half of his savings on studio time, beats, and production. He had no idea that cutting a record would be so expensive, and the worst part about it was he wasn't even finished with his demo yet. He had no idea that the studio was overcharging him. He was just excited to be in there making his dream a reality. He didn't stop to think that the studio's manager had probably stereotyped him as a hustler because of the expensive car and all the other material items that most dope boys possessed. Maybe it was because he wasn't involved in the game, so he wasn't concerned with the attention he attracted. But, whenever someone was bold enough to approach and ask him about work, he would reply by saying, "I'm not into that, dirty."

Before Sean knew it, six more months had passed him by and he still wasn't through with his album. Either the beats weren't hot enough or the production wasn't handling their part. He was striving for perfection, and he wasn't about to settle for less. It didn't matter to him how long it took to put it together or how much money it took, he just wanted to make that good first impression because he knew just how important it was and what it could do for his career.

With two thousand dollars left to his name and still jobless, he knew he had to find employment fast, so he was out on a daily job hunt. Although he hated to, he was forced to leave the studio alone. It had been two months since his last involvement in a recording session and being away from that environment was really getting to Sean. It was like he was experiencing studio withdrawals. Deep in his heart, Sean knew he was destined to do the music thing, but it took a resource that he desperately lacked. Money.

Being that the stash house was paid for, which he found out after doing a little research, Sean didn't have to worry about a place to stay. Not that he had to worry about that, anyway, because he always had mom's spot, but he was more of the type that believed in having his own shit. If he wasn't there alone, he was more than likely enjoying the company of one of his beautiful lady friends.

There were four very dependable women in Sean's life. His mother, which of course was number one, who needed no explanation. Then came Meloney, who was Sean's little schoolgirl honey. He knew with the determination, ambition, and drive she possessed, she was destined for greatness. Ever since they first met on the Greyhound bus, she had his nose open. baby girl had him completely open. Due to her studies, they were not able to spend as much time together as they'd like to. Since he'd managed to learn and master the art of patience in prison, he was willing to wait for her. Good things always came to those who waited. If he was lucky, he got to see Meloney once a week, but if finals were coming around and the only thing he knew to expect from her was a phone call, which was also cool.

He and Meloney's relationship was mainly built by phone communication, so he became accustomed to their daily conversations. In the beginning of their friendship, they would carry on like typical teenagers, talking on the phone until the wee hours of the morning. Meloney knew staying up late would probably affect her performance in class, but she didn't care. It was as if Sean's conversation and voice was a magnet drawn to her ear. She clung to every word he spoke. Not only was the sound of his voice hypnotizing, he was also a very good listener. He would always inquire about her day and her well-being. Knowing that his words were truly sincere caused her to melt like butter whenever she talked to him.

Sean never once brought up the topic of sex in any of their conversations. There was times when Meloney would wonder if he was actually interested in her in a romantic, intimate way. He explained to her that when she was ready to move to that next level, it would be by her decision alone, not his influence. Until then, they should use this time to really get to know one another, on a deeper level. Of course, he really wanted to make love to her, but he also wanted much more than just a physical thing with her.

Most men had often said that it was the chase that kept them interested, which was somewhat true. However, for Sean, it was always about the woman that was in the chase. See, what most women failed to realize was just like men, they, too, tended to get very lax in a relationship. A good woman constantly reminded herself that there was always another woman that was willing to compete for a good man's love and affection. This thought, alone keeps her constantly on her toes, thinking of different, exciting ways to keep her man happily at home. That was the type of woman Meloney was. She wasn't afraid to be adventurous with the man that she cared for.

She loved the fact that it wasn't all about sex with Sean. Truth be told, she found him irresistible and didn't know how much longer she could carry on with the good girl role. It was extremely hard for her to keep her composure while in the presence of him. A couple of times while they were alone, she thought about stripping off all of his clothes and climbing on top of him, but she just didn't want to give him a bad impression of her. In her heart, she honestly felt that Sean would be a good husband one day. However, at that moment, it was all about school and graduating. That was number one in her life.

Then, there was Maxeen. She was also a good woman with a decent head on her shoulders. He liked the fact that she was very outspoken, held no punches, and had zero tolerance for nonsense. It was obvious that she had been through her share of problems, so it was hard for someone to pull the wool over her eyes. At first, he thought that she was just another fuck until he really got to know her. He found out very quickly that she was nothing like the woman he'd met the day he came home from prison.

Matter of fact, after that night it took him close to three months to receive any type of sexual healing. She later explained to him that what she did for him that night was like a coming home present. The next time she decided to do something, there would have to be feelings involved. That included both parties. Since the sex was so good, he had no choice but to play by her rules, if he wanted to get more of it. In the midst of playing her game, he found himself catching feelings for her. He soon found out that Maxeen was a hell of a hustler, as well, when it came to boosting high priced clothes.

It was nothing for her to go into a high dollar store and walk out with nothing but expensive, fly shit. Since she considered Sean her man, although neither of them had actually worded it in that manner, she kept him laced from head to toe. Sean thought the only downfall about her was the fact that she had to put up with a fake ass, wannabe thug baby daddy. For some reason, he just couldn't accept the fact that it was over between the two of them. Therefore, until she got that situation fully under control, Sean planned to continue feeding her with a long handle spoon. When he began to back up off her that only made Maxeen want him more. He knew she was also breaking her baby daddy off a little something something to keep him from clowning, but he also knew that she wanted to be with him.

Last, but surely not least, there was Monae. She was the one that was satisfying Sean's every desire when it came to sex. But, that was it. She was like a high-powered drug. Very addictive. What he really liked about Monae was the fact that she came with an extended feature, Adrian! She was what Sean considered a freak-a-zoid that came at his every beck and call, willing to serve him up.

Whenever he was feeling extra horny or had a taste for two women, he'd call up Monae. Being that he wasn't the type that faked the funk, Sean kept it real with each of the women, letting them all know he had other female friends. That way, there could never be a misunderstanding. So, if any unexpected visitors came into play, no one could get upset about it because they already knew the deal. As far as unexpected visitors or just popping up uninvited and unannounced, all of that was out of the question. Sean established that during the beginning. It was all about respect, which was exactly what each of his female friends displayed. They respected his wishes by calling first, mainly to avoid confrontations.

Sean still hadn't figured out what he was going to do with the nine kilos of coke that was still hidden in the pool table. He told himself if he were to sell them, it would have to be all at once. There was no way he was going to work the streets again. No amount of money was worth that. Too many bad consequences had resulted from being involved in the game. First, he was stripped of his freedom. Second, his only child and his high school sweetheart lost their lives because of the game. Last but not least, he'd also lost his best friend. Not necessarily to the game, but the circumstances of his death were surrounded by the game. Those losses were invaluable.

# Chapter Six

Finally, after countless hours of job searching, Sean got a call. A job offer came through for a service station clerk at a Vickers service station on the south side of town. Since he was literally down to his last few dollars, he accepted the offer and started working immediately. Working the three to eleven shifts wasn't the shift he really wanted, but since he desperately needed the ends, he took it. While on the job, he met and became friends with an employee name Gerald.

After getting to know Gerald, Sean found out that he, too, recently came home from doing a bid. He did five years in the feds for possession with intent to distribute. Being that they had so much in common, Sean instantly took a liking to Gerald. Mainly because he reminded Sean of Derrick. They were the same height, had the same complexion and Gerald even sported his hair in dreadlocks, like Derrick. However, they weren't as long as Derrick's.

The two of them began to hang out after work, doing

things that friends did. Sean introduced Gerald to Adrian, and the two hit it off instantly. Gerald was one of those guys that knew personally, or could tell you, about every well-known street hustler in the Lou. Let him tell it, before he went to the feds he was serving them all. There may have been some truth to part of Gerald's story, but Sean knew somewhere along the line like most convicts did while telling their version, Gerald put a remix on it.

While at work, Sean did witness various people approach Gerald quite often asking about work. He would play it off and act as if he hadn't seen nor heard anything. He wanted Gerald to think that he was green to the game. Sean put two and two together, and came up with his conclusion that Gerald had to have been selling drugs out of the job. He never actually saw a hand-to-hand deal, but the signs were obvious.

That was how Sean found out that there was a drought going on. He overheard Gerald telling someone that the drought had everything all fucked up. Little did Gerald know, the answers to all of his problems were right in front of him. Sean thought about turning him onto the product he had, but decided against it because he knew Gerald couldn't possibly afford to buy it all, let alone a single kilo. Besides, Gerald was entirely too careless and sloppy with the way he handled business. That would only lead to the both of them going back to prison. And that was not part of the plan.

After a month of watching all the cash that came and went, which could've been in his pocket, Sean brainstormed and came up with an idea on how to get it. All he had to do was figure out a way to bring his proposal to the table and not offend Gerald at the same time. Sean knew that most hustlers tended to carry an ego complex and weren't too fond of the idea of working for someone close to them.

It was rather a delicate issue to tackle being that he had convinced Gerald that he was a square cat from the county, whose people happened to be well off. When they were sharing stories about their lives, Sean failed to mention his criminal behavior.

"Hey, Gerald, what's up with all those cats that be coming up here talking to you? What you up to? I mean, if you feel that it's none of my business, that's understandable, too. I just like to know the kind of company I'm keeping and what I'm around."

"There's no need to worry yourself, county boy, I'm not gone get you in trouble," he said, laughing, "Nah, but seriously, though. I used to hustle with them lil' niggas before I went to the feds. They just be checking with me trying to see if I have any work. But, you being from the county and all, you probably wouldn't know nothing about that," he joked.

*Nigga, I've probably than sold more dope and seen more drug money than you've seen in your entire career,* thought Sean. It was hilarious to him how Gerald thought he was some major boss hustler.

Unlike Gerald, Sean had tucked his ego away a long time ago. He knew how to separate personal issues from business, which was exactly what he was about to do. He knew he had to come clean about the drugs he had if he ever wanted to get rid of them. And, it was the perfect time to do so. He decided to have a serious talk with him that night after work at the place he felt the most comfortable at, his spot.

"So, what was so important that you had to discuss it tonight, my nigga?" he asked Sean after he walked into his crib.

"Damn, nigga, sit down, have a drink with me. We'll

get to it." After filling two shot glasses with Hennessy, Sean took a seat across from Gerald. Gerald pulled out a sack of weed and a box of cigarillos. "Look, man, I have to fess up about a few things, dirty. First of all, I lied to you about some things." In the middle of rolling a blunt, Gerald stopped and looked up at Sean.

"Ah yeah, about what?" he asked with an inquisitive look on his face.

"You remember when I told you that I was out of town for the last ten tears? That wasn't exactly true. The truth is, I was in the pen on drug charges." Gerald had a strange look on his face. One that Sean found uncomfortable. "Why you looking at me like that?"

"You must think I'm stupid or something, huh? What, you thought I didn't already know that shit? You think I'd put my business out in the streets like that and not know the company I'm keeping? I didn't just start doing this shit, dirty. I was just waiting on you to come clean." His comment had caught Sean totally off guard. It never occurred to him that Gerald might have done a little investigating himself.

"Nah, man, it's just that I've lost a lot fucking around in the game. I was trying to let the past stay the past, you feel me?"

"I can understand what you're saying, and I respect it, but real friends don't keep shit like that from one another."

"Yeah, I know. That's why I had to holla at you. I been overhearing you talking to yo' cats about it being a drought. What if I told you that I could produce rain? What if I told you that I could get my hands on some A-1 yay yo?"

"My only response would be what's the fuckin' hold up, playboy?"

## The Hustle

"Hold up now. Listen, I'm only doing this to get the rest of the money to finish up my album. After that, I'm out, man."

"A'ight, a'ight, I catch yo drift. Now, like I said before, what's the hold up?" he replied with a huge grin on his face.

"The only thing about it is my people is asking for thirty a key since it's a drought. Now, before I place a order, can you handle that price?"

"You said it's A-1, right? Well, we good then."

"Okay. Since I'm off tomorrow, just meet me here when you get off work. I should have a brick for starters. And, don't forget to bring a scale, too."

"What! Now you trying to rush a nigga off? You must got something poppin' tonight."

"Some'n like that. I got Meloney coming through. I'm hoping to finally get some action tonight."

Damn, nigga, you still haven't tapped that ass yet? Let me find out yo ass is fo' real one of them game drunk country boys." They both laughed.

"Nah, but fo' real though, that's my boo, dirty. I wasn't trying to rush shit. But, a nigga in desperate need of some sexual healing. So tonight, I'm 'bout to say fuck all that gentlemen shit; I'm trying to crush some'n!"

"Alrighty then," Gerald said, gathering up his weed and blunts, and putting it back in a plastic baggy. "I'll get at you tomorrow then, my nigga."

Once Gerald was gone, Sean let out a relieving sigh. Then, a devious smile came across his face as he thought about the possibilities of knocking off all nine kilos without having to personally distribute a grain of the dope. He would finally be able to finish off his long awaited album.

Staring out of his living room window, Sean watched

Gerald get into his crème colored convertible 5.0 mustang. He was hoping that he hadn't made the wrong choice by hooking up with Gerald. There was no turning back now that the line had been crossed. All he could do was play his hand and hope in the end that he came out a winner.

One hour later, Meloney walked in looking stunning as usual, working the shit out of a tight fitting, sky blue Chanel dress with a pair of matching six inch Chanel heels. Sean had informed her that they would be visiting an upscale restaurant and that she should wear something nice, but comfortable. She was hoping that she hadn't over dressed for the occasion. Little did she know the upscale restaurant he said they would attend was in fact his house.

Looking at how truly sexy she was made Sean's mouth water. She looked tastier than his favorite dish. He loved the fact that she decided to wear her hair up because it catered to her exotic facial features.

"Hey, baby." she said excitedly as she embraced him.

"Damn, boo. You looking and smelling good as a mafucka! What perfume is that you rocking?" he said after their embrace was broken.

"Ahh, just some Chanel No. 5. Why, you like?" she replied nonchalantly.

"Hell yeah! Baby girl, you smell good enough to eat!"

"Boyyy, you know you silly," she cooed.

"Well then, just call me a silly, serious mafucka 'cause I'm dead serious, ma," he replied, pulling her closer in his arms. The two instantly began to indulge in a passionate kiss, and then all of a sudden she pushed back.

"What's wrong, baby?"

"Nothing. I...I just thought we were going out to dinner."

"We are. Everything is taken care of, c'mere," he said, taking her by the hand to lead her into the kitchen where he spent the last hour preparing their delicious looking meal. Her face lit up when she saw the feast they were about to enjoy.

"So, you been in here bur... I mean cooking, huh?" she said, laughing.

"Okay. Now you got jokes, huh?" he said, pulling her into his arms again.

"You know I'm just playing, baby. It smells and looks good. Or, maybe I'm just hungry," she joked again.

"Well, maybe that's it because from the looks of those skin and bones on your body, you sure could use a bite, or two, or three to eat," he joked back. "Ouch!" he squealed after she punched his arm. "I was just playing, sweetheart," he said, kissing her soft lips, "Go on in the living room, make yourself comfortable, and I'll call you when it's ready, okay?"

"You probably just don't want me to see the containers that the food came in," she joked as she walked out of the kitchen.

"Un-un, ma, I cooked this myself. That's on my son, may he rest in peace," he replied.

"Sean, what did I tell you about saying all of that!" she said, sticking her head back into the kitchen. "I believe you, baby. I just be joking, that's all. Damn, don't you know me by now? I know what it is, you have me mixed up with those other females you be seeing." Knowing exactly where the conversation would lead, Sean decided to stop her before she went there.

"C'mon now, Meloney, don't go there. You know

we've already discussed this a million times. Whenever you tell me you're ready to take this relationship to that next level, my female friends are out of the picture, okay?" he said, walking over to where she stood.

"I know, I know. Now, go on finish playing chef 'cause I'm hungry, baby!" she said, pushing him gently toward the kitchen.

"Okay, with yo' lil hungry ass," he stated, causing her to burst into laughter.

"Boy, you are so silly! Have you ever thought about becoming a comedian?"

"Man, you just on fire tonight with yo lil' jokey jokes, huh?" he commented, and then kissed her lips one more time.

"C'mon now, baby. I'm hungry fo' real." She was pouting.

"Okay. Okayyyy!" When Meloney turned to leave, Sean playfully slapped her on her behind, and then watched it jiggle as she walked away. In the back of his mind, he was hoping that he finally got some of her good loving because he was in desperate need of it.

For their dinner, Sean prepared steaks medium well smothered in onions and mushrooms with baked potato, cheese, and sour cream. He also prepared a Caesar salad, which was devoured as soon as he sat it in front of Meloney. Thanks to the help of his mother that coached him over the phone, everything had been cooked precisely.

"So, what do you think about the food, do you still think it's take out?"

"Nah, baby. I know you cooked it, and it's delicious," she managed to ease out after swallowing what was left of the food that was inside her mouth. "I must admit that you didn't strike me as the type of person that could cook."

"Why is that, because I ran the streets all day hustlin'?"

"Something like that. I mean, every Black man I know who hustles, they're usually the ones who's always looking for a woman that can cook."

"The thing about me that you'll soon find out is, I'm nothing like any of those other guys. Matter of fact, I'm positive that you'll never meet another man like me in this lifetime."

"So tell me, Mr. Martin, what makes you so different and what makes you unique?" She put her fork down and gave Sean her undivided attention. While gazing into his dark brown eyes, she felt like he was slowly hypnotizing her. All she could focus on was his sexy, full lips that seemed as if they were moving in slow motion. She struggled to catch the words that were coming from his mouth. She was too busy being turned on by his lips. She wondered what they would feel like kissing all over her body.

"Meloney, Meloney! Did you hear what I just said?" he asked, breaking her trance.

"Of course, I heard you, baby. You said the difference between you and other guys is that you were put on this earth especially for me and that we're soul mates." She fired back without missing a beat, letting him know that he has her undivided attention. "Baby, you have to excuse me. I have to use thebathroom." Before he could reply, she got up and walked toward the bathroom.

"A'ight, sweetheart. I'll be in the living room putting in a movie," he yelled out to her.

A few seconds later, she snuck up behind the love seat Sean was sitting on. She leaned over and kissed his cheek. In an instant, his nature began to rise. He suspended the thought because he figured it would only be a waste of time. He had become very familiar with Meloney's infamous dick tease. By then, he was used to it so it really didn't matter anymore. Although he was willing to wait, he felt that the waiting game was getting old. He sure didn't think taking it slow meant six months of nothing- no sex, no oral pleasure, nothing. He desperately wanted to make love to her.

Recently, he had made up his mind to give her another month, and if nothing happened by then he'd back up off her so she could see what she'd be missing without him. Sensing a little resistance, Meloney leaned in and kissed him again. That time on the lips. Sean instantly detected a difference in the second kiss. It felt like she was more into it that time. He braced himself, waiting for the resistant wall she usually put up. To his surprise, she didn't stop.

Seconds later, she was sitting on his lap straddling him as they continued to kiss. Then, she did something she'd never done before; she began to explore his body, starting with his chest. All of a sudden, she stopped and got up off his lap. She could tell Sean was about to get upset by his facial expression. Then, when she pulled him up off the sofa by the hand and started walking toward the bedroom, he knew that something was about to go down. If she had looked back at his facial expression, she would have noticed the huge smile on his face. I'm 'bout to tear this pussy up, he thought as he slapped her on the ass.

As soon as they stepped foot into the bedroom, she threw Sean down on the bed. "Who are you and what have you done to Meloney?" he joked.

"I'm sorry, but she's no longer with us. Kiss me and tell me if you could tell the difference between the two of us," she replied. Sean was at a loss for words. He knew he was about to enter a world he'd longed for, for so many nights, but had never been invited.

"You talking to me?" he asked in a playful manner while pointing to himself.

"Yeah, silly! And, you better hurry up before Meloney decides to show up and ruin the party."

Sean pulled her on top of him and immediately devoured her lips. The energy between the two of them was out of this world. For many different reasons Meloney held back her affection from Sean, but she planned to let go completely. While entangled in a passionate kiss, she began to tug at his fabrics as if she was trying to rip them off his body.

Sean was also busy exploring. His hands caressed every inch of her temple, equally satisfying every part it touched. Her breasts were like a music instrument in which he eagerly began to play. Throughout the midst of their tongue love, he ended up on top of her. Removing her dress, Sean gently planted kisses on her upper body, slowly working his way down to that beautifully manicured island between her legs. Reaching her mid section, his tongue danced to its own rhythm around the outer surface of her belly button. The coolness of his tongue caused her body to quiver.

As he came to her love nest, he was made aware of the degree of her wetness because her juices had erupted like a volcano and overflowed onto her inner thighs. While watching Sean work his magic tongue, she firmly planted her hand on top of his head. The more intense it got, the deeper she tried to bury his head inside her womb. It seemed like forever since someone had touched the spot she considered sacred to her. The feeling was so wonderful that she began to let out tears of joy. Right then and there, she made up her mind that Sean would be the only man privileged enough to touch her body for as long as she lived.

The pleasurable sensation she received had proven to be more than she'd expected, "Oooh! Oooh shit! Stop! Sean, please, stop," she requested, but at the same time pushing his head further into her vagina. All of that confused the hell out of Sean. He didn't know whether to stop or keep going.

"Damn, Meloney, what's wrong now?" he said in a slightly aggravated tone.

"Nothing. I'm sorry. I don't really want you to stop. It just feels so good that I got confused," she said, gasping for air, "Sean, I love you. I love you so much. I want you to make love to me right now, baby." Those words sounded like magic to Sean's ears. He'd been waiting to hear Meloney say that for the longest time. He, too, felt as if she was the right one for him.

Making love to Meloney was truly heaven on earth. It was everything he'd dreamed it would be and more. They made love for hours, giving each other pleasure beyond measure. Every time Sean would climax, he was so turned on that his manhood would instantly become erect again, causing his sexual performance to seem like a miraculous act. After their love making session was complete, they both just laid there silently listening to each other's heartbeat while holding one another, savoring the moment.

# Chapter Seven

The next morning, Sean woke up feeling fresh and rejuvenated. Almost like a new man. He understood that he could never love another woman the way he loved Cynthia, but he strongly believed that he could learn to love Meloney just as much. He was grateful that it was Saturday because he planned to do nothing but lounge around the house and enjoy his company. It was a beautiful Saturday morning, especially waking up to a woman as wonderful as Meloney cooking breakfast in nothing but one of his tee shirts.

A cool breeze flowed freely through the open kitchen window. The strong smell of bacon nestled the air, causing his stomach to react with a growl. "What you call yourself doing?" he asked, sneaking up behind and wrapping his arms around her. Being caught completely off guard, Meloney jumped at his touch and the sound of his voice. She thought he was still lying in bed asleep.

"Dang, baby! You scared me!" she said as she turned to face him. Before she could say another word, he kissed her. The kiss was so intense it nearly took her breath away. "So, you finally decided to wake up, huh?"

"Yeah. I would've been up, but I was sleeping so good I didn't want to get up. Last night was the best sleep I've gotten since I've been home, thanks to you," he replied while gently grabbing her face with both hands and kissing her on the forehead.

"I should be the one thanking you. The way you put it down on me last night, it was long overdue!" They embraced each other. "Wait a minute! Did you just do what I thought you did?

"What are you talking bout, baby?" Sean asked with a puzzled look on his face.

"Did you just kiss me on the forehead?"

"Girl, quit playing. You had me going, thinking I did some'n really wrong."

"I told you not to take everything serious all the time, baby. But, fo' real, though, I can't get my mind off of last night. Speaking of doing something wrong, I can't recall that. But, I can tell you what you did right," she said, grabbing his crouch.

"Oh yea, and what's that, lil' mama?"

"The way you sucked on this pussy and caused me to have multiple orgasms. I think that was just a once in a lifetime, lucky shot. I bet you can't do that again!" she challenged.

"Oh! So, you're challenging the kid, huh?" he said, pointing to himself and imitating a wrestler.

"Yeah! Put yo money where yo mouth is...or better yet, put yo tongue where my pussy is."

"Ding! Ding! Ding! Sounds like a round two coming up. I was hoping I get to punish that ass before you left for Kansas City this afternoon." By that time, he had both of his hands all over her ass cheeks, caressing them.

"First, we have to eat breakfast, then we might, and I strongly state might, have time for a little somethin' somethin'," she replied with a smile on her face. The truth of the matter was, Meloney knew she wasn't about to go out of town for two weeks and not get another dose of that good dick before she left.

"Speaking of breakfast, I'm hungry as a hostage, ma. What you done hooked up anyway? It smells kinda good?"

""Well, let's see, I got some pancakes, bacon, and eggs."

"Cool. I'ma go hop in this shower and..."

Meloney kissed his lips and stopped him from speaking another word.

"I thought you said you wanted to go another round? Let me find out you really can't handle this nookie!" she playfully stated.

"I do wanna go another round. I just kinda got the feeling that you'd duck rec because of the way I had you practically scaling the walls last night." They both laughed.

"Shiiit, boyyy! It's been a long time since I've had some, plus Yo' thing all..., I'm cool now that I know what to expect. I just gotta relax my, then it's all good."

"Well shit, let's go then!" he suggested, grabbing ahold of her waist.

"Wait a minute! First, let's eat some breakfast, then we'll make love?" she said, kissing his lips.

"Whatever you wanna do, ma."

"Baybee, now you know since we crossed over to the next level, we're together, right? I mean, that's the way I would like for it to be because I'm not trying to share you with your other little friends. I've been hurt far too many times in my life, Sean, so I'm letting you know right now,

I'm not about to put up with no bullshit from you, nor no other man ever again. I can do bad by myself." The look on Meloney's face was stern and serious. The pain was clearly still there, but Sean was determined to heal her broken heart.

"Slow down, baby," he spoke while gently touching the side of her face. "I've been hurt before, too, and I know how it feels. I can promise you that I'll never bring your heart any more pain."

"As long as we got an understanding, we straight, boo. I don't want to sound like no control freak, but as far as those other females, I'll give you the time you need to get that situation straightened out. 'Cause I'm definitely not trying to share my man nor catch any thing, you feel me?"

"Of course, I feel you, baby! But, what I really wanna feel is your insides again," he stated softly in her ear.

After they finished breakfast, Sean and Meloney made love intensely for 45 minutes straight as if that was the last time they'd be together. Once they showered, he drove her to the Greyhound bus station downtown on Cass Avenue. They arrived five minutes before her bus was scheduled to depart, so there was really no time for long goodbyes. Meloney boarded the bus with a duffle bag full of her personal belongings that her roommate was generous enough to drop off while Sean was still sleeping. She never planned to spend the night last night, but after they made love there was no way she could just up and leave. The mood felt too right.

Now that she was about to board the bus, she was having second thoughts about leaving. Especially since she admitted her feelings, she knew she was very much in love with him and she didn't want to spend another day, let alone two weeks, away from him. Her thoughts and feelings were really making her departure very complicated.

\* \* \* \* \*

When Gerald arrived later that evening, Sean had the product already sitting on the kitchen table, waiting to be prepared and bagged for sales. Gerald was completely in awe when he inspected the coke and saw how good the quality was. It was nothing like the product he was used to getting. Most of the dope he'd gotten his hands on was cut at least four to five times before it even reached him. He knew the product was as close to grade A as possible, which only meant the crack dealers and the smokers both were about to go crazy over it .

"So, what's up? What you think?" asked Sean, finding it hard to read Gerald's facial expression.

"Damn, Sean, what the fuck you do, go to Cuba and get this shit?"

"Nah, G, my peoples just come through like that, know what I mean? But, get this, dude said he only got like eight more birds left, and how fast we move this one will determine if he'll save 'em for us."

"Shit, you ain't gotta say no mo', this mafucka'll be gone like tomorrow night 'round this time," Gerald enthusiastically stated.

"You sho? 'Cause if I tell 'em that, then that's exactly what he'll be expecting."

"Don't sweat the small stuff, homie, this shit is gone already. We just waiting on niggas to come pick it up, you feel me?" he replied with confidence.

"Okay then, this is how we gone play this. Since I'm not the type that likes to keep all of my eggs in one basket, I'll give you eighteen, and I'll keep the other half. So, when you're done with those, just hit me up then I'll swoop through, collect, and drop off, 'cause this is the last time we'll meet here, a'ight?" Sean replied, afterwards noticing that he was starting to sound more and more like the old Sean that was once heavy in the game and giving out orders.

"I'ma be real with you, dirty, thirty a key is high as fuck, but since it's a drought I'll roll with it. Plus, it looks like it's some fire, so we all good. Oh, I forgot to tell you that I'm vicious with the whip game, so I'm probably gone stretch this eighteen into 24, if that's cool with you. And, don't worry about the scratch because the first eighteen I make, I'm shooting it straight to you."

"That whip shit is all on you, G. Just as long as you handle business, I'm good with it. What we'll do is split the profit in half after we deduct the thirty. You know I gotta make some'n. Look, I know how niggas feel as far as working for another nigga and shit, but it's not like that between you and I. I don't think I'm better than you or no bullshit like that. It's just that you seem to have all the clientele, you will probably be moving mostly all the work. But, don't get it fucked up; I'm not fucked up about getting out there making it happen. It'll just take longer, and by then those other bricks will be gone. And, I'm sure that you can use the extra ends just like I can. We friends first and foremost, so don't let this business come between that. I've seen a lot of genuine friendships get torn apart over this white bitch right here," he said, pointing at the kilo that sat on the table. "I don't want us to fall victim to this bitch as well."

"You don't have to worry about that shit with me. Them type of niggas was suckers, no disrespect to yo old partners, but I'm not cut like that, Sean," he said, looking directly in his eyes. Sean sensed truth in them. So, he decided to be truthful as well.

## The Hustle

"I believe you. Plus I did my homework on yo background, so I already know you's a stand-up type of dude, and you're used to getting it big. So, I'ma be honest with you, too. After these keys are gone, I really don't know if there will be more, so take that info and run with it, a'ight?"

"That means I have to get on my grind, then. By the time we get done pumping all this shit, I should have well over enough ends to do my thang, so I'm cool. But, what about you? Will you be able to finish up that record?"

"I don't know. Hopefully, I'll have enough money to finish it, and then I can put all of this bullshit behind me."

"Well then, what the fuck we still sitting around gossipin' like some old ass ladies? Let's get this shit weighed up in halves and wholes so I can do what I do best!"

"That's what I'm talking 'bout!" Sean stated, giving Gerald dap. He never figured meeting Gerald would be a blessing in disguise. The big gamble he was making just had to pay off.

Forty-five minutes later, they had half of the key bagged up and ready for distribution. The fumes from the powder lingered in the air so heavy that they both had to wear facemasks to keep from catching a contact. In addition, to keep the substance from entering their system, they decided to wear protective Latex gloves. Gerald told Sean he decided to knock off the first key in order to build clientele, and then he'd whip the rest up so that he could see a profit.

As Sean continuously scooped a playing card into the white mountain of coke that was spread out all over the glass kitchen table, he thought back when he used to weigh up bird after bird in his mother's basement. That

97

was the only place where he didn't have to worry about being bothered. The hundreds of hours he'd spent dealing with the illegal substance brought back memories, both good and bad. It caused him to remember a promise he'd made to himself and recently broke. He promised himself that he'd never touch dope again. However, he never anticipated nine keys being practically dropped in his lap, either.

Losing Derrick was devastating. Day after day Sean has had thoughts about that night at the club. He wished he could somehow rewind the hands of time and bring him back. Since that wasn't possible, he knew he had to hold it down for his best friend. Thinking about all that had transpired since his release had him teary eyed. But, the main reason why he was about to shed tears was because he realized that the streets had somehow gotten ahold of him once again.

"What's up, dog, you a'ight?" Gerald asked, noticing the spaced out look on his face.

"Shit, I'm cool. Here, finish weighing up this shit, I gotta use the bathroom." He then handed Gerald the playing card that was in his hand. Since the bathroom that was adjacent to his bedroom was closest, he decided to use it. Upon entering the bathroom, he immediately thought about Derrick, wondering if he'd ever slept in his bed or was this house used exclusively for stash purposes only.

After relieving himself, he washed his hands, and then took a handful of water and splashed it on his face. The cold water was equivalent to a hard smack in the face. It instantly woke him from the daze he was just in. Leaving the restroom, Sean felt like a new man. When he entered back into the living room, he was glad to see that Gerald was just about finished bagging up the dope.

## The Hustle

He liked the fact that Gerald didn't indulge in any drugs, whatsoever. If he had, there was no way he would've trusted his freedom with a user. He didn't knock users, but he knew when it came to making decisions, the drugs always distorted the user's decision-making skills. He just couldn't take a chance on someone like that. In addition, that was truly unacceptable, especially with what he was trying to accomplish.

After the product was bagged, Gerald wasted no time. He immediately began to make calls to potential customers. When he got off the phone, he told Sean that he had some business to take care of and that he'd get with him later. "A'ight G, be careful and umh, call me when you get to where you're going to let me know you made it there safe, a'ight?"

"A'ight, my nigga. What, you in for the night or somethin'?"

"Yeah, man. I think I'ma just chill and check out these lil' flicks I rented. Shiiit! I might just call Maxeen and see what's poppin' with her," Sean retorted, thinking back to the last time they were together intimately.

"A'ight, be easy!" Gerald said right before closing the door.

Once Gerald was gone, he went right to work cleaning his kitchen table and anywhere else, he thought drugs might have somehow escaped to. He had no plans of leaving any type of drugs or paraphernalia lying around where he rested. Satisfied that his place was clean and kosher, he called Maxeen.

"Hello," she answered in her sweet, sultry voice. Sean had no idea that a man could actually fall in love with a woman's voice. That was, until he heard Maxeen speak.

"Hey, sexy, this Sean. S'up with you, did I catch you

at a bad time?"

"Naw, you okay. Actually, I was kinda hoping that you'd call. I called you last night, but you didn't answer so I figured you had company. I wanted to talk to you about something."

"Well, here I am, baby. I'm listening."

"Naw, not over the phone. Is it okay if I stop by?"

"Is that the only reason you wanna see a nigga, just to talk?"

"That, and the fact that I miss you and I need some of yo Mandingo lovin'. Isn't that more than enough reasons?"

"Let me think..."

"Boy, quit playing! I'll be over there in an hour, okay?" Sean quickly noticed the slight agitation that she displayed in her tone. That made him wonder what she wanted to talk about.

"Damn, Maxeen, baby. You know a nigga was only fucking with you. Get them panties out of yo ass, and come on through and give Big Daddy some lovin'!" he playfully commanded, easing the tension between the two of them. She couldn't help but to crack a smile on the other end of the line.

"Why I can't never stay mad at you?" she replied, blushing.

"Because you know sooner than later, you gonna be wanting some of this good ass dick."

"You so nasty, Sean. I'ma call you when I'm a block away from yo house, alright?"

"A'ight, baby girl. I hope you know I'm layin' here naked as a newborn waiting on you, so hurry up," he stated right before disconnecting the line.

An hour later, Maxeen walked through Sean's door looking phat. "Damn, you looking good, boo! So much for playing hard to get," he announced as he greeted her at the door asshole naked as if he had on a complete outfit.

"Un-un! I know you didn't."

"I didn't, yet, but I'm about to when you bring yo ass in here!" grabbing her by her slim waist. It amazed him how such a huge ass could be attached to a tiny waistline.

"Uhhh! You better get that snake looking thing off of me!" she barked as soon as she felt Sean's rock hard dick rise and poke her in the stomach. It was obvious that she was only playing because of the way she was massaging it. As they shared an intimate kiss, Sean instantly notice that the kiss didn't come as near as close to the one he and Meloney shared before she left for Kansas City. But, it still was good.

The only thing he didn't like about Maxeen was the fact that she smoked. He found that to be very unattractive in a woman. However, the fact that she respected him enough not to do it around him or in his presence was a plus. The only way he knew that she was actually a smoker was because the scent always lingered on her and sometimes stayed in her clothes, and it always seemed to be very strong whenever she came to visit. "Max, baby, can I ask you some'n?" He had her pinned up against the door. She loved whenever he cornered her like this.

"Of course, baby. What's up?"

"Why do you waste your time smoking them nasty smelling ass cigarettes when you're not even a real smoker? I mean, you and I have spent entire weekends together and there's been times when I haven't seen you smoke one cigarette. A real smoker couldn't go that long without smoking a cigarette."

"I know, I know. I'm trying to let it go completely. But, as far as why you haven't ever seen me smoke a cigarette, I'm just respecting my man. I mean, your wishes. You told me you don't like the smell of smoke, so when we're together, I leave that habit in the streets. Now, I want to ask you a question."

"A'ight, shoot!"

"Why do this thing keep poking the hell out of me? Do it have the Parkinson's disease or something?" she joked, looking down at his dick. He was making it jump up and down like it had hydraulics.

"Shiit, my only guess is he's excited. He acts like that when he knows he's about to get some good coochie. I don't know, maybe you should ask him, he can talk." They both laughed. "But anyway, how you gone come up in my crib with all them damn clothes on?"

"Boy, what are you talking 'bout, I only have on this thin ass dress!" she barked, and then lifted it over her head, taking it completely off. Underneath she was totally nude. Her pubic hair looked as if she had spent hours grooming it. It was manicured and trimmed perfectly in the shape of the letter V. Looking at her thick, toned thighs, Sean could tell she was into fitness.

"Max, it seems every time I see your body naked, it looks more toned and defined than the last time. You spending some serious hours at the gym, ain't you?" he stated, matter of factly, while watching her ass sway as she made her way over to the sofa. He was hot on her heels.

Plopping down on the couch, she stated, "Shiiit, I have to! Looking at all these video hoes and models make a bitch step her game up! It's called motivation, love. I be damn if I let a bitch steal my man because she looks good in a pair of boy shorts."

"You don't have to do all that sweating and working out in nobody's gym no mo', because I got the perfect thing for you that's gone keep that ass in tip top shape. All you have to do is faithfully use this D.D. Workout plan daily. You can't fail with it."

"D.D. Workout plan? I ain't never heard of that! What is it on, DVD or something?"

"Girl you ain't never heard of the D.D. Workout? The daily dick workout? That shit is guaranteed to keep that ass lifted and in shape," he said, pulling her up on his lap.

One of the many characteristics she liked about Sean is his spontaneity. Whatever came to mind, he'd act up on it without giving it a second thought. He was the complete opposite of her daughter's father. Her baby daddy was nothing but a lazy ass bum that constantly tried to mooch off her. Sean was a true go-getter that made his own way. Although she never asked him for anything, it was nice to know that if she ever needed something, she could probably get it from him. She wasn't sure if he was ready for a serious relationship with a woman that had a child being that he lost his son, but she knew he desperately wanted to have more children because he always talked about it. She just didn't know if he wanted her to bear them. Those were some of the thoughts that were going through her mind while they were engaged in foreplay on the sofa.

"Damn, Max, what's up, you a'ight? I'm feeling like I'm doing this all by myself. You want me to stop?"

I'm sorry, baby. I was just thinking about how strong my feelings are getting for you. What are we doing, Sean?"

"What do you mean what are we doing?"

"I mean us. This thing that we're involved in. This so-called relationship, slash, friendship. How far is this thing between us gone go?"

"Look, Max, you know I'm feeling you, too, but I can't honestly tell you that I'm ready to settle down. I can't say it'll just be me and you from this point on because then I'll be lying. You understand what I'm trying to say, don't you?" That was when she got up off his lap. The conversation wasn't going the way she hoped it would go.

"Yeah, I understand. You basically saying that I have to wait until you decide you've had enough of those other hoes before you commit to me!" she snapped with an attitude.

"Damn, why can't we just leave things the way that they are? Why you wanna complicate shit, Maxeen?" he replied, matching her attitude.

"Because I can get this same treatment from my good-for-nothing ass baby daddy, Sean!" she stated while slipping her dress back on.

"Then, why the fuck you not with him, MAXEEN?"

"Because I'm in love with yo' black ass, okay? Is that what you wanted to hear?" Tears began to fall from her eyes.

"Look, I'm sorry, baby. I didn't mean to upset you. I just don't want anyone to get hurt, you nor me." He grabbed her and held her in his arms. "You understand where I'm coming from?" he questioned, as he gently lifted her face with his hand until their eyes met each other's gaze. Then, he kissed her. When he kissed her softly on the lips, once again, he captured her attention. At first, she tried to resist him, but her will power proved to be no match for his affection. Her lips slowly parted, allowing her tongue to explore his mouth in search of its mate. She wasted no time in removing her dress once again. The all access invitation was available to Sean. As things began to heat up, they both realized that the sofa wasn't roomy enough for the things they planned to do, so they slowly made their way to the floor.

"Sean, I'm sorry for arguing with you. I don't want to argue anymore. I just want you to make love to me, please," she whispered softly and submissively. At that very moment, Sean felt as if he was obligated to give Maxeen what she wanted. Before he got started, he grabbed a remote that was sitting on the end table, pushed a few buttons, and then on came the CD player with Usher singing about taking it, Nice And Slow.

Sean made passionate love to Maxeen like never before, as if he was madly in love with her. Deep in his mind, he knew this would probably be the last time they shared that intimacy, so he was determined to leave a lifelong impression on her. What started in the living room on the carpet continued all throughout the house, finally ending inside the bedroom. As exhausted as they both were from all of that aggressive lovemaking, they could do nothing but fall peacefully asleep in each other's arms.

# Chapter Eight

"I told you we'd be knocking this shit off with the quickness! Mafuckas loving this shit, Sean! It's hard to believe that we ran through five bricks in the past four days, ain't it?" Gerald stated with excitement while counting out the recent twenty eight thousand dollars he'd made that day.

"Yeah, you right. I didn't believe that shit would be jumping like this, my nigga. That's what we needed, though," he agreed.

"So, how much you need to finish that album up?"

"Altogether, about 90, 000. Why, what's up?"

"I was just wondering, 'cause I know you're only making thirty six thousand out of this whole deal, right?" asked Gerald.

Sean had no idea where Gerald was going with the whole conversation, but he knew it was leading to some place he didn't feel like traveling to. To him Gerald had just broken a cardinal rule in the hustler's handbook guide. Never under any circumstances, count or question

# The Hustle

another hustler about his/her money. "Damn, nigga, you got my paper counted down to the very last dime, what's up with that bullshit? What you gone do next, try to take it from me?" he snapped.

"C'mon, man. You know it ain't like that! I was just tripping off the fact that you'll still be like fifty four thousand dollars short. From the way you've been talking, 'bout starting yo own label, you're more like a hundred and fifty four thou short...to be honest with you; I did my homework on you, too. I heard the story about yo' peoples and how he got hit up at the club the night you came home. Now, if I'm right, which I usually am, I'm guessing that the work we've been moving came from yo deceased homie. That's kinda strange that he happens to get killed the day you get out of prison and it leaves you access to God only knows how much blow. But, the bad thing is you're out of tune with the streets and you're scared to take a chance at moving it, ending up right back where you just left. So, that's where I come in at. Look, I don't have no problem helping you move this shit, you see I've been all the way straight with you. But one favor deserves another. You gotta come down on the prices, Sean. I've been giving you thirty for every brick I've moved."

"So, what you saying, Gerald?" Sean questioned with uncertainty but the last sentence struck a chord with him.

"I'm saying let a mafucka make a lil' change out the deal, too, so both of us can be happy. See, most of the lil' money I've made so far from putting my whip game down is practically gone. I had to straighten out a few past due bills," he lied. "I'm just hoping that after you finish with what you got, you gone shop one mo' time and front the keys to me at a decent price, that way we both can have enough money to do what we need to do. Plus, I'm sure you could use some extra loot to hit yo homeboy's people off with to make sure they straight since he looked out for you, right?"

*You think you so fuckin' slick, don't you?* thought Sean. *You probably stayed up all night plotting this little scheme.*

Nothing else Gerald said before the last sentence meant shit to Sean. However, the last sentence struck a chord with him. So, in reality, he was right. If it weren't for Derrick, things wouldn't be as easy as it was. Sean told himself that whenever his label got off the ground, he'd take good care of Derrick's family. But, what if it never got off the ground? What if I put all of the money I have into the label and the album flops? He asked himself. Right then, he knew he had to come up with a plan B. After he thought for a minute, he knew what he had to do.

"Okay, G, we gone flip this shit one mo' time, then after that, you're on your own. I don't care, but I hope you save some money this time because this is it."

"Now, that's what the fuck I'm talking bout!" Gerald stated with excitement. "Let's get this paper, my nigga!"

Being that everything was out in the open and no more secrets were being kept, Sean decided that it was time for him to get his feet back wet in the game. He didn't want to become too dependent on Gerald just in case he decided to get some bright ideas. Rule number two, never underestimate or over trust a hustler.

For the next couple of days, Sean spent most of his time reaching out to old clients, hoping to reel them back in. In doing so, he found out that not very much had actually changed in their world. That went for the ones that he'd managed to contact. The ones that he failed to contact were because they were either dead or locked up in jail.

Even though he'd practically turned to hustling full time, he still managed to continue to work when he was scheduled. Gerald showed him how to put the whip game on the last of the bricks in order to stretch the profit. Since they put the mix down, Sean suggested that they sell ounces for a thousand instead of the 12 they'd been charging.

\* \* \* \* \*

Over the next few days, Sean and Gerald were starting to become close friends. Not only did they hustle together, they also kicked it as well. Their clientele on the south side

was starting to grow rapidly. At the job, Gerald got things fixed where he and Sean shared the same hours and off days. That way, none of the other employees could come in between their business.

So far, things were going smooth for Sean and Gerald. At the job, they began to develop a system with moving their product. To Gerald, it was practically flaw proof, but Sean thought otherwise. He didn't like the fact that Gerald was starting to get extremely comfortable and careless while hustling out of the job site. In his eyes, that was a big mistake. Since it involved his freedom and well-being, Sean knew it was vital that he speak about it. One day as their shift was coming to an end, he decided to say something. Like every other fool that thought they had it all figured out, Gerald told him that he had everything under control and for him not to worry. He went on to tell him that he was just being paranoid, that nobody knew what was going on.

Seeing that it was no use to bicker back and forth,

Sean left it at that. He told himself if he didn't see any changes in his movement in the next couple of days he was going to disassociate himself from that potential time bomb waiting to explode. He was the type that believed in giving everyone their fair chance, so that meant he'd continue to trust Gerald, at least until he gave him reason not to.

\* \* \* \* \*

As Sean sat on the sofa counting money, he still couldn't believe he and Gerald were moving the work as fast as they were. He was down to his last ten ounces and that was only because he didn't feel like leaving the house to go deliver it. They were able to knock off one hundred and forty ounces in a week's time with no problem. Being that he'd agreed to Gerald's proposition, Gerald helped him sell the rest of the dope free of charge.

With the profit of 180, 000 dollars from the first six kilos and 140, 000 profit from the remaining three kilos, that would bring his total up to 320, 000 of cold, hard, blood money. Sean was in desperate need of a major plug. He knew that amount of money could easily get an entire family wiped off the face of the earth .So it was a must that he was careful and wise about whom he inquired to. Handling that much loot again had him feeling as if he'd never left the streets for 10 long, hard years. As he sat back on his sofa after freaking a Black n Mild, he lit the cigar and thought about how good it felt to be back on top.

\* \* \* \* \*

While out in the streets making his daily runs before his shift started, Sean began to think about Asia, wondering how she was doing. He hadn't heard from her in a few months. The last time he talked to her, she seemed to be holding up well, but he knew she was still grieving over Derrick. Thinking of her brought a sense of guilt over him because he knew he was at fault for not reaching out to her. He made a promise to his best friend that he'd take care of her if anything were to ever happen to him, and he hadn't kept his promise. Being that he was a man of his word, Sean knew he had to do something about that.

Since he wasn't that far from her house, he decided to give her a call just to see how she was doing and if she needed anything. "Asia, what's good lil' sis? How you and my niece doing?" asked Sean after she finally answered. He didn't think she was home because it took her so long to answer the door.

"Hey, Sean. We okay. Thanks for checking on us. I was just thinking about you the other day, wondering was you okay. So, how are you doing?"

"I'm good. Hey, I got a little some'n for you all, and I don't want to hear that, 'we good,' shit. I'm not too far from the house. Is it okay if I stop over?"

"Of course, c'mon through. Have you talked to momma Brown lately? She hasn't been feeling to well."

"Naw. But, I'll go check on her later. Right now, I'm close by you, so I'll see you in a minute," Sean announced, and then disconnected the call before she had a chance to protest. He figured that Asia was an independent chick that didn't like handouts or being pitied.. She owned her own beauty and nail shop, and was very capable of earning her own living. But, none of that made a difference to Sean. What meant something to him is the promise he made to Derrick.

When pulling up in front of Asia's house, Sean noticed a young, handsome guy, who looked to be in his early twenties, get out of a rimmed up Ford Explorer that was parked directly across the street and walked right into the house like he paid the bills. Immediately, Sean felt a sense of anger come over him as he thought about how Asia was blatantly disrespecting Derrick and the residence they used to share. Being that she was extremely beautiful, Sean knew that there would always be someone in pursuit of her, but he didn't think that she'd be starting to date so soon. Not when the supposed love of her life had passed away a little less than a year ago. Sean got out of his car with a mean mug on his face and malice in his heart. He was about to check Asia and the nigga she was calling herself seeing. As he came up to the door about to knock, he heard Asia speaking to the guy that had just entered the house.

"Look J.R., you're my little brother and I love you, so that means you are always welcomed in my house. But, if you're bringing drugs up in this house, you can't stay here. I mean it! I got too much to lose!"

"Damn, Asia, why you trippin'? You know I wouldn't do you and my niece like that!"

"Well, tell me why did I find that damn scale in the room you been staying in? I know Derrick didn't leave it there! Now, you know if I didn't allow him to bring that shit in here where our daughter sleeps, I'm definitely not gone let my little brother do it, are we clear?" she snapped. Sean stood on the opposite side of the door with a huge smile on his face. He was feeling the way Asia handled her household.

"Yeah, a'ight, Asia!" her little brother retorted in an aggravated tone. Satisfied with the response he'd just heard, Sean knocked on the door.

"J.R. would you get the door for me, please?" she asked, sounding as if she hadn't just chewed his head off seconds ago. Without even asking who was there or peeking through the peephole, the door swung wide open. "What up, who you looking fo', player?" he asked, giving Sean the ice grill.

*Fuckin' youngsters*, Sean thought to himself, "Asia. Can you tell her that Sean is here, and, lil' homie, here's a word of advice. Next time make sure you know who's on the other side of the door before you yank that mafucka open like that."

"Yeah, whatever! Asia, some cat name Sean is here to see you!" he yelled loud enough for the entire block to hear. "Damn, sis, you ain't tell a nigga you done met somebody new," he replied as she went to the door.

"That's because it wouldn't be none of yo business, and don't even go there with me! Now, you know won't no other nigga ever get to enjoy nothing that me and my baby Derrick shared together! And, for yo info, this is Derrick's best friend! Sean, this is my nosy ass lil' brother, J.R.," she clearly stated, making sure that Sean didn't have the wrong idea.

"What up, playboy?" J. R. spoke, changing up his whole demeanor.

"Ain't shit, dirty, what's up?"

"Sean, come on in the kitchen with me. I was just in there fixing dinner, we can talk in there." A quick glance around the spotless living room assured Sean that Asia was still taking care of things around the house. Matter of fact, the place looked even more beautiful than the last time he'd been over.

"So how you holding up, Asia?" he asked as he took a seat on one of the island stools.

"I'm okay, but to tell you the truth, Sean, it's hard. I keep waiting on Derrick to come through that door... but... my baby's never... coming back," she broke down in tears.

"I know, Asia. I know," Sean replied while cradling her in his arms, trying to console her as best as possible. "I know it's hard, but the thing is you don't have go through this alone. Anytime you need me, I'm here for you and the baby. But, I want you to do me a favor," he whispered into her ear.

"Wh-what?" she asked, wiping her tears away.

"I need you to get out and meet new people, and try to move on with yo life. I know that is what Derrick would want."

"Sean, that's what everybody keeps telling me I should do, but it's not that easy for me when all I could think about is Derrick. I miss him so much, Sean!" She could no longer hold back her tears.

"C'mon now, baby sis. You have to remain strong for not only Derrick, but also for your daughter. Here, take this." He then handed her a paper bag. "It's like thirty thousand in there, go buy you and the baby a whole new wardrobe, and then put the rest in your bank account."

"Thank you, Sean." After wiping her eyes with the back of her hand, she took the bag out of his hand. "You're the only true friend that Derrick really had. Every other so-called friend has been busy trying to fuck me. I wish they'd get it through their heads that I'd never go there. Besides, what Derrick and I shared was real love, can't no other nigga compare or come close to him!" By the strength in her words and the sincerity in her voice, Sean knew Asia meant every word she said.

"I know you're still mourning your man, but Derrick would want you to be happy. So, take all the time you need to grieve, and then try to get on with your life. You're young, beautiful, and intelligent. It's never too late for you to start over again. Now, wipe yo eyes and let me see that strong, thorough chick that my nigga introduced me to the day that I got out of prison! But look, I got a few things I need to take care of before I go to work," he said as he broke their brotherly, sisterly embrace. "If you need me, remember that I'm only one phone call away. I don't care if you're just calling because you feel the need to talk, just holla at yo big bro."

"Okay, Sean." They hugged one more time before Sean left. His heart truly went out to her. He knew exactly how she felt losing a loved one. As he pulled off in his car, he thought about all of the events that had taken place since his release from prison. Losing his only son, his best friend getting murdered over some senseless shit, and being torn between three beautiful women, two of which he'd developed strong feelings for, and last but not least, getting sucked back into the game.

He finally realized just how true the saying "never say never" really was. When he made the decision to get back into the game, all he could see was the big picture, finishing his album and getting his record label off the ground. Everything he wanted was in arms reach; all he had to do was hustle a little to make it happen, starting with re-copping. Being that the city was still relatively dry as far as coke, Sean knew it was time for him to make a move quick before everybody got back in pocket. Nevertheless, there was still one big problem standing in the way. He lacked a connect!

# Chapter Nine

It was Friday morning and Sean woke up in an extremely cheerful mood. Mainly because he knew that Meloney was due to arrive back in town. The two weeks she'd been gone seemed like an eternity to him. The only time that his mind wasn't on her was when he was busy entertaining his other female friends. While Monae was nothing more than Sean's personal playmate, he considered Maxeen to be something different. The thing he had for her was much more serious.

Now that Meloney was back, he knew that he'd have to make a decision as far as who he really wanted to be with. His heart had already chosen Meloney, but his body was craving Maxeen. After a long, hot shower, he walked over to his closet to pick out an outfit that best described his mood. It was in between comfort and casual.

He decided to go with a pair of blue Paper Denim jeans, an old school orange and white striped Rugby Polo long sleeve shirt with a pair of white and orange Air Force Ones. Once he slid into his freshly pressed jeans, he

116

unconsciously stuck his hands in all four pockets, an old habit of his, and discovered what was left of a business card. Since the jeans had recently been to the cleaners to be washed and pressed, the name on the card was kinda faded, but the number was still visible. For the life of him, Sean couldn't remember where the card came from. He couldn't even remember the last time he'd worn those jeans. He sat there wrecking his brain, trying to solve this mystery but his mind drew nothing but a blank.

Then, all of a sudden, it hit him! The last time, he'd wore those jeans was the night of his release when he and Derrick were at Club Liquid. That was when a vision of Felix, Derrick's friend, appeared in his mind. "That's who this card belongs to," he said to no one in particular. Although Sean could clearly visualize Felix's face, he couldn't remember his name. It, too, had been faded in the washer. Therefore, Sean figured he'd just use the pager number and wait on a call back instead of calling the direct line.

While getting dressed and ready to go pick up Meloney, Sean wondered what exactly should he say and hoped that the man hadn't forgotten who he was. In the middle of all the deep thoughts he was having, his cell phone suddenly began to ring. "Hello."

"Yes, this is Felix. Did someone from this number page me?" his Spanish accent was very noticeable.

"Ahhh, yeah. Felix, this is Sean, Derrick's friend. Remember, we met at your club, the night that Derrick got killed?

"Okay, okay! Yes, I remember chew now! How are you, my friend?"

"I'm good. I'm good. But, I could always be better. I was wondering if I could meet with you?" Silence fell over the line. Sean thought that Felix had maybe hung up, so he called out his name. "Felix, you still there?"

"Oh, yes! I'm sorry, of course we can meet. Actually, I'd expected you to call me long time ago. Derrick told me you'd come around soon." Sean smiled at the fact that Derrick knew him almost as well as he knew himself.

"I just been trying to put my life back together. You know, recoup from that long ass vacation I came off of."

"Oh. I see. So, now we back to normal, eh?"

"Yeah, we good now."

"Okay. So, you remember where me club is, no?"

"Yeah, I remember where it is."

"Okay, meet me there tonight at eleven thirty. I have VIP waiting for you, okay?"

"A'ight. I'll be there at eleven thirty, and thanks, Felix."

"No problem. I'll see you tonight," he replied, before disconnecting the call.

When Sean hung up the phone, a huge smile spread across his face. All he could think about was the quality of the product Felix had, which brought him to the conclusion that only someone well connected would have access to something that pure and good.

\* \* \* \* \*

Since Sean started back hustling, he'd been driving rentals more often than his own vehicle. There was no way he could drive the city streets peacefully in a Beemer while delivering drugs without the possibility of getting harassed. He knew most cops lived for an easy bust.

Leaving out of the house heading to pick up his baby, all he could see was that pretty face of hers and that sexy smile.

Thinking about how street smart she was and how quick she'd draw her own conclusion, Sean decided to play it safe and drive his own car to pick her up. The last thing he wanted was for her to find out he was back in the game. Meloney's bus was due to arrive at twelve thirty, but he had plans to be there waiting for her at twelve on the dot. He knew she loved little things like that. Although she would never admit it, little things like being there early waiting meant a great deal to her. She always expressed to Sean how the little things meant more to her than anything else. He loved the fact that she wasn't materialistic or high maintenance.

The weatherman had predicted a slight chance for showers, but so far, it was turning out to be a beautiful day. There wasn't a rain cloud in sight. Although it was about 75 degrees outside, the humidity and heat that was trapped inside his car had it, feeling like it was well into the nineties. After he hopped into his ride, he quickly put the key into the ignition, rolled down all four windows, and turned the air on high, attempting to force the hot air into the outside atmosphere. Since his house was right at I-70, it took him a little less than ten minutes to get to the Greyhound Bus Station. Pulling up on the small parking lot instantly bringing back memories of when he first came home.

Sitting in his car in a trance-like state, Sean carefully watched his surroundings. Looking at strangers meet and greet their loved ones as they entered and exited the bus was truly a wonderful sight to see. He thought about how happy Derrick was to see him, and the warm embrace they shared. As he began to go into the I shoulda, woulda, coulda stages, his thoughts were interrupted by the ringing of his cell phone. "Hello." He answered on the third ring.

"What up, playboy?" Gerald yelled through the receiver.

"You! What's really good, G? Where you at?"

"Ahhh, you know me. I'm out in traffic. Why, what's good with you? We ready to rock and roll or what?" That was the code way of asking Sean did he hook up with the connect.

"Not yet, but I'm supposed to see my aunt tonight. You feel like riding with ya boy, or what?"

"Shiiit, you know I'm with that!"

"That's what's up! Right now I'm at the bus station waiting on my baby girl to get in town."

"Yeah, that's right. You did tell me that Meloney was coming back today. Do she still got you on pussy punishment or did you finally tap that ass before she left town?" Gerald said, laughing at his own joke.

"C'mon with that bullshit! Now, you know this pimping is way too strong! See, the difference between me and you is I have patience, you don't! The sooner you realize that patience is the key to everything in life, the better off you'll be, my brother!"

"Yeah, a'ight! But, on the real, though, I'll catch up with you later, so call me when you get back to the crib."

A'ight, fool! The bus just pulled in anyway, nigga!" hanging up before Gerald could reply.

\* \* \* \* \*

Knowing that Sean got in the last word really irked Gerald. He was always the type that felt he had to have the last word. He could do nothing but smile to himself, thinking of how Sean had beat him at his own game. After he placed his phone back into the middle console, he reached into the ashtray and pulled out a perfectly rolled blunt. Next, he pushed in the cigarette lighter and held it until it automatically popped out, and then lit the tip of the blunt and deeply inhaled. The aroma of the weed quickly filled the car. "I'm back, mufuckas! I told you I was coming back!" Gerald shouted at the top of his lungs to no one in particular. To him, it felt damn good to be back on top of the game.

As he cruised down Natural Bridge Road in his brand new sky blue Lexus ES400 weaving through traffic like, he never noticed the all black Ford Excursion with heavily tinted windows following him. It was Terrell, an old business partner of Gerald's who was looking to settle.

The last Gerald had heard about Terrell, who mostly went by the name Tu, was that he'd lost out in trial and received thirty years. Since Tu couldn't reach out to Gerald, he had his people constantly calling hoping to collect his money. If Gerald didn't recognize the number, he wouldn't answer. Or, if he were caught off guard, he'd simply give whoever called the runaround. Since Tu's wife, wasn't personally around to collect his doe, Gerald basically said fuck it.

However, once Tu received the lengthy 30-year sentence, things changed in Gerald's eyes. To him, Tu was officially assed-out on the fifty grand he owed him. Even if he wanted to pay him, at the time he couldn't. The truth of the matter was, Gerald was nothing but a trick that flossed and spent money like he actually had shit loads of it. The only thing that ever made Gerald look as if he was doing good was his appearance. But, that was just a façade. Since he kept nice jewelry, new clothes, and something fly to ride in, the average hustler or person would think he was sitting on some change. But, he wasn't.

It had been almost two years since he'd last seen or dealt with Tu, so it was safe to say that Tu was the last person on Gerald's mind. He had no clue that Tu had filed for a direct appeal right after his trial, and never in a million years did he think that Tu would end up reversing his sentence. In his second trial, his lawyer proved, beyond reasonable doubt, that his client was innocent, and all charges against him were bogus, so the DA was left without a choice. He had to drop the first-degree assault and armed criminal action because of lack of evidence. The only charge Tu was rightfully convicted of is a class C felony of possession, which only carried one to seven years.

Hungry for a conviction, the DA proposed a deal to Tu and his lawyer. The deal was if Terrell Jackson AKA were to leave the court room a free man  he'd  still be placed on 1 year probation for the class 'C" felony of possession .That was basically the DA's way of keeping him in the system .He was confident that Tu would violate within that year. That was a week ago. Now back on the streets, Tu was out to collect what he felt was rightfully owed to him. Even if it meant killing for it!

# Chapter Ten

When Meloney got off the bus, she was so elated to see that her man was right there waiting for her. The entire time she was at home with her family and friends, all she could think about was Sean and how wonderful it was when they made love. She spoke highly of him to her family and friends. Matter of fact, he was all that she talked about the whole time she was there. There was no doubt in her mind that Sean was the man she wanted to start a future with.

Being that Meloney and her mother were extremely close, she told her all about Sean. She even shared with her just how good he put down between the sheets. That was just how comfortable she was when it came to conversing with her. She also expressed to her how she felt about him. In past relationships, there was a time or two when she actually thought she was in love, but looking back at it now she realized that it was only infatuation. What she felt for Sean was definitely love.

Sean had her nose wide open and Meloney knew it.

Her only hope was that he was feeling her just as much as she was feeling him. All her life, she'd dealt with smooth talking guys like Sean. Some were genuine and sincere, and some were frauds. At that moment, she couldn't tell which was Sean, although she was hoping for the latter. Until then, she planned to keep her heart under twenty-four hour watch. At least, that was her intentions.

Meloney came from a bloodline of hustlers and players, ranging from her grandfather's father all the way down to her brother, who'd recently changed his lifestyle. So, there wasn't too much game she couldn't recognize. Coming from her line of family, she had practically seen and heard it all before. However, like every woman that was eager to be loved, she, too, happened to fall victim to some two-bit player. After really getting to know Sean, she quickly began to see that he was speaking a different language. The language of love, something she was hoping to learn to speak fluent. Walking toward Sean, all she could think about was how she hadn't been this happy in a long time.

"Damn, I missed the shit out of you, girl!" Sean revealed as he embraced her tightly.

"I missed you, too, boo," she replied right before they shared a short kiss.

"You know I couldn't get you off of my mind, don't you?" he said, telling what most people would call a half truth, since he was keeping company with Maxeen and Monae in her absence.

"It seemed as if two weeks took forever! I know I probably drove my mother crazy talking about you," she exclaimed while walking hand and hand with him toward his car.

"You been talking to your mom's about me?"

"Yeah, and she said she can't wait to meet you." All

of a sudden, the conversation from Sean ceased completely. Meloney didn't say anything about his quietness until they were seated inside the car. "Why you get so quiet all of a sudden, Sean? Did I say something wrong, baby?"

"Nah, I was just thinking."

"Thinking about what?"

"What if I meet yo moms and she didn't like me, Meloney? That's one of the problems I had with my son's grandmother. She didn't seem to think I was good enough for her daughter. She didn't like the fact that I hustled, and to make it worse, her husband was in the same line of work!"

"Well, you don't have to worry about that with my momma! Plus, all that illegal stuff is in the past, right? I'm going to tell you the same thing I told my brother, selling drugs is like living in a box. All you have to do is step outside the box and there's a whole world waiting.

"Yeah, I know," he agreed while staring directly onto the highway he was driving on. He feared if he looked into her eyes she might discover the truth. He hated the fact that he had to keep lying to her because he knew he'd eventually get caught in one, so he decided to change the subject. "So, are you hungry?"

"Yeah, I could use a bite to eat. Why, did you cook for me again?"

"Not this time. But, I will if you want me to." he said as he looked over at her.

"That's okay, baby. You don't have to cook for me today. To be honest, I don't care what I eat as long as I'm with you," she replied as she leaned her head on his shoulder.

"Is that right?" he questioned, smiling. At that moment, Sean knew Meloney meant exactly what she said. All she wanted was to be in his presence. "Well, I was thinking that we could hit up the Old Steak House on Grand. Is that cool?"

"Sounds good, baby," she stated, and then kissed his cheek.

After they got their eating arrangements settled, Meloney began to tell Sean all about her trip back home. Sean loved the fact that she always had something interesting and meaningful to say. That was one of the many reasons he fell head over heels for her, she knew how to carry a conversation like most teachers, and she could talk for hours about any and everything. Good old fashion conversation like that was very hard to find nowadays.

Pulling up on one of his favorite eating spots brought back a lot memories for Sean. He thought about how he and Cynthia used to frequent the place. Although those memories were sacred, they were also painful. That was the reason why he quickly brushed those memories out of his head, replacing them with dreams that hopefully involved the woman that was sitting beside him. Even though it seemed as if it had been forever and a day since he'd last visited the spot, he noticed that little had changed.

Walking inside, Sean was instantly taken back by the food aroma. He was really looking forward to sinking his teeth into one of their infamous Porter House steaks. Now that he was inside, he did notice a few changes that had been made in the restaurant. The small, stuffy restaurant he remembered it to be was no longer that. It was spacious and much more roomy. He noticed the back wall where he used to always sit had been knocked out and a whole new section was added. The renovation that was done gave the place a more youthful vibe.

# The Hustle

The thing that hadn't changed was the long ass line of hungry, anxious, no nonsense people that faithfully spent their lunch hour there. Workers and pedestrians from all around came to experience some of the great tasting food The Old Steak House had to offer. Even though Meloney's school was right down the street, she'd never visited the eatery. Sean couldn't believe she hadn't been in the restaurant once. "Baby, are you serious? You're honestly telling me that you've never been in here to eat before?"

"I'm serious, baby. I didn't even know there was a decent restaurant this close to the school. I've become so accustomed to Wendy's and all the bull crap they serve in the school's cafeteria."

"Well, sometimes you have to step outside the box, baby. There's a whole world waiting to be explored outside of that campus." They both laughed.

"Ahhh, so now you're turning my advice around and giving it back to me? I like that," she said, stealing a quick kiss on his cheek.

"What was that for?" Sean questioned while holding the exact same cheek that her lips had just touched.

"That was for being the wonderful man that you are. The love of my life. Why, do I have to have a reason to kiss my man?"

"Nah, I was just wondering what I did to deserve that and hoping that whatever it was, it was also worth some coochie, too."

"Boy, you are so silly!" she said, and then they both burst into laughter.

Finally, after a fifteen minute wait, the hostess led them to a cozy table for two in the far left corner where two menus sat waiting for them. Ten minutes after they placed their order, their food arrived to the table piping hot and looking scrumptious. They both went with the lunch special, which consisted of the eight ounce Porter House steak, two over easy eggs, and fries. Once they were finished eating, Meloney suggested they take a drive downtown to Union Station and walk through the mall . Being that he hadn't seen her in two weeks, he figured it would be a good idea to spend a little quality time together. Meloney loved every second that she got to spend with Sean. To her, that was better than any store bought gift.

Just walking through the mall with her man, holding hands, and spending quality time was what she considered priceless. The attention she received from Sean was what she'd been longing for in a relationship. Now that she'd finally found a loving, kind man that was willingly offering love, she wasn't about to let him go. Strolling through the semi-crowded mall, they looked like the perfect couple.

Meloney felt like a school girl with a huge crush, falling deeper and deeper in love by the second. But, she wasn't the only one in the relationship feeling that way. The only problem was, Sean kinda felt as if he was feeling Maxeen just as much. That had him seriously pondering the future decisions he knew had to be made. But, all of those mixed emotions changed after spending the entire day with her, and then making love that evening. He had officially made his mind up about who he wanted to be with, but he told himself he'd spend one more day with Maxeen.

# Chapter Eleven

Bright and early the next morning, Meloney had her roommate pick her up from Sean's residence. Before she could fully plant herself into the passenger's seat, Rachel shouted, "Bitch, yo' ass is in love, ain't you? Don't try to deny it, either, because it's written all over your face!"

"Nuh unh!" Meloney replied, avoiding eye contact with her friend.

"Look at you! You like a sick puppy! You can't even look me in the eye and answer my question." They both started laughing.

"Is it that obvious, Rachel?" Meloney questioned, finally admitting her guilt. "Girl I've never felt this way about a man before in such a short time span."

"Shiiit, you all been seeing each other for almost a year now! What did you expect, Meloney? I once dated a nigga for three short weeks and swore I was madly in love with his ass. At least I thought so until that muthafucker hit me up for some money and never came back!"

"Rachel, you're silly!" Meloney stated after their

laughter subsided.

One of the reasons the two became so close was because of their similar backgrounds. They both were straight out of the 'hood, aiming to better their situation. As soon as they met, the girls clicked instantly, becoming inseparable on campus. Both Meloney and Rachel's fathers were ex-hustlers, so they were both raised with street smarts. The only difference between the girls' fathers were Meloney's dad was deceased while Rachel's dad was busy doing a twenty-seven year bid. The two young ladies were much more different from the rest of their class mates. They didn't come up in the sheltered life like most of them. While college was nothing but a party to the majority of the students there, the girls took their education serious. They both knew it was basically the key to getting out of poverty and staying out.

The girls understood each other very well and knew from their families' past experience that the streets had nothing to offer.

"I just hope he's feeling me as much as I'm feeling him, girl," Meloney stated, breaking their silence. "I don't think I could take my heart being broken again."

"Gurrrl, don't even sweat it. I will personally fuck that nigga up if he ever thinks of playing you!" They both burst into laughter, which caused Rachel to jerk on the steering wheel just to prevent from side swiping a parked car.

"Girl, you know you crazy!" Meloney blurted out.

"Yeah, I might be, but I'm also dead serious, too! I know how to handle situations like that." The look on Rachel's face told Meloney that her friend was telling the truth. She was serious.

\* \* \* \* \*

# The Hustle

After witnessing Meloney ride off, Sean hit the shower to get ready for his meeting with Felix. He made sure to text Gerald and tell him the exact time and location they were going to meet so he wouldn't be late. Since it was only nine thirty five, he took a long, hot shower instead of his usual quickie.

Stepping out of the shower, he dried himself off with one of the big, expensive Polo beach towels that Maxeen had recently bought, or maybe stole, for him.

After fifteen minutes of debating on what to wear, Sean finally decided on a grey linen Hugo Boss two piece suit, a navy blue silk shirt, and navy blue gators with matching belt and fedora.

Admiring himself in the mirror and seeing that he was truly dressed to impressed, Sean was ready to meet up with the big man, Felix. Being that Gerald was always preoccupied entertaining some female, Sean was almost sure that he'd be somehow running late. Stepping out of the door, he inhaled a huge chunk of the night air. The spring breeze felt soothing as it caressed his body. The weather was just right. Not too cold, not too hot. Perfect for the outfit he had on.

While on his way to the club, the sounds of Rick Ross' *Maybach Music* pumped through his subwoofers. Listening to Ross spit that fire, Sean began to seriously think about his rap career, something that he had also neglected tremendously, and how he'd been sidetracked by the streets once again. At that very moment, he made a promise to himself that after he flipped the money he had, he was finished with the game and back into the studio.

Pulling up behind Union Station brought back the new memory he and Meloney had just created earlier that day in the same parking lot. He couldn't believe his ears when she suggested that they have sex in the car. He loved the fact that she could also be spontaneous. While sitting in the car waiting on Gerald to show his face, a lot of different things ran through his mind. His life and what direction it was heading, his relationship with Meloney, Monae, and Maxeen, his son's death, and his future was just a few of the thoughts that bombarded Sean's mind.

After about fifteen minutes had passed, coming to the conclusion that Gerald was pulling a no show, Sean decided to go on in without him. As soon as he stepped out of the car, out of nowhere a car came speeding around the corner like a bat out of hell bumping the Isley Brothers' *Between the Sheets*. It was Gerald, and it was the first time Sean had seen his new car. He just smiled to himself because he'd expected something like that out of him.

"Nigga, can you leave them hoes alone and be on time for once?" Sean asked Gerald after he hopped out of his ride.

"My bad, dirty. I was fucking that bitch, Adrian. Every time I got ready to leave she would start sucking on my dick, trying to persuade me to stay the night with her ass!" He just couldn't stop cheesing.

"Damn, you still fucking with that bitch?" Sean questioned. He was actually trying to see if she and Monae was giving up the same treatment as they used to give him.

"Every now and then. Ahh, yeah. Before I forget, she told me to tell you Monae wants you to call her. That bitch is so in love with you, homie!"

"Man, she cool and all, but I can't stand to be around her ass for a long period of time. She too fuckin' annoying. That's why whenever we're together, I make sure to keep her mouth filled with dick just to keep from hearing her talk," Sean stated, as he and Gerald walked toward the club's entrance at a slow pace. They both burst into laughter.

"On everything, my nigga, that bitch do have a squeaky, high pitched, annoying ass voice, don't she?" Gerald replied, calling money on Monae's voice.

"But, she do got that fire twat and head, though!" Sean countered as he gave Gerald dap.

When they reached the club's entrance, Sean announced to the bouncer who he was and who he was there to see. After throwing Felix's name in the mix, he was greeted with the utmost respect and allowed to go right in. Just like the last time when he and Derrick were there, he and Gerald walked straight in as if the half block line of people didn't exist. Upon entering the club, he was immediately approached by Stacy, the same fine ass waitress he first met with Derrick.

"Long time, no see, stranger! And, just think, I'd just about gave up hope on seeing you again. Anyway, how are you doing?"

"I'm good, ma. A nigga just been going through some things since I lost my brother, but I'm good, though. What about you? I see you still looking good."

"I have to. Don't nobody want no busted ass waitress all in their grill trying to take their order." Sean couldn't help but to laugh at her humor. He found it attractive.

Gerald just stood there dazed, wondering how much game he'd have to spit to get the fine ass waitress in the sack. Not the type to keep wondering and guessing, he decided to shoot his shot. "Damn, Sean, can I get some type of formal introduction or somethin'!" Determined to get to know her, even if he had to trick off his last few thousand with her. To him, as fine as she was, he was sure she'd be worth every penny.

"My bad. This is..." Sean drew a blank when he looked into her eyes.

"Stacy!" she replied, disappointed that he'd forgotten her name. "Yeah, Stacy." Sean stated matter of factly as he continued to stare into her captivating eyes. Stacy matched his stare without blinking once. For that mere few seconds, it seemed as if the two were frozen in time. Gerald instantly picked up on the chemistry the two had. He didn't like the fact that Stacy was showing more interest in Sean,

"Damn! Why don't y'all just get a room!" he replied in a joking, but slightly sarcastic, manner. Realizing that she was acting out of character, Stacy snapped out of it.

"Felix should be here any moment. He told me to have you wait in VIP and order whatever you like. It's on m... I mean, the house." With that being said, she lead them both to the VIP section. Walking through the mass amount of club goer's, Sean suddenly began to feel a sense of deja vu came back over him. The spot was packed to its full capacity, and there was still people standing outside in line with high hopes of making it in the club. "Do you all know what you want? And, I'm only talking about drinks or anything on the menu!" she informed, figuring she'd straighten Gerald out before he thought about poppin' slick or getting out of line. It was obvious that she was used to getting that type of attention. She knew how to put a guy in his place and still be lady-like about it.

"Yeah, let me get an Incredible Hulk," Gerald stated real snobbish like. He figured since she wasn't interested in him, fuck her. It wasn't that he was ugly or that she didn't find him attractive, because she did. It was just that she already had her sights set on Sean, which was who she intended to get to know better.

"And, what can I get for you?" she questioned, diverting her attention back to Sean.

"Just give me the same as my homie, baby."

"Coming right up!" she replied, and then casually sashayed away, giving him a display of her meanest walk.

"Damn, she got a sexy ass walk on her! Don't she, G?"

"Hell yeah! I wouldn't mind hitting that, but it don't seem like she fucking with a playa. Shit like this don't usually happen to a nigga like me."

"Yeah. I bet it don't," Sean said, attempting to bandage up his friend's ego. "Anyway, it's too many fine bitches up in here to be tripping off of some broke ass waitress!" Sean continued.

"Shiit, you ain't know? I might fuck around and pull me a couple bad bitches tonight, but I think you should try yo hand at ole girl, Stacy. It seems to me like she's feeling you, and since she is, you have to give her what she wants."

"Man, my plate is already full as it is dealing with Meloney and Maxeen that's why I backed up off of Monae. I'm already having a hard time deciding between the two of them. A yo! Speaking of Monae, this is where I met her and Adrian at!"

"You bullshitting! Now I know I'm 'bout to bag me a deuce banger! But, as far as yo' situation, if I was you I'd keep 'em both and add ole girl to the stable. They say the more the merrier. At least, that's how I'd play it," Gerald said with a huge grin on his face.

"But, see that's the difference between you and me. I can be satisfied with one woman, you can't. You have to have as many women as you can possibly get in order to make you feel like a complete man, and I don't."

"Nigga I don't need no bitch to make me feel complete. Anyway, ain't nothing wrong with having yo cake and ice cream, too!"

"Yeah, I bet it ain't! That's probably the reason why yo ass be broke all the damn time because you full of cake and ice cream," Sean joked.

"Man, fuck you! I ain't never been no trick for no bitch," Gerald stated, knowing damn well he was lying through his teeth.

The potential argument came to an abrupt halt when the boys spotted Stacy heading back in their direction. Since Sean wasn't the type to front his boy off in front of a female, he let it go. "Felix is in his office now, Sean. He told me to come get you and escort you there." She couldn't look at Sean without smiling and blushing.

Sean turned to Gerald and said, "I'll be back, my nigga. Do what you do best, mingle with the females a little," he replied, and then walked off, trailing Stacey.

Just watching her walk was a total turn on for Sean. From head to toe, she reeked of sex appeal. As he continued to watch her big, apple shaped ass bounce up and down to its own rhythm, with each step she took, he felt an erection slowly coming on. She really wore her uniform well. As they got to the DJ booth, he noticed a set of spiral stairs to the left that led to the second floor.

"Right up there, baby. And, this time, please, don't leave without saying goodbye, okay?" she said in more of a demanding tone than a request. Sean just smiled and headed up the steps.

Upon completing the flight of stairs, he observed two doorway entrances less than twenty five feet away. Walking down the corridor, he could feel the bass from the music vibrating the floor beneath his feet. The thick plywood door let Sean know that he was at the right door. As he stood motionless at the door, he wondered what laid behind it. Would it be a bright future or the road to destruction? He knocked three times.

"Come in, me friend!" a familiar voice suggested from the opposite side of the door, just enough to be heard over the muffled music sound. Entering the door, Sean's eyes instantly began to scan the medium sized office until he spotted Felix sitting behind his big cherry oakwood desk smoking an expensive cigar.

The office was tastefully decorated from the thick, plush, cinnamon color carpet down to the oil paintings of old jazz artists such as Miles Davis, Sonny Rolling, and Charlie Parker all doing what they loved to do.

"How you doing, Felix? Thanks for seeing me."

"No problem. I've heard so much about you from Derrick," he said, making the sign of a cross from the top of his forehead to the middle of his chest. "I"ve been waiting for you for quite a minute now, Sean. I was beginning to think that you were serious about going straight."

"Yeah. I thought I was done with the game, too. But, the circumstances changed when Derrick got killed."

"Si. That's very understandable. So, tell me what can I do to make your situation better, me friend?"

"Well, as you already know, when Derrick got killed he still had most of the product he copped from you. So, with me being the only person close to him that knew where the stash was, it left me stuck with it."

"Oh, so you want me to buy it back from you!"

"No! No! It's already gone," Sean corrected him. As he continued, he ran it all down to Felix all the way up to his current status. While he talked, Felix kept direct eye contact, he was searching for any sign of weakness in

Sean's character. As far as he could see, there was none. When it came to spotting weaknesses, Felix was usually on the money. He already knew what type of guy Sean was, with his drive and ambition, they could make a lot of money together.

"So tell me, how do you want to do business? Will you just buy from me, or do you want it on consignment?"

"Well, I got three hundred thousand to work with right now."

"Okay," he said, grabbing the calculator that was on his desk. "That's thirty at ten thousand a piece, plus, I'll give you ten more, which you'll owe me one hundred twenty thousand, is at okay?" Quickly adding the figures in his head, Sean noticed that Felix was taxing him an extra twenty stacks, but he didn't say anything about it. He figured it to be a test of faith.

"Yeah, that's cool. I can work with that," he said with a smile on his face. He was smiling at the fact that he was about to make a lot of money. Forty kilos at eighteen thousand a pop, that was seven hundred and twenty thousand, minus one hundred and twenty, came to a total of six hundred thousand dollars. *That's what's up*, Sean thought.

"Good. Then, we began our business venture tomorrow. Someone will call you in the morning with directions. No talk, no questions. Just follow, understand?" he stated He stood and shook Sean's hand, sealing the deal. After his business venture was set, Sean was ready to leave the club. Ever since Derrick's murder, he really wasn't into partying anymore. He headed towards VIP to find Gerald.

With every step he took, Sean either bumped into or accidentally brushed up against some strange female. He figured it had to be ladies night the way the women were out in attendance.

What's good, my nigga!" Gerald stated excitedly as Sean entered the VIP room. "I thought you got kidnapped for a minute. I was just about to come looking for yo ass!" he stated in a loud, drunken voice, surrounded by four lovely young ladies.

"Shit. Everything is everything. It's all hooked up for tomorrow. I'm 'bout to roll out, go home, and get some sleep. Which is some'n I advise you to do!"

"Mannn, it's too fuckin' early to turn in. Stay and have a drink with yo boy."

"Nahh, you do you. I'll just get up with you tomorrow, a'ight?"

"We wanna go," replied two beautiful ladies that were sitting next to Gerald. From the time that Sean stepped foot in the VIP room, they were clocking him.

"Sorry, ladies, but I'm involved with someone right now."

"So are we, but they asses ain't here right now!" the dark complexioned sister announced as she and her girlfriend laughed and high fived each other.

"Maybe next time," Sean politely stated, leaving her and the rest of the horny women with puzzled looks on their faces. Then, he turned back around and spoke, "Hey, just give yo number to my partner and I'll get at you." The honey with the light eyes couldn't believe she was getting rejected. Not the way niggas constantly hawked her. Sean knew when a man played hard to get it, only intrigued women that much more. And, since baby girl was no different from most women in the club, she decided to play his game, she gave her number to his partner like he suggested and waited her turn.

"A'ight, dirty," stated Gerald, talking with that

drunken slur. "I'll get at you tomorrow."

"In the morning," Sean replied while walking towards the exit of the VIP room and into the crowd of people. Before he could make it out, Sean ran into the beautiful Stacy.

"Ahh, so you was just gone leave again, huh? Look, let me tell you something, Sean. You are fine ad all, but I'm not gone keep running up behind you like some desperate lil' puppy!"

"It's not like that, ma, I..."

"Good!" she said, cutting him off. "I'm supposed to get off at three, but I'll tell Felix I'm taking off early. Now, my question to you is, will you be out there waiting when I come outside?

"Damn! Since it doesn't sound like I really have a choice, I guess I will. Now, my question to you is, how are you so sure that he's going to let you off early?"

"Don't you worry about Felix, I got him. Besides, that's my father's best friend, which means he's like an uncle to me, so he's not a problem," she confidently stated with a devilish grin on her cute face. "Plus, don't you have some business with him?"

"Yeah, some'n like that. But, where did all that come from?" Sean didn't like the fact that he was being questioned by a woman that he didn't know.

"It's nothing," she said, brushing it off. "Anyway, let me holla at Felix to let him know I'm about to leave so he could get someone to come cover my station."

"A'ight. And, don't be taking all day, either!"

"Boy, I'll be out there in a minute. You driving that black Beemer, right?" she stated before walking.

Damn! How in the fuck do she know what car I'm driving? Sean said to himself as he watched her throw her hips from side to side as she walked. Stacey was a very beautiful woman. Everything about her was gorgeous, from her shoulder length sandy brown hair to her oval shaped almond brown eyes, down to her model-like slim waist and big round sexy ass.

Sean had no knowledge of the fact that her father was once one of the richest hustlers in St. Louis who'd recently caught a twenty year fed bid. Since his daughter had been basically raised in the streets, he taught her the ways of the game, which is the reason why she worked the club with Felix. She was the type that liked to be hands on with each and every business venture she had going on, legal and illegal. Right before her father was indicted, he and Felix purchased an old warehouse that was located right behind Union Station and turned it into the hottest night club on the Missouri side of the river.

# Chapter Twelve

At the present time, Stacy wasn't romantically involved with anyone. At least, not seriously. The last serious relationship she was involved in was with her estranged husband. That was a few years ago. After her husband caught a large amount of time in prison, she realized she wasn't strong enough to stand by a man that was doing a tremendous amount of time behind bars. She knew if her husband was to ever, by some miracle, get out of prison, she would more than likely be in grave danger. But, the fact was with the charges he had on him, getting out within the next twenty years just wasn't happening. So, she figured why should her life stop and be placed on hold just because his was? The only man she communicated with daily was Felix. It wasn't that she didn't desire male companionship, because she did. She just couldn't seem to find a man she felt was worth the time and energy. So, she opted for the next best satisfying thing. Money! She once told a guy who she was seeing that the only orgasm she received came from counting money.

Even though she knew Sean was fresh out of prison and really didn't have shit, she knew his potential worth, thanks to Derrick. Besides that, she was also physically attracted to him. But, Stacey wasn't the type to jump off a cliff for a man. Just because he had her attention didn't mean he was capable of keeping it. So far, she was getting good vibes about him. She was hoping that they could get to know each other better and take it from there. She wasn't really looking for anything serious. Her mind was basically on scratching the itch that was between her thighs, and possibly putting Sean down on the team at the same time. Last but not least, she was praying that he wasn't anything like her husband, overly possessive and very abusive.

When Stacey stepped foot out of the club, Sean was in complete awe. He couldn't believe how much more beautiful she looked in her regular attire. Although he knew he was looking at the same woman he'd just finished talking to moments earlier, in some ways, she looked completely different with her hair down.

He was really feeling her entire being. The way her hair hung gracefully down her back and onto her shoulders made her look that much more stunning, as if that was actually possible. When he first saw her in the club, he figured her hair to be long by the way she had it pinned up. But, he had no idea it was so long. For a minute before she came out, Sean actually contemplated leaving because he knew what was about to go down. Something that he wasn't quite ready for.

Anyone that had ever experienced lust or deep infatuation could have easily seen the sexual attraction that Sean and Stacey shared for one another. Although he very much wanted to indulge in Stacey, he really didn't want to get involved with another woman. He was already going through his own personal crisis juggling the two he had, now with a third coming into the mix, he was about to find out that everything that looked good wasn't always good for him.

"What up? Is everything okay?" he asked as she entered the passenger door and sat down.

"Yeah. Everything is good. I told you, Felix isn't a problem. I got that handled," she said, smiling. The moment she got into the car, her sweet smelling perfume instantly took over, smothering the fresh leather smell that new vehicles carried.

"Damn, you smell good! What's that you're wearing?" he asked, attempting to make small talk.

"Why thank you. It's called Mystic. I picked up a bottle last month when I was out in London. "So, you like it, huh?" She couldn't help but to blush at the compliment he'd given her.

"Yeah baby, that shit's the bomb! Plus, I'm loving the fact that you didn't over saturate yourself in it. So, since it's obvious that you're the one in charge here, can you please tell me where I'm suppose to be driving to?"

"Well, since you put it that way, I figured we'd go to my spot for a few, and maybe have some drinks and talk. Is that cool with you?"

"Yeah, that's cool," he stated nonchalantly. "By the way, where exactly is that?"

"I stay on 4th Street. Not too far from here."

"Where on 4th Street?" he questioned. The only houses he remembered to be on 4th was some expensive condos. On 4th and Locust, to be exact.

"On 4th and Locust in those high rise condos," she proudly stated.

"Damn. Go head lil' momma! Not to be all up in

yours, but I know them spots run a pretty penny."

"Yeah, something like that. That's just one of the properties I own in St. Louis."

"Damn, you said that like you got outta town spots and shit," he replied as he continued to drive in the direction of her condo.

"Hell, I do! What? A bitch can't stunt like y'all niggas do? Y'all better wake up and realize it's the new millennium! Bitches is grinding harder than most dudes nowadays. And, before you go jumping to conclusions, didn't no man do shit for me except my father. And, all he did was supply me with the proper connect. I hustled myself, built my own clientele, and made myself rich."

What the fuck! thought Sean. He couldn't believe he was sitting next to a kingpin bitch. The story was getting more interesting by the minute. Most of the females he'd ever fucked with depended on him to take care of them. He was always the breadwinner in the relationship.

Now that he'd finally met a woman that was earning her own keep and holding shit down in the streets, he felt himself being turned on by her sense of power. During his prison stay, he often dreamed of finding a beautiful, independent, strong woman with a business mind that would be able to offer something besides sex. A woman with those type of characteristics was most likely every man's fantasy girl. Especially if he'd done a bid with some no-good ass bitch.

As he reached Stacey's parking garage, a booth equipped with a large, white swinging arm that lifted and lowered kept him from entering the underground garage. Usually there was a guard working the booth, but since none was present occupants of the building had to use their key card to gain entry.

Sean thought about how he'd passed that building

numerous times, but never actually acknowledged its existence. After riding up two levels, Stacey directed him to her personal parking space that had her name painted in it. Upon exiting the car, she lead Sean to an elevator that was less than fifty feet away. Neither of them had spoken a word since they exited the car. Both of them appeared to be lost in their own thoughts. For some reason, Sean was kind of nervous. That was unusual for him, especially being in the company of a female. Tired of the silence, Sean decided o speak out.

"So, how long have you been living here?"

"Well, as of yesterday, two years now. I know you probably still think I'm stuntin' in somebody else's shit. But, I'm not. What you see is all me, but you'll know exactly how real it is tomorrow."

"To be honest, that thought did cross my mind. But, I also learned never to underestimated anyone, male or female. And, most importantly, never judge a book by its cover."

"You're a smart man. I like that," she said, smiling. "Before I moved in here, my girls and I used to pass by this building all the time while we were on our way shopping. I used to tell them that I was going to buy a condo in here one day. The very next day, my girl, Shaundra, called me up telling me she had something to show me. So, I get in the car and ride with her, and that heffa brings me down here saying that she scheduled me an appointment to look at the available condos that were open in the building. After I saw the place, I instantly fell in love with it," she stated as the elevator came to a stop on the eighth floor where her condo was located. "Since my dad and Uncle Felix had purchased Liquid and it was in the downtown area, I knew I couldn't pass up on the place. Especially with me not liking to drive. "That is, unless it's about money." She smiled as she exited the elevator. Sean had no idea what to think about this woman. She was a mystery that he was eager to solve.

As they entered the condo, the coziness and warmth the place provided quickly wrapped its arms around Sean, giving him an at home feeling. "Make yourself at home while I find something more comfortable to put on. The kitchen is down the hall to the left," she said, pointing in its direction.

Once she was out of sight, Sean began to explore her living quarters starting with the formal sitting room. Looking at the sixty inch television, he could not help but think about how hard of a time the movers must have had traveling eight flights of stairs because there was no possible way it could've fit into the elevator. Thankful that he wasn't involved in the task, he moved on.

Next, he admired the grey marble and glass coffee and end tables, and how it complimented the grey leather furniture that rested on top of thick, aqua blue carpet. With each step he took, he noticed how his feet sank at least a half inch into its fibers. The art that decorated the walls looked as if it all had been created by the same individual. Someone that was very abstract and unorthodox, who also possessed an unlimited amount of talent.

Walking over to the entertainment system, Sean picked up one, of the many remote controls that laid lifeless on top of it. One touch of the power button brought the system to life with Mary J. Blige eagerly singing her heart out.

"Would you like something to drink?" Stacy asked, startling Sean.

Quickly regaining his composure, he replied, "Yeah, that'd be nice. What you got, ma?" He was hoping that she didn't see him flinch when she snuck up behind him.

"Shit, whatever you want, I got it."

"Well then, just give me whatever you're drinking, ma. I'll be cool with that." When she walked past him in her tan silk, loose fitting pajama boy shorts that slightly revealed her ass cheeks, white wife beater, and fully erect nipples, she instantly grasped Sean's attention. With one good glance, he noticed every detail about her body. The tan silk shorts she had on blended well with her caramel skin complexion. From the way her nipples stood out under the cotton fabric she had on, he could tell that they were unusually long. His dick was hard as nails. He didn't know if he was about to get some action, but he sure as hell hoped so.

It didn't take her long to return. With drinks in hand, she sashayed over to the sofa he was sitting on and took a seat right beside him and handed him his drink. He couldn't help but to focus on her toned, muscular legs as she crossed them, wondering just what she could do with them. He envisioned her wrapping them around his waist tightly as he made passionate love to her.

"Damn, Sean! You eying my legs like you want to eat them up. Ummmh, I'm scared of you."

"Baby, you definitely don't have a reason to be scared of me. The last thing I'm trying to do is hurt you," he replied, smiling.

"Ummmmh, anyway! I made us vodka and cranberry juice. Is that okay?

"Yeah. That's cool, ma," he stated with lustful guilt written all over his face.

"Boyyy, quit looking at me like that."

"Like what?"

"Like you're ready to fuck the shit outta me," she amitted, before taking a sip of her drink.

# The Hustle

"What? Is that what you want me to do? Because if it is, it could be arranged. I hope I didn't just offend you with my honesty."

"Nahhh, you good. I like the fact that you keeping it real with me. Since we being honest and all, I gotta tell you that I've been feeling you from the first night I met you. But, I figured I'd give you time to mingle and do you since you just got out of prison. Actually, Derrick talked and bragged about you so much, I was practically sold on you even before I seen you." Her last statement shocked the hell out of Sean, but he didn't reply on it.

"So you've been feeling me since the first night we met, huh? I like the fact that you understood my situation and decided to give me a chance to do me. You don't find too many women like that nowadays." As the vodka and cranberry juice took effect, Sean found himself slowly but surely letting his guards down. Although he had two beautiful, reasonable women on his team that never questioned or judged him and were crazy cool and very satisfying, he still wanted to test the waters with the woman that was sitting next to him. Even if it was only for one night.

"I'm not your average woman, Sean. I already have everything I could possibly desire. All I need now is a good man with determination that's faithful to me. If I get that, the possibilities are endless. The sky's the limit for us."

"Shiit, a good man isn't hard to find. You just got to know where to look," he said, obviously talking about himself.

"Are you sure you can be faithful, Sean?" she questioned, placing emphasis on the entire sentence. Feeling that the mood was right, Sean leaned in and kissed her while softly speaking in between each peck,

"Don't worry, I got you, ma." Stacey couldn't help but to give in to his soft lips and sensual kisses. Before she knew it, their tongues were exploring each other's mouth. Stacey was the type of woman that knew what she wanted, she had no problem going straight for it. So, without missing a beat, she unloosened his belt, and then went for the button that held his jeans in its place.

Sean unconsciously lifted his body up a bit to make it easier for her to pull them down while still engaged in a heated kiss. As they slid down to his knees, she maneuvered her hand down to his crotch area and began to rub and massage his penis through his designer boxers. Sean, himself, was busy filling up on every piece of her uncovered flesh until his hand made its way between her legs. Stacey moaned and sign the second he stuck his finger inside of her. At that very moment, there was one or two things Sean was sure of. Either it has been a while since she last had some dick or she was the great pretender.

His hunger for her was getting stronger and stronger with each passing second. "Let's go to my room," Stacey finally suggested, speaking in a soft, whisper like tone. With her speaking so seductive and being extremely close to his ear, he felt the warmth of her breath. It almost caused him to lose his load right there on the spot. When he stood to follow her, he relieved himself from his shirt and the jeans that were holding his ankles captive.

Completely naked, he followed her down the long corridor up a flight of stairs and into a luxurious bedroom. At that point and time, he was so caught up in her rapture that she could have easily led him straight to his grave and it probably wouldn't have mattered to him. Stacey always felt a sense of control whenever she was inside her bedroom. She was the master and Sean was now her slave. She ordered him on the bed and straddled him as if he was a Stallion. The way his body shivered when she touched him was confirmation to her that she had him right where she wanted him. She smiled, thinking to herself how pussy was always a man's biggest weakness.

When she began to perform oral sex on him, she sucked and licked his dick as if it was a lollipop. Looking at the beautiful woman and how she took pride in using her mouth to satisfy him pushed him to the brink of climax. But, he couldn't come just yet. He wanted to feel inside of her first, which was why he stopped her and decided to return the oral pleasure. He wanted her to get a taste of his technique so that she'd know how a professional pussy sucker really got down.

# Chapter Thirteen

Back at the club, Gerald was still posted in the VIP section having the time of his life. He was surrounded by five drop dead gorgeous women that were all tipsy and practically down for whatever. But, there was one chick in general that he was really feeling. She had recently joined his entourage of women. To him, hands down, she had every chick in the room beat in personality, plus, she had a body to die for. Baby girl was real. He was so caught up in the rapture of things he didn't realize that one of the women was working for the enemy.

Tonya was simply carrying out orders that were sent down by her boyfriend, Tu. Those orders were to get up under Gerald by any means necessary, get him nice and drunk, and convince him to leave with her to a designated hotel, in which Tu would be there to surprise him. For Tonya, following Gerald was the easy part. The complicated part came in when she saw him pull up to the club because she knew she would have to compete for his attention against a bunch of sack chasers. But first, she had to get the okay whether or not she could enter the club from her man.

Tu didn't care what it took for Tonya to persuade Gerald to leave with her. Just as long as she made it happen. The only thing he knew was the next time she called, she had better been saying she and Gerald were at the spot. Tonya knew Tu was a married man, but it didn't stop her from falling in love with him. First, she viewed him as only a quick come-up, so she was willing to do whatever it took to reel him in. But, over the course of time, her feelings somehow got involved.

Since Tu was always testing her love and loyalty, she figured it was just another test to see if she was a down enough bitch to be on his team. The other four women that were sitting next to her were no comparison at all. They all had hidden agendas, but Tonya's agenda was totally different from the rest of the woman. She was willing to fuck Gerald for the sake of her man while the other girls were willing to fuck him for the sake of a few dollars.

There was no way she was about to let any one of those females come between her plans, so when she noticed they were actually willing to do whatever, she turned her freak image on full blast. "Fuck these other bitches, baby," she whispered in his ear. "I'm trying to leave with you, and go to my hotel room and fuck all night long! That is, if you think you can handle this," she said, letting her last words linger on her tongue. Just mentioning the word fuck captured Gerald's undivided attention. Looking at the bad, thick ass redbone, picturing all the nasty, freaky things he could do to her, Gerald was ready to leave the club.

This shit was easier than I thought! Tonya thought as she smirked while they made their way toward the club's entrance to exit. "My car is over there, baby," she said, pointing at the black Pontiac Grand AM. "Follow me, okay?"

"Yeah, that's cool," he replied with a slight slur in his speech as he made his way to his car.

"I hope this trick ass nigga don't crash before we get to where we're going! Tu would be mad as hell," Tonya said to herself after looking back and seeing Gerald stumble a little. She then hopped into the car that Tu had purchased for her two months ago. In the past, she'd dealt with plenty of guys like Gerald before, so she knew just how to handle him. When Gerald pulled up beside her, for the first time she noticed just how handsome he really was. For a second, she played with the thought of becoming his girl, then quickly shook it out of her head. There was no way she could ever leave Tu. In the short period of time that she'd know him, he'd managed to do more for her than any other man she'd ever been involved with. That alone answered any "what if" questions she may have had about she and Gerald. There was no way she was willing to risk losing what she knew she had for something she knew nothing about.

Following Tonya through the downtown streets heading toward the expressway, Gerald finally figured out just where she was heading to. Super 8 Motel. With it being right by Interstate I-70, he considered that to be easy access to dip on her ass once she fell asleep after he wore that ass out. Practically the entire ride over to the hotel, he could see that she was conversing on her cell phone. For a minute, he wondered just who was she talking to. Then, he chalked it to her probably giving her man some bogus excuse about why she wouldn't be home. Suddenly, he began to laugh out loud, thinking about all the other women he'd once had in that same predicament after leaving the club with him.

"Fuck that nigga! You don't owe him no explanation, baby! Don't worry, after I finish beating up the pussy, I'll send yo ass home cum drunk!" he continued, laughing. Gerald was always like that. He never took anyone's relationship or feelings into consideration. To him, it was all about Gerald.

When they finally pulled up on the hotel's parking lot, she motioned for him to park while she pulled to the entrance to rent the room. Gerald smiled to himself when he saw her go into the office to pay for the room. Only if he knew his old friend Tu was the one gracious enough to pick up the tab. While Tonya was in the club working her magic, he decided to get the room and have everything all set up for her. All she had to do was go inside and get the key. Once the fake transaction was completed, she pulled her car right beside Gerald's and got out.

"We all good, baby. Let's go," she announced.

"Anybody ever told you, you favor Free from 106 & Park?" Gerald asked as he trailed behind her.

"All the time. But, let's get one thing straight, ain't shit here free unless I want it to be!" she said, switching her ass a little harder.

"Oh, okay, it's like that, huh?" The entire time, he was thinking to himself how in the end, the only thing she'd be left with was a mouth full of nut and dick mints on her breath.

"You still drinking or what?" Tonya asked.

"Shiit, I'd like to, but we'd have to go across the water and I ain't feeling that there. But, I got a lil' some'n in the trunk of my car," he replied eagerly.

"Well, what you waiting on? I'll be right here in the room." Without saying another word, he headed toward his car. Tonya was thankful for that little break because it would give her time to call Tu and update him on what was going on. Before she could get her phone out of her Coach purse, Gerald was entering the room. In one hand he held a portable cooler and in the other a fifth of XO Hennessey.

"Lock the door," she said, seeing that he had left it unlocked. The minute he turned toward the door, she stuffed the phone into her pocket. "I'll be right back, I have to use the bathroom," she continued. "Why don't you go down to the ice machine and get us a bucket of ice, daddy?" she spoke in her most alluring, sexiest voice. Before she could get another word out, Gerald had the ice bucket in hand, heading for the door. The minute he was out of sight, she rushed into the bathroom and turned the shower on full blast just in case he came back, so he wouldn't hear her conversation. "Yeah, baby, it's me...We in the room now. Yeah. Un huh, it'll be unlocked, daddy. Love you, too."

Just hearing Tu admit his love and how proud he was of her put a huge smile on Tonya's face. She was very much blinded by love, so when he told her to give Gerald head or fuck him, whatever it took to keep him there, it was no problem to her. It was all about her man, Tu. She would do anything to please him. She began to strip down to her panties and bra, proceeding with the plan that Tu so heavily embedded in her brain. There was a knock at the bathroom door.

"A, you a'ight in there, baby girl? You gone stay in there all night or are you gone come out here and fuck with yo boy?" yelled Gerald from the opposite side of the door.

A few seconds later, Tonya opened the door and posed in the doorway with her hand on her huge hip. "So, do you like what you see?"

# The Hustle

"Damn skippy! Ummn!" he said, licking his lips. As he walked toward her, she decided to meet him halfway. They began to kiss each other aggressively as if they were starving for one another's intimacy. While entangled in the lustful embrace, Tonya began to take control, backing him toward the bed. When Gerald's body made contact with it, he fell instantly with Tonya in his arms. She then lifted his shirt and began to plant soft kisses upon his chest.

The further down she went, the more tensed Gerald's body became. Then, all of a sudden, she stopped. "What's wrong, ma?" He asked, his facial expression showed confusion.

"Could you please grab some towels and a wet wash cloth out of the bathroom?," she replied.

At first, Gerald thought that she may have smelled the sex scent he had on him from earlier, but then he remembered how well Monae had washed him off before he left her spot. He wanted to admit to Sean that they were fucking, but he wasn't sure how he felt about her. Since his dick was hard as steel, he was willing to do whatever Tonya requested, just as long as she was willing to satisfy his sexual urge. He had no idea she only requested the towels so that she could unlock the door.

When he returned from the bathroom, Tonya was totally nude lying cross the bed, looking as if he she was ready for whatever. Gerald smiled at the sight of her, and then quickly began to remove his clothing. Standing there naked, he admired every inch of her body right before he dived into the bed. Tonya had to literally grab ahold of him just to keep from falling off the bed. As she hungrily clung to him, the two began to pick up where they left off. It didn't take her long to make her way back down to his weak spot. Gerald just laid there while she had her way with his manhood.

She ran her tongue across his shaft until it became hard and swollen. Since giving head was her specialty, she put it down to the fullest, using nothing but mouth and a massive amount of saliva. Not once did Gerald feel a single tooth graze against his joint. Baby girl was all pro! Each time she felt that his orgasm was building up, she would slow down her motion. What Gerald didn't know was she was only trying to time Tu so that she wouldn't have to fuck him. With the television volume up halfway and his eyes closed tightly enjoying the blow job of a lifetime, Gerald never heard or noticed Tu and his partner when they walked through the door.

"Well, well, well! If it ain't slick ass Gerald! What up, nigga. I just know you got some'n fo' me, right?" Tu exclaimed, making it sound more like a statement rather than a question. Gerald recognized his voice immediately. As soon as he heard Tu speak he was up out of the bed, attempting to put some clothes on. He definitely didn't want to go out like that.

"He...Hey, Tu! What up, my nigga? When you get out!" Gerald nervously asked. He was trying his best to conceal the fear he was feeling.

"What's up, huh? Shiiit, if I didn't know better, I'd think this nigga's happy to see me, Duke!" Tu said to his partner. "The fuck you mean, what's up, when did I get out? Mafucka, you wasn't worried about all that when you heard the news about me blowing trial, was you?"

"I...I..." Gerald stuttered.

"I...I...What? Now yo ass is tongued tied, huh?" Before he could say another word, Duke had managed to ease up on the side of him, catching him square in the jaw with a hard right cross. As the punch connected, a loud deafening sound of bones being broken could clearly be heard over the volume of the television. The force of the punch knocked him off of his feet. Laying in a fetal position, his only reaction was to nurse the aching jaw bone he had. He cupped it with his right hand while squirming around on the worn out carpet. By that time, Tonya was fully dressed. She proudly took the position on the right side of her man and stood there calmly, waiting for him to finish handling his business.

"When you disrespected my people, you disrespected me, ma'fucka! But, you never expected to see me again, huh? Life's a bitch, ain't it? But, check this out. You know that change that you owe me that you neglected to pay? You can keep it. I don't even want it anymore. Matter of fact, just give it to your mother as a gift from me. That's the least I can do to make sure she bury her son in style. Duke, smoke this piece of shit!"

"Baby, baby, I thought you said you wasn't gone hurt hi..."

Before Tonya could finish her sentence, Tu stuck a seven inch blade into her abdomen, and then twisted the knife and yanked it out of her. She fell to her knees, grabbing her wound. Blood began to quickly seep out of her wound at an alarming rate. Gerald could do nothing but lay there watching. He knew his fate had been decided when he saw Duke pull out a 9mm Beretta with a silencer attached on the end of it.

"Tu, please don't..." Gerald pleaded for his life through a clenched, broken jaw. But, his cries fell upon death ears. Phew! Phew! Phew! Was the muffled sound that Duke's gun made as he pulled the trigger. In a matter of seconds, the once decent hotel room had been turned into a murder scene. "Duke check that fool pockets, see if he has any money in em .This nigga's known for high-cappin " Tu demanded .He looked down at Tonya's lifeless body and shook his head , "So beautiful, but yet so naïve. Duke, I hate to admit it but I'm gone miss that tight young pussy." he stated, stepping over her corpse with his right hand man on his heels. "Just another casuality of war big homie." Duke replied as he calmly closed the door behind him.

# Chapter Fourteen

As the rays of the sun peeked through the venetian blind, Sean was just starting to wake up from a steamy night of lovemaking with the beautiful Stacey. In his eyes, she had proven herself to be more woman than he expected. The many ways she sexed him all night and how good she gave head had his nose completely open. Before he started getting dressed, he decided to take a quick shower. As he laid next to Stacey's sleeping body on her queen sized bed gathering his thoughts, he couldn't help but to think about Meloney, wondering if he was making the right decision by choosing to commit to her. Watching Stacey, noticing just how peaceful and serene she looked, had him wishing that he could somehow enter the world she was in.

Spending a night with her had truly given him a bunch of mixed emotions as far as what he thought he felt for the other two women in his life. He tried to convince himself that last night was a one time deal. Meaningless sex that happened between two consensual adults. Nothing more, nothing less. But the more he stared at this beautiful creature sleeping so peacefully, the more he pondered the thought of what it would be like to have a serious relationship with her. As he gathered his clothes to head for the adjacent bathroom, he glanced at the digital clock that at on her nightstand. It read ten twenty seven a.m. Realizing that he had serious business to take care of, he knew he had to bounce.

"Hey, baby," Stacey spoke in a sleepy voice. "You taking off on me?"

"Yeah, I got some business to take care of this morning."

"Don't we?"

"You telling me you was serious?" he stated mystified. By that time, he was back seated again.

"Ahhh, so you thought I was joking, huh?" she replied as she sat in an upright position, exposing her voluptuous breast. "You'll see just how serious I am when I meet you at two o'clock at Crown's Soul food restaurant on Jefferson and Delmar."

"Yeah, a'ight. We'll see," he said in a playful manner. "Anyway, I know you have an extra toothbrush so a nigga can get his grill, right?"

"Yes, baby. Look in the medicine cabinet, it should be one in there." Sean got up and headed towards the bathroom.. "Sean," she said while opening her legs, revealing her perfectly manicured pussy. "You sure you don't want to go another round before you take that shower?" Stopping abruptly , he turned and spoke,

"I wish I could, baby, but unfortunately, I have things to take care of. Can I take a rain check on that offer?"

Although she wouldn't have mind getting some

more of that good dick of his, Stacey was more than fine
with his answer. If it would have been any different, she
would have took that as a sign of weakness, something
that was a complete turn off for her. She only respected a
strong man, that was the only type she was willing to
surrender her heart to. For her, a man had to choose
business over pleasure. As she watched him walk off, she
was starting to view him as potential boyfriend material.
Ten minutes later, Sean came out of the bathroom fully
dressed and looked rejuvenated. Stacey walked him to
the door and sent him on his way with a kiss.

The first thing Sean did after walking through his
front door was check his messages while fixing himself a
fresh cup of coffee. He knew he had a big day ahead of
him. First, he had to double count the money just to
make sure it was all there. He didn't want to make a bad
first impression by giving Felix a short count. Next, he
had to call Gerald to make sure he'd be available to lend
his assistance once he got the work. Now that he had his
check list in order, all he had to do was wait on the call
from his connect, so he relaxed at the kitchen table and
listened to his messages while sipping coffee. "Hey, baby,
it's me, your future wife. I was just sitting here thinking
about you so I thought I'd give you a call, but obviously
you're not there. So, just give me a call whenever you get
back in, okay? I love you, Sean." Hearing Meloney's voice
brought a huge feeling of guilt over him, from what he
did with Stacey.

"Hey, Sean, it's Maxeen. First of all, I wanted to
apologize for our last little argument. Please, call me
when you get in. I need some, baby. Call me." Maxeen
always had a way with words. The way she used them so
seductively sent chills up Sean's spine. It had him
seriously thinking about returning her call first to see if

they could get together later on. Thinking about how intense make-up sex could get had his mind in a frenzy. At least, until his cell phone rang, interrupting his thought process. Looking at the caller ID that read unidentified caller, he knew it had to be Felix.

"Hello," he answered on the second ring.

How are you, my friend?" Felix replied. It was obvious he was in a very good mood. But, who wouldn't be? Especially if they knew they were about to make over a quarter of a million dollars in one move.

"I'm good. What's up, are we ready to rock and roll?"

"Si. Can you meet my friend at the Soul Food restaurant on Jefferson and Delmar, at let's say, two o'clock? And, don't be late."

"No problem. I'll be there." Sean stated before hanging up the phone. Instantly, his mind went back to those exact same words, but with Stacey saying them. It wasn't that he didn't want to believe her. It was just that he'd never met a woman that was deep in the game to that magnitude. For Stacey to have access to fill the order he placed, she had to be well connected. A few seconds later, he noticed that he was still holding the receiver in his hand. "Damn! This bitch wasn't bullshitting!" he stated as an afterthought. A smile then flashed across his face. He knew there was nothing better than fucking the connect.

Twenty minutes later after taking his second shower of the day, Sean was dressed to impress and ready to take care of business. He made sure to keep it casual for the occasion. Since he didn't want to come across as the thug or street hustler, he decided to sport a button down white and tan striped Izod shirt, a pair of tan colored khakis with a pair of soft brown Steve Madden loafers.

# The Hustle

When he arrived on the scene, the place was pretty busy for two o'clock in the afternoon. Intentionally, he arrived a few minutes early because he didn't want to keep Stacy waiting with that amount of drugs on her. He knew he'd be pissed, had someone kept him waiting while he was in possession of a life sentence worth of narcotics. As he nervously sat inside his car reflecting on his life, he thought about all the promises he'd made to himself while sitting in prison and how he managed to break all of them so far. He hadn't even been out a full year and was already starting to let his goals and dreams wither down the drain. So again, he made a mental to hit the studio as soon as he and Gerald sold a nice portion of the work he was about to receive.

The three-hundred thousand dollars that was resting in the passenger seat in a black army duffle bag was well over enough to do what he needed to do. But, when you were addicted to da hustle, enough was never enough. Sean kept telling himself after he and Gerald finished this deal, he was completely done with the game. At least, that was what he thought.

What he didn't know was he'd have to handle this and every other deal all by himself, that there would be no more drug dealing for Gerald, thanks to Tu. Sean had no idea that his partner's body had been discovered earlier, along with one of his female companions, by the cleaning lady as she made her rounds after check-out time.

Right as he was about to call Gerald to inform him of what was going down, he observed a grey Ford Expedition pulling up on the lot. Inside it was Stacy and an unknown black male. After Stacy's driver pulled beside Sean, he got out of the car to greet her. She, too, got out.

165

"Hey, baby," she spoke as she hugged Sean and gave him a quick peck on the lips. She then replied in a no nonsense like tone, "You got something for me?"

"Damn, you get right down to business, don't you?" he shot back.

"With forty kilos in back seat of my truck, what do you expect? This is business, not a date, Sean," she bluntly stated.

Seeing that she was all about business, he, too, put his business face on and attended to the matter at hand. Without saying another word, he reached into the passenger's window and grabbed the duffle bag that contained the money, "It's all there, three-hundred K. You can count it if you like," he stated sarcastically.

Once the bag of money was in Stacy's possession, her driver quickly got out of the truck, opened the driver's side back door, and tossed the bag of money on the floorboard. Then, in one swift motion, he grabbed two duffle bags that were also on the floorboard and tossed them inside the open window of Sean's vehicle. It all happened so quick, one blink and you could've easily missed the whole transaction. Then, out of nowhere, Stacy walked over to Sean and French kissed him, and then asked if she could see him later after work. She was back to acting like the chick he'd kicked it with the night before. Of course, his ego was boosted again, so he decided to play hardball with her.

"I'ma have to get back with you on that, let me check my schedule." He then got into his car, started it up, and drove off without so much of a goodbye. In his eyes, he figured one cold shoulder deserved another. Especially since he was handling business like she so blatantly put it.

It felt good to finally be heading back in the

direction of home. So far, it seemed as if everything was going in his favor. He hadn't even seen a single police car since he picked up the drugs. But, as soon as that thought crossed his mind, while sitting at a red light out of nowhere appeared a police vehicle approaching right behind him. Instantly, Sean's heart began to beat at an abnormal rate. Beads of sweat started to take its form on his brow. Sean told himself over and over not to panic, that they wasn't even worried about him. But, all the pep talk in the world still couldn't calm his nerves. The only thing he could manage to think about was prison and how he didn't want to go back. There was no way he intended on pulling over willingly, not with forty bricks in the car. That would be the equivalent to taking the gun that he now had his palms wrapped around, and putting it to his head, pulling the trigger. A straight sucker move. The only logical thing he seen himself doing was holding court in the streets, something that he was praying it wouldn't come to.

So, with a Glock .10 under his right leg and forty kilos on the passenger floorboard, Sean faithfully obeyed each and every traffic law, hoping and praying that the lawman would continue to mind his own business. But, it didn't seem like he had intentions of doing that, not with the way he swooped in behind Sean. The moment Sean witnessed the officer talking into his cb radio, he knew he was in trouble. Next came the siren followed by the cherries. Sean decided that he would pull over, only for the sake of possibly getting a head start in the chase he was about to initiate. He figured as soon as he saw the cop exit his vehicle, he'd floor it, leaving the cop on the side of the road.

Keeping a cool head, he began to pull to the shoulder of the road. He was sweating much more profusely than before. He wasn't sure how the situation would play out, but his mind had it all figured out. To his surprise, the cop car swooped around him instead of behind him, hightailing right past him as if he didn't exist, leaving Sean shaking on the side of the road. With that much blow, if convicted, which he was sure he would have been, Sean knew he'd never see the streets again unless he was willing to take the rat way out. That wasn't an option for him. He rather die a respected man than live as a snitch. He was willing to try to shoot his way out of trouble, if necessary.

Watching the rear end of the police car as it disappear, heading to fuck someone else's day up, he couldn't help but to smile knowing that he'd just dodged a bullet. One thing for sure was he knew he wouldn't he getting hauled off in that particular police car. Now, all he had to do is make it home. Dodging that bullet was indeed a sign to Sean. He knew he had to make a drastic change for the better before time ran out on him. The rest of the ride home was event free. The second he pulled into his garage, he knew he was in the clear. As he entered it, he reached into the middle console and pulled out his cell to give Gerald a call. It went straight to his voice mail.

After he and the product were secure inside the house, he reached into one of the bags and pulled out a kilo to give it his initial inspection. It passed with flying colors. It was the exact same blow that Derrick left him with and the most coke Sean had ever possessed at one time. Looking at all those bricks that he'd placed on the table and how they were professionally wrapped in saran wrap and duct tape had him wondering just how far had the cocaine traveled from. He then thought about all the brothers and sisters who lost their lives or sold their souls for less than one percent of what was on the table. He was starting to get nervous just by looking at all of that cocaine. As he picked up his cell to call Gerald again, it began to ring. It was Meloney.

"What's up, baby? Why haven't you called me? I'm beginning to think that you're playing me to the left now that you got what you wanted."

"Nah, baby. It's not like that! I just went out to the club with Gerald last night and today I kinda been running errands for my moms," he lied.

"You must have had a real good time last night because I've been calling all morning and couldn't get an answer," she replied, fishing to see if he'd spent the night in someone else's bed.

"It was a'ight. But, you know that club scene really isn't my type of hype. I only went because I let that fool Gerald talk me into it. As far as the phone situation, since I knew I wouldn't be able to hear it in the club, anyway, I decided to turn to it off, and I didn't realize it was off until this morning when I woke up."

"Ahhh, okay. So, what's up for tonight, do you have to work?"

"Unfortunately, yes. Why, what's up? You trying to see ya man or some'n when I get off?"

"Maybe!" she replied, with a touch of sass in her voice.

"Well, if you decide to come through, there's a key waiting for you inside the mailbox. Just stick yo hand all the way in the back, it's there. I should be home around twelve thirty, a'ight?"

"Okay, baby. I love you, Sean."

"Love you, too...And, ummmm, have some'n sexy on that's easy to take off, a'ight?"

"Boy, gone and go to work. I'll see you tonight!" she

stated right before hanging up.

Since Sean had an hour left before his shift started, he quickly stashed the coke in the pool table stash spot with the exception of one. The kilo he kept out, he broke it down into four quarters just in case Gerald decided to have some of his clientele stop by the job. Even though he really didn't like the idea of doing illegal business out of the job, he knew Gerald would most likely do it, anyway. Who was he to tell a grown man what and what not to do? Since most of the money was going in his pocket, he was cool with it. Besides, there was no one but he and Gerald at the store during those hours, so it was basically all good. Right as he was about to walk out of the house, he thought about calling Gerald once more but decided against it, being that he knew he'd see him at work.

# Chapter Fifteen

Pulling up on Vicker's parking lot, Sean's eyes scanned the area for Gerald's Lexus. It was nowhere in sight. His first assumption was Gerald was late because he was too busy chasing pussy, as usual. As he walked in to relieve Mrs. Turner, the AM worker, he noticed that she was still busy counting the cash drawer for her shift. That was an indication that he was a little early because she usually had her drawer counted and ready to go by the time he and Gerald arrived.

"Well, hello, Sean," she spoke as she continued to count the store's take for her shift without looking up from her task. Mrs. Turner was an older white lady that was married to a black man. For her to be approaching her fifties, she still looked damned good.

"Hey, Mrs. Turner! Has Gerald called in or some'n?"

"No, he hasn't. But, he better have his ass in here! I think the district manager may be stopping by the store between the hours of four and five," she said, finally looking up, taking a short break. Mrs. Turner was kinda hip for a white woman. Her character was a prime example of the affect a black man had over his woman. Most women, regardless of color or nationality, usually took on traits of their significant other.

That was about all he knew about Mrs. Turner and her husband. Whenever he saw either of them, it was only in passing. After counting her drawer, she left one hundred and seventy-five dollars in the cash register for Sean to begin his shift with, and then put the remaining amount in a manila envelope and dropped it into a hidden floor safe. Then, she was gone.

Twenty minutes into his shift and still no sign of Gerald, he decided to give him a call just to see what excuse he'd use for being almost an hour late. After about four rings the phone was finally answered, but it wasn't Gerald. Sean's first reaction was to hang up after hearing someone's voice other than Gerald. He figured that maybe he had the wrong number. "Hello!" the stranger replied for the second time, but with more persistence.

"Yes, is Gerald around?" Sean asked, attempting to disguise his voice.

"May I ask who's calling?" the stranger replied. Right then, Sean knew that it had to be a cop on the other end of the line. At least, that was what his gut feeling was telling him. Usually, his gut feelings were right. Good thing that he decided to use the store's phone line instead of his cell.

"Yes, this is Mr. Martin, the manager over at Vicker's service station. I'm calling to speak with Gerald to see why he didn't show up for work tonight."

"Well, Mr. Martin, this is Detective Jones from the homicide unit in First District and unfortunately, Gerald won't be coming back to work. I may need you to stop by the station to answer a few questions, or I could just stop by the job if it's more convenient for you." Sean didn't know what to think, but he knew either one or two things had happened. Either Gerald was the homicide victim or he was the culprit. He knew the drill all to well and how the system worked. He knew the officer was in the first stages of his investigation, fishing for any little piece of evidence he could gather. He also knew that being deceptive would only cause problems in the long run, so he agreed to speak with the officer. Whatever the case was, he knew he had nothing to do with what had happened, so he felt he had nothing to worry about.

"Well, as of right now I'm currently at work, Detective Jones, and unfortunately, I don't get off until midnight. So, how do you want to do this?"

"I tell you what, why don't you just give me the address to where you're at and I'll come to you." After Sean gave the detective the address to his job and hung up the phone, he went ballistic. "Fuck! Gerald, you stupid mafucka!" he said as he frantically paced the small area behind the counter. "What the fuck am I gon' do now with all this work?" he questioned himself out loud. Although he and Gerald had managed to become somewhat close friends, he suddenly realized that he really didn't know Gerald at all. The situation was much different in the prison environment, where one was able to get to know each other on a personal level, because you're around each other constantly.

He quickly found out how most people were only willing to disclose the side of them that they wanted you to know. But, if a person was constantly around those same individuals, sooner or later, they were bound to slip up and reveal their true identity. Being that he and Gerald only spent a limited amount of time together, he knew very little about his true character and his past. The truth of the matter was, he and Gerald had become close, but not as close as he and Derrick were. So much of his focus was on Detective Jones and the fact that he'd be arriving soon, that he was too selfish to realize that he'd lost a friend.

With each customer that came into the station, Sean felt a sense of panic come over him. He had no idea what to expect out of the unwanted visitor. Finally, at around six thirty, in walked a huge white man that looked as if he could have passed for an NFL linebacker. He stood about six feet two in height, and three hundred pounds easily with very broad shoulders. One glance and it was obvious to Sean that he was Detective Jones in the flesh. Sean studied the man carefully, hoping to feel him out, but he was unreadable. Although, he did have a serious asshole, racist look about him, Sean figured his story was typical. A college athlete who's dreams of going pro were shattered due to some serious injury ,was more likely his story.

Detective Jones possessed very strong facial features, kind of like an old action figure. As he waited for the customer in front of him to be served, his eyes constantly scanned his surroundings looking for clues.
"Mr. Martin," he stated as he stepped to the counter. "We spoke earlier on the phone, I'm Detective Jones." He then extended his hand. Sean gave him a firm handshake. Lord knows he really didn't want to shake the hand of the one whom he considered to be the enemy. Even though it wasn't Detective Jones personally, Sean still felt as if he was somewhat responsible for taking ten years away from his life.

"Yes, I remember," he stated dryly.

"I can see that you're rather busy this evening so I'm not going to take up a lot of your time," he spoke confidently while looking Sean directly in the eyes. After the formal meet and greet process was done, the questions began.

Basically, Detective Jones was fishing, hoping to learn more about Gerald's character. He also wanted to find out if he and Sean had a relationship outside of their work environment.

Thirty minutes and twenty questions later, he seemed somewhat satisfied with the answers he received from Sean. Sean told the detective he and Gerald only knew each other through work, nothing more. But, Sean would soon find out that Detective Jones was no rookie when it came to a homicide investigation. He thoroughly did his homework on both of their backgrounds.

# Chapter Sixteen

By the time Sean's work shift was over, he was extremely exhausted both mentally and physically, not to mention stressed. He was so busy worrying about the detective, the dope he'd just scored, and his future, he totally forgot that he told Meloney to meet him at the house. When she greeted him at the door with only his bathrobe on, he smiled and took her into his arms.

"Poor baby. You look like you had a hard day," she stated as she embraced her man. "I did, boo," he replied, "Some detective came by the job about Gerald," he said after they broke their embrace.

"Are you serious? Is he okay?"

"I'm afraid not, baby. I mean... the detective didn't actually say what happened to him, but he told me that Gerald was found dead in a hotel room this morning. He came over to the job questioning me, looking for a lead to go off of. He probably was trying to see how I'd react to all of the questioning."

"Was everything okay between you two?"

"As far as I know, baby. I mean, we was at the club together the night before last. He didn't act like nothing was wrong. In my eyes, he was having a good time."

"Did you tell the police that?"

"Hell nawl! If I would've told him that, he'd be looking at me as a suspect, watching me."

"So what," she snapped as she followed him into his bedroom. "You don't have anything to hide! I mean, you're not hustling anymore, so it shouldn't matter, right?"

"You're right. But, baby, I just didn't feel like being bothered with his ass. While he was in there harassing me, cats was coming through the job looking at a nigga all sideways and shit. Like I fucks with the police or some'n."

"Sean, you're a grown ass man! Why are you still worried about what some street thugs think of you? The whole point is your friend just lost his life, Sean. Don't you think that's being a little selfish on your part? Look, I'm not saying help the police do their job, but you could at least tell them the truth, baby. I think you owe Gerald that much since you two were friends." Watching him strip naked was turning Meloney on big time. As she sat on the edge of the bed next to him, she literally had to use all of her will power to keep from sexually assaulting him.

"Mel, a lot of people's friends get killed practically every day, the police don't get their help. So, what's the difference?

"The difference is, more than likely your damn number is all on his phone records, Sean. Do you know that's the first place they're going to look for potential suspects?"

"Damn!" Sean stated out loud as an afterthought. "The one thing the detective did say is he wasn't alone."

"Somebody else must have gotten hurt as well,"

Meloney added.

"Yeah. And, knowing Gerald, nine times out of ten, it was probably a female because that dude was like a dog in heat, he stayed chasing pussy."

"Baby, just to be on the safe side, I think you need to call that detective back and tell him that you and Gerald used to go out from time to time after work for a drink. That way, he won't be looking at you funny when he finds out from Gerald's phone records that you two communicated frequently."

Realizing that Meloney was right, he decided to follow her advice. "You're right, baby. I'll call him tomorrow while I'm at work," he said as he stood up about to head into the bathroom. As he rose from the bed, Meloney parted her legs slightly, revealing that she was totally naked under the robe. That instantly grabbed Sean's attention. "By the way, Ms Lady, what exactly are you doing with my bathrobe on?" he questioned while pulling at the garment, attempting to open it.

"Stop it, Sean!" she said in a playful manner. "And, for your info, I just got out of the shower," she replied, snatching the robe out of his hand. "Why, you want it back?" she asked as she stood up and seductively began to ease it off of her in a strip tease kind of way, revealing parts of her near perfect body. Sean couldn't help himself, he had to touch her.

From that point on, no words were spoken because they were both literally tongue tied. The way Meloney touched Sean as if he was the only man that existed on this earth, sent chills throughout his body. If he didn't know anything else, he knew Meloney's feelings for him were as real as it got. At that very moment, she was the only woman that existed in Sean's world. The feelings that he got whenever they were together was much stronger than lust. It had to be love.

Meloney eagerly took control. Her body ached for his affection and she couldn't wait to become one with Sean. The two began to explore each other's body as if it was their very first time making love. Sean was extra gentle, but at the same time, very attentive. He gave Meloney's body the VIP treatment of love. As time slipped away in the midst of the night making way for the a.m., they fell sound asleep in each other's arms. The next morning, Sean was awaken by the sound of his cell phone as it sung profusely.

"Hello!" he finally answered in a groggy, half sleep voice.

"Hey, you. Did I wake you?" a familiar voice called out from the opposite end of the line. It took Sean a second to register the voice. Once he realize who it was, he eased up out of bed. "Nah, I'm good. What's up, Asia, is everything okay?" he said after he closed the bathroom door. It wasn't that he was trying to hide something from Meloney, he just didn't want to disturb her sleep. Especially since it looked as if she was in a deep, peaceful state.

"You think you could come through when you're out and about?"

"Of course. Why, is everything okay?" he replied with deep concern.

"Yeah, everything is good. I just need to holla at you in person, that's all."

"Alright."

"And, Sean, don't forget," she stated matter of factly.

When Sean reentered the room, he sat down on the edge of the bed and began to stare at Meloney. He loved the way she made him feel. It was like whenever he was with her, he was always at peace. The comfort level was through the roof. Although love was a complicated emotion, she made it seem so simple. It was crazy how easily she was able to transform a tension filled evening, replacing it with passion and love. Before he got up to shower, he leaned over and gently kissed her forehead. After seeing her slightly squirm from his touch, he was tempted to wake her and make love to her one more time, but he decided against it. Instead, he headed for the shower.

The steaming hot water was like a renewed source of energy. He exited the shower totally nude to discover Meloney had awakened. By the aroma from food being cooked, he knew exactly where she was.

As soon he entered the kitchen, the first thing he spotted was Meloney's shapely ass cheeks. They were so round and voluptuous and it was hard to conceal them under the tee-shirt that she had on. Sean thought she looked super sexy standing over the stove cooking in just a tee-shirt. Every part of her body looked enticing. When he embraced her from behind she stuck her ass out, indicating that she wanted to feel his manhood up against her flesh. But, what she didn't know was Sean was naked.

"A'ight now! Don't start nothing you can't finish!" warned Sean.

"Who says I can't finish?" she asked, reaching her hand around grabbing a hold of his dick. "We still got about forty five minutes." By that time, she was face to face with Sean, stroking his dick.

"I don't know. But, there's only one way to find out," he replied as they began to kiss.

Somehow, in the midst of all the kissing, he managed to maneuver her around to where she was pinned against the island that was located in the middle of the kitchen. Sean picked her up in his arms and sat her on the island stool. His rod was now hard and ready to explore the depths of her love tunnel. She positioned her body as close to the edge of the stool as possible to allow him access to her goodies. The moment he entered her cave it became extremely wet, as if she'd had an instant orgasm. With each thrust, she began to moan louder and louder while holding on the edge of the island as if her life depended on it. This wasn't like the gentle love making session they had the night before. And, she was loving every minute of it!

Once they finished, she headed to the bathroom to wash up while Sean ate his breakfast. A few minutes later, she came back into the kitchen with a soapy towel and began to wash her man's private. Sean loved the attention he was receiving. She washed and cared for him as if he was unable to care for himself. After she finished, she gave him a peck on the lips and left the kitchen to go get dressed.

By the time she was fully dressed, make-up included, Rachel was parked out front waiting. Sean walked her to the door and gave her a passionate goodbye kiss. It was so hot and steamy, even Rachel got a little wet looking at them. Meloney is definitely the one, thought Sean as he watched her walk toward her friend's car. As soon as she was gone, he figured he'd pay Asia a quick visit just to see what she wanted.

Since her house was only a hop, skip, and a jump away, in exactly eight minutes he was on her door step knocking at the front door. Right in the middle of knocking, the door swung open.

"Seannn! Why didn't you call to let me know you were on your way?" she blurted out in a surprised tone of voice. Sean's first assumption was she was doing something that she had no business doing. After realizing that he was being somewhat judgmental, he erased that thought.

"I told you that I'd be stopping by before I went to work, remember?" he replied as he entered her domain.

"I know, but I would've had my little brother here waiting. He asked me to try to get at you to see what was up. Here, sit down while I call 'em," she demanded, directing him to a seat on the sofa.

"Where's my goddaughter?" Sean asked as soon as she re-entered the room.

"She's over at Derrick's mother house. She'll be home tomorrow," she stated, and then plopped down on the couch right next to him. That was the first time Sean had ever seen her without makeup. Her beauty was natural. He definitely understood his best friend's reasons for wifing her. She was wifey material.

"He should be here any moment. I just texted him to let him know you're here."

"Do I know your little brother?" he asked while searching his memory bank at the same time. Actually, he was just trying to keep conversation flowing so he wouldn't have to focus on this beautifully breathtaking woman that was sitting extremely close to him. Before any unnatural thought of his best friend's girl could subside in his mind, he forcefully willed it out of his head.

"Yeah, don't you remember him? He was the one that was here when you stopped by that one time. He answered the door."

""Ahhh, okay. Now I remember! But, what does your little brother want with me?" he asked, playing the dumb role. He knew he could only want one thing.

"He wants to discuss some business with you. That's all I know. I try not to get involved in his affairs, but lately he's been crying about how he's been getting beat by guys that's selling garbage. I told him that maybe he should holla at you because you and Derrick always dealt straight up. Well, at least that's what Derrick used to always say. It had to be true because my baby had most of the city on lock," she said, smiling. "I wasn't sure if you were back in the streets or not, but I figured if you wasn't you'd probably be able to lead him to someone you trusted. Would you like something to drink while you're waiting on his slow ass?"

"Yeah. You got some orange juice?"

"Of course, boy! My baby loves orange juice. I have to keep that in this house. I'll be right back," she said, and then got up and sashayed into the kitchen's direction. Sean couldn't help but to look at her ass as it bounced with each step she took. If they were under any other circumstance, he would've definitely tried his hand with Asia. But, since she was Derrick's baby mother she was considered off limit. That was final!

No one said that he couldn't harmlessly admire her all around beauty. Just as long as he didn't act on it he figured there was no harm in admiring. Right in the middle of his thoughts, Sean was interrupted by someone at the front door as they unlocked it and let themselves in. He immediately recognized the stranger to be Asia's little brother.

"What up, playa?" he spoke, and then carried on toward the same direction his big sister had walked in. Sean just hit him off with the old head nod. It was always easy to tell when someone wanted something because they tended to get nice all of a sudden, which was exactly how dude acted. The tough guy role he once displayed when they first met had changed completely.

As Asia was exiting the kitchen with a glass of O.J. in hand, she was greeted by her brother. "What you cooking, big sis?" he stated as soon as they locked eyes.

"What ever happened to speaking to a person when you enter their house, J.R.?"

"My bad, you right. What up, big sis, what you cooking today?" he said, smiling. Asia just smiled back and shook her head. She knew it was J.R. being J.R.

"Nothing today because Tia is at her grandmother's house," she stated while on her way back into the living room where Sean was waiting. "Here, Sean. Well, I'ma leave you two alone to talk. I'll be in the basement finishing up my laundry. Sean, holla at me before you leave, okay?"

"Fo' sho!" Sean replied after taking a sip of his drink.

Once Asia was out of ear shot, J.R. began to speak his peace. "I just basically wanted to holla at you to see if shit was all good as far as the work situation. My sister said she didn't know for sure if you were doing anything. But, I told her to call you, anyway, because I figured, if you didn't have it, you could probably plug me in with someone who does."

Before Sean answered, he thought for a second about which approach he wanted to take. He knew he needed someone's help in moving the dope he'd just purchased, so he really didn't have the luxury of turning down this potential business proposal. "Exactly how much work do you be fucking with? I mean, I don't have it myself, but I got a partna that's doing some thangs. The only problem is, he don't fuck with nothing less than a quarter brick," he announced. He basically just wanted to make sure the deal would be well worth his time if he decided to deal with J.R.

"Shiiiit, that's gravy then. 'Cause every time I shop, I'm copping nothing less than a half. Plus, I got four other partners that do the same every two days," he stated proudly.

"Oh, yeah?" Sean inquired while secretly adding up the figures in his head.

"But, yo people wouldn't have to worry about dealing with no one but me. I know how that shit goes."

"Good, because that was the next thing I was about to say. Matter of fact, my man is leery as hell. If he don't know you, he won't deal with you, I don't care how much you spending. So, until I could talk him into agreeing to meet with you, you'll more than likely have to go through me."

Looking at Sean, J.R. had the strong feeling that it was probably his work all along, but he kept his thoughts to himself. As of that moment, he could give a fuck less whose work it was, just as long as it was right and affordable. Truth of the matter is, he needed a connect desperately. So desperately that he was willing to do business anyway Sean suggested. So, when can you get with yo peoples? 'Cause me and my guys are ready like yesterday!"

"Okay. Give me yo number and I'll contact you after I talk to my man, a'ight? Just make sure you have that paper correct and ready."

"Just say the word, big homie, and I'm ready," J.R. replied with excitement while giving Sean dap. He thought about asking him when should he expect his call, but decided against it. He didn't want to press the issue or get Sean paranoid about dealing with him.

# Chapter Seventeen

Sean left Asia's house overwhelmingly excited about his new business venture. It was the type of clientele that was needed to move the huge supply he was sitting on. He'd already managed to accumulate a few good customers on his own, and even met a few more through Gerald on the job. But, that wasn't enough. All of those customers combined only equaled to selling close to four kilos a week. That kind of clientele would be an average dope dealer's dream, but Sean was way above average, plus, he wanted out of the game like yesterday. He smirked, thinking about how much faster he'd move the work with the help of J.R.

He played with the thought of calling in sick so he could handle his business, but since he was halfway there he said fuck it. When Sean got off of interstate 55 exiting onto Jefferson Avenue, he made sure to buckle his seat belt and turn down the sound system to a reasonable tone. Gerald had pre-warned him about 3rd District police department. The last thing he needed was a confrontation with the law while he had four quarter keys stashed in the spot over the glove compartment.

There was no way he was about to let a traffic cop gain stripes off of his arrest. Pulling up on his job's parking lot, he thought about how he could've easily knocked off half, if not all, of what was in the stash had it not been for Detective Jones blowing up the spot the day before. As soon as he pulled up and parked, a young cat that went by the name Fat Mike pulled up to the gas pump in his burgundy color Nissan 300z.

Fat Mike was one of Gerald's best customers when it came to consistency. One thing was for sure, his name fit his description to a tee. Standing at a full height of five feet eight, Mike had to weigh at least three-hundred fifty to four-hundred pounds. To be that big, the cat carried his weight very well. He wasn't the lazy, physically drained type. He moved around as if he was a hundred and fifty pounds.

One time, he and Gerald met up to do a drug transaction on a Shell service station when rookie cops pulled up on the lot right as it was going down. Since Gerald's car was nowhere near a gas pump, and he and Fat Mike, both, had their heads down they looked suspect. This instantly caught one of the officier's attention. Spotting the cop car out of the corner of his eye, Fat Mike became very nervous. He was like a deer caught in headlights and he didn't know what to do. When Gerald looked up, all he seen was a uniformed officer heading toward his car with his gun drawn. He just knew he and Fat Mike was busted. There was no way he'd have time enough to stash the dope, especially since he just gave it to Mike. He was so caught off guard focusing on the cop that he hadn't seen what Mike did with the two ounces. All he could pray and hope for was that Mike took his weight and kept his mouth closed.

When he looked over at Mike, he could see him fidgeting, like he was attempting to hide something. By that time both cops were at the car, pulling on the door handles quicker than Gerald could say, "Shit!" As they both were getting ushered out of Gerald's vehicle, all he could think about was how he knew Fat Mike had more than likely dropped the dope somewhere in his car, leaving him the case. After about twenty minutes of searching, the cops finally came to the conclusion that they were clean. They had no choice but to let them go free. After the incident, the two parted ways without so much as a goodbye. The next time Gerald met up with Mike, he asked him where exactly did he hide the dope because he remembered seeing the cops search him several times. He showed Gerald how easily he was able to tuck and hide the two ounces up under a roll of his disgusting fat where his breast was. Sean was blown away when Gerald told him the story. All he could think about was trying to convince Fat Mike to stay down on the team. Lord knows he needed him!

As he got out of the car, Fat Mike stopped him short before he could enter the door. "What up, Sean?" he spoke.

"Shit, what's good, Fat Mike?

"Man, I heard the news about the big homie Gerald. Somebody murked him and his bitch at the Super 8. That's fucked up, dirty."

"Yeah, it is."

"Damn, and that nigga told me everything would be everything today. I was really looking forward to that," Fat Mike replied, hoping that Sean would be able to help him out. Seeing where things were heading, right where he needed it to, Sean walked over to Fat Mike so he wouldn't have to yell out what he wanted to say. He had to be careful of who was listening.

"Was you trying to get down, or some'n?" he said in an almost whisper like tone.

"Yeah...I was looking for a quarter. Why, you cool?"

"Peep game. I'ma go in and start my shift, so I need you to swing back through in about twenty minutes 'cause I can't do shit in front of ole girl," Sean stated, referring to Ms. Turner.

"I tell you what," Fat Mike said, reaching into his pocket to retrieve a card with his info on it, "just give me a call when it's cool to come back through. I have to go snatch up the change, anyway."

"That's what's up!" Sean replied as he gave the card a once over.

As soon as he walked through the door, Mrs. Turner began to rattle on full force. "Baby, did you hear what happen to Gerald? I told his ass about messing with all those strange women! But, he just wouldn't listen! It was all over the five o'clock news when I made it in the house yesterday! Soon as I got in the house, my husband started telling me all about it!" She managed to say in one breath. She was so amped, she was practically yelling.

"Yeah, Mrs. Turner, I know. A detective answered his phone when I called to see why he was late for work." Right as she was about to start motor-mouthing again, Sean's cell phone began to ring. Thank God for modern day technology, he thought. "Hold that thought, Mrs. Turner," he stated, and then walked off without giving her a chance to reply. "Yeah," he answered on the second ring.

"Damn. Is that how you answer your phone?" questioned a familiar voice.

"Sometimes. It all depends on what type of mood

I'm in. Since I just arrived at work, a place I really don't want to be right now, I'm kinda feeling like a dry ass yeah."

"I feel you. Shit, sometimes I don't feel like fucking with the club either, but I go. It's important to keep a job, Sean. Being there keeps a person out of a lot of shit at the end of the day," Stacy replied.

"So, you finally decided to call me, huh? I was beginning to think that you just used me. You got what you wanted and just kicked me to the curb. I kinda felt like a whore." They both laughed.

"Boy, you silly! But naw, it's not like that. I just been handling my business. You just have to be patient, baby. Patience is a virtue, remember that! Plus, I'm not trying to have you all sprung out and shit too quick. But, don't get it fucked up, it's going to happen," she stated matter of factly. "I just need you to keep your mind on business first. Because if you don't, you'll find yourself getting lost in me. No pun intended," she said, laughing at her own little joke.

*Who the fuck do this bitch think she is trying to school me?* thought Sean. He let her have that round, but round two would definitely be his. "You right," he reluctantly stated. "But, what makes you so sure you won't also be sprung?"

"Because I was born to spring, not get sprung. Anyway, was everything cool with that?" she said, referring to the product she'd sold him.

"Of course, sweetheart. Believe me, you would've heard from me if it wasn't."

"Okay. Okay... well, that's all I wanted to know. Oh, and one more thing, can you stop by the house when you get off work tonight?"

"Uhhh, I don't know. Tonight might be a bad night

baby, I got some business that I need to take care of. But, I'll see what I can do, though."

"Well, if you can't make it, can you please call me to let me know? If that's not asking too much," she continued.

"I think I can handle that, Ms. Stacy. But, ummh, let me get off this phone so I can start my shift." When Sean finally hung up, Mrs. Turner was just about to walk out the door. Before she could leave , Sean called out to her, "Mrs. Turner, could you please watch the store for a second while I run out to my car and grab something?"

"Sure, baby. Go on and do what you have to do."

Sean hurried to the car and snatched up the work that he had stashed in the stash spot. He wanted to make sure he'd be prepared when Fat Mike called. That way, all he had to do was come through with the cake. Being that Mrs. Turner was very observant, border line nosy, He knew she'd be looking to see what exactly he had retrieved from his car. Reasons like that was why he chose to keep a gym bag handy in the car. After stuffing the work in the bag, he made sure to grab the small portable CD player he used while working his shift. When he walked back inside, Mrs. Turner handed him the phone receiver. "It's for you," she stated. "It's a detective," she continued, but that time whispering as she covered the receiver with the palm of her hand.

Mrs. Turner knew how close Gerald and Sean were, so she figured it was only a normal formality for the leading detective to want to speak with the victims' closest friends. If it wasn't for Sean waving her off, she would have stood there the entire conversation. "This is Sean Martin speaking. How may I help you, detective?"

"Mr. Martin, I was wondering if you could come down to the station and answer a few more questions?"

he stated with a pinch of an attitude. Sean caught it instantly.

"I already told you everything I know, detective. What more do you want from me?" It was clear to the detective that Sean was irritated by his call.

"Ahh, okay. So, now you wanna play games, huh? You lying little fuck! How come you forgot mention the fact that you two were at the club together the night he got murdered, huh? That right there alone puts your black ass in the suspect category! Now, I'm giving you one more chance to come clean with me. You're only making it harder on yourself, bud!" Detective Jones snapped.

"Now, let me tell you some'n, you big, white, racist, steroid shooting mafucka! If you have an arrest warrant, I suggest you do yo damn job! Other than that, I don't have shit else to say to you! Unless, my lawyer is present." After speaking his peace, Sean ended the call.

"Fuckin' nigger bastard!" Detective Jones stated to himself as he placed the receiver back in its cradle. He knew he really didn't have anything on Sean except for the fact that he and the victim were seen at the club together. But, upon further investigating the matter, a waitress employee said she witnessed Gerald leaving the club with a woman whom fit the description of the second murder victim. The waitress also confirmed that Sean didn't leave the club until it closed, that gave him an air tight alibi. Only if the detective knew the waitress he spoke with was romantically involved with Sean. "I know your ass is involved somehow, you fuckin' dope dealing sonofabitch! Soon, you'll slip, they always do," he spoke as he stared at Sean's mug shot. "And, you can bet your ass I'll be there!" he continued, as if he was still talking to Sean.

# The Hustle

After receiving a text from Sean, Fat Mike made his way back to the station to complete the transaction. When he pulled up to the station, he walked in with a Burger King bag full of blood money, figuratively speaking. Sean had already placed the quarter kilo in the trash can, in the restroom, so there would be no hand to hand shit caught on tape. He wasn't worried about other customers going into the restroom because the store's policy was to keep it locked at all times. So, in order to gain access to the restroom, one would have to have a key to get in, which was in Sean's possession.

When he first started at the job, Gerald put him up on the camera situation and how it operated, rotating constantly. So, when it was time for the money transaction to be made, all he had to do was time the camera, waiting for it to point in another direction, then pocket the loot. He didn't have to worry about it picking up sound because it wasn't equipped for that. As soon as Fat Mike gave Sean the dough, he, in return, placed the restroom key in Mike's hand. "What the fuck is this for?" he asked confused.

"Go to the bathroom, playa. What you looking for is in the trash can in the restroom," Sean replied.

"Ahhh, okay. And, that's seventy-five hundred instead of seven. The extra five I owed to Gerald from the last deal."

"Okay. Good look. It's always good to see that there's still a few honest crooks left in the game," Sean said, and then laughed.

Fat Mike walked to the back of the store to where the restroom was located to retrieve his package. It was wrapped up in a brown paper bag. Mike could tell that it was that fire! Whenever he would holla at Gerald, the dope would be okay, but Mike always had a feeling that it was much better before Gerald got his hands on it. It didn't bother him because he was still able to make his.

Now that he was finally getting A-1, he couldn't wait to put his whip game down on it for a change. When he finally came out of the restroom, he had a huge smile planted across his face. That was a tell-tell sign for Sean that he was pleased with what he received.

"Is it a'ight if I stop back through before you get off? Because this shit is already gone," Mike said, smiling, revealing a mouth full of gold fronts.

"Yeah. Just don't bring nobody with you, and call before you slide through, a'ight?"

"No doubt," Mike stated right before walking out of the station.

After he left, Sean began to think about Detective Jones and the verbal threats he made against him. He knew it was all a crock of shit because if the detective really had something on him, he would've been arrested already. Now that he was knee deep back into the game, Sean had only one mission. That was to move the work he'd just spent his money on as quickly as possible. The evening rush hour was just starting to kick in for the service station. It was quickly beginning to fill with customers of all sorts.

Most were working class people who just finished putting in their daily eight hours, coming to get cigarettes and gas up their vehicle for the next work day. Then, there were those who were purchasing other miscellaneous items. Last, but not least, there were dope fiends and hustlers of all sorts in the premises as well. Sean began to serve a few more of his deceased friend's customers as they came in asking his whereabouts. He couldn't believe they hadn't heard the bad news. But, then again, he knew most street niggas were too heavily involved in the streets to have time to sit at home watching the news.

When Sean broke the tragic news to them, most of them didn't seemed phased in the least bit. All they cared about and wanted to know was who was handling shit now. That was just how niggas in the streets were. If a person wasn't putting paper in their pockets, to hell with them. The few he decided to serve only brought an ounce or two. The ones he didn't serve, for whatever reason, he told them to holla back in a day or two.

With all the heavy activity that went on that day, at the end of his shift Sean went home tired, exhausted, and twelve thousand dollars richer. On the way home, he continuously thought to himself that there was something he knew he forgot to do. As the sweet sound of Jill Scott's voice filled the car's atmosphere, it began to quickly sooth his body and mind a well. About halfway through the tune he suddenly remembered he was supposed to get back at J.R., so he decided to give him a call.

Being that it was a quarter after midnight, he figured J.R. to be laid up with some female or still out on the grind. That was, if he was a serious paper chaser. Sean told himself if the young cat was still out grinding, it only indicated that lil' dude was hungry for the paper. But, if he was laid up with some chick it may mean that his priorities may be in the wrong place, like Gerald. Sean wasn't sure if he wanted to get himself involved with another Gerald, being how the end result turned out. It wasn't anything personal, it was about business. What he was trying to accomplish he needed some around-the-clock, hustle type niggas on the team.

The phone didn't get a chance to ring a full ring before it was answered. "Who dis?" J.R. answered in a confident, cocky manner. It was evident that he was waiting on a call.

"This Sean. What up, playboy?"

"What's up, pimp, I thought you forgot about us small people?"

"Naw, lil' homie, I could never do that. I just had to get at my dude first, you feel me? Since he said it was a go, we ready to roll now. That is, unless you in for the night. If so, we can hook up tomorrow in the a.m."

"Naw, OG, I'm out in the streets doing me. Just say where and I'm there."

"That's what's up then! Peep this," Sean said, thinking of a good, safe spot to hook up at, "Meet me at that Amaco on Grand and Natural Bridge. I'll be there in ten minutes." He instructed, although he really had plans of showing up five minutes early. That was the norm for him. "Don't worry about the change." Sean interrupted, "We'll take care of all that later." he added before ending the call.

When he pulled up on the lot he quickly took notice how packed the station was for that particular time of morning.

The lights from the station and the full moon made the paint on Sean's black Beemer twinkle like the stars in the sky. The people of the night that lingered around the gas station couldn't help but to stare at it and the man driving it. With a ride as expensive and nice looking as that in a neighborhood like theirs, he was instantly pegged as a drug dealer in their eyes.

"What's up, man. You working?" one crack head asked as he rushed toward Sean at a fast pace. His clothes were filthy and his face resembled the color of grey ash that looked as if it was in desperate need of a strong dose of Proactive.

"Sorry, homie, I don't fuck around," Sean replied. Being that he still had on his Vickers work shirt, the crack head brought his story. That also prevented the rest of the fiends from approaching him with the same question. Little did they know, Sean had half a brick sitting on the floorboard of his car.

While Sean was at the counter paying for the Mr. Pure orange juice he had in his hand, he could hear heavy bass coming from the parking lot. He knew right away it had to be J.R. Looking out of the store's window, Sean witnessed the junkies as they bum rushed J.R. in the same fashion as they'd just approached him moments earlier. Being that J.R. was the young, aggressive type, he wasn't as nice as Sean had been while speaking with the baseheads.

"Fuck naw! Didn't I just tell yo ass I didn't have shit? Now, get the fuck outta my face!" he yelled as he shoved the man he was talking to in his face.

"Damn, youngster, slow yo roll. You don't need to bring that type of attention on yourself, especially since you out here every day," Sean stated as he came out of the store. "Follow me. We need to shake this spot."

"My bad, OG. I tried to tell this stupid fuck I wasn't doing anything," J.R. justified his actions as he trailed behind Sean heading toward his truck.

"It's all good. A, my man!" Sean called out to the guy that J.R. had just assaulted. "Here, go take care of that monkey that's on yo back." he replied while placing a twenty dollar bill in the stranger's hand.

"Thanks, man, good looking out," the crack head stated, revealing a rotten toothed smile. J.R. stared out the window of his truck, wondering why Sean just gave the crack head money knowing damn well what he was about to do with it.

Once Sean reached Grand and Broadway, he pulled over and motioned for J.R. to come to his car. After he was seated, Sean hit a few corners and began to give him his spiel. "I know you're probably wondering why I gave that base head some money, right? It's because that's how I came up in the game. See, I was taught that the game is fair to those who's fair in it. Whether it be the users or the sellers, don't ever adopt the attitude of being above or better than any of these mafuckas out here. Sometimes, you have to give away something from the heart with no intentions of receiving anything back. You never know when you might need somebody. Let me give you an example. Say if you're out on the block pumping and all of a sudden you catch a problem with the law. Now you need a safe place to duck off in, just until shit cools off. Now, remember you got a block full of fiends that you've constantly been pushing around and doggin' out. Do you actually think these mafuckas gone let you camp out at they spot until the heat rolls over? Fuck naw! They gone let yo ass get busted! You don't need that type of problem when you trying to cake-up. You need all the friends you can get, homie. You feel me?"

"You right, OG. I never looked at it in that type of way." That was all J.R. could say as he held his head low from the guilt and embarrassment he was feeling.

"It ain't shit, it's all about learning. The thing is, you have to learn fast and from other people's mistakes because all it takes is that one wrong mistake and you're done. You just have to think before you act in this game. Shit can get wicked real quick like. Now, getting back to business. There's a half a brick in this bag. I need ten for this deal, but I'm asking twenty for the whole thing. My people told me to inform you that if you buy five or more at one time, the price will drop. Personally, I'd like to see you and your crew cop five or better. Let me remind you, my nigga is real fickle when it comes to this here shit, so stack yo cheese. There's no telling when he might decide to just up and shut shit down, you feel me?" J.R. nodded.

"Good. Now let me get up out of here, so I can go home and get some much needed rest, a nigga tired as fuck." Sean said as he pulled up right behind J.R.'s truck.

"A'ight, big homie. I'll get at you tomorrow to give you the cake."

"Be careful. And, ummh, what's that you got in your shit, fifteens?"

"Yeah," J. R. answered proudly.

"Keep that bullshit down. You got too much to lose. Hit me on the cell when you reach the spot to let me know you made it there safe." He then handed J.R. a piece of paper that had his contact number written on it. Taking precaution, Sean waited for J.R. to pull off in his truck before he decided to leave. He knew J.R. had no clue as to where he stayed and his plans were to keep it that way. As soon as he hopped on the interstate going east, his cell began to ring, "Hello," he answered on the second ring.

"What's up, baby, are you still coming over?" It was Stacy.

"Yeah," he reluctantly stated after a brief second, "I'm on my way now." It wasn't that he didn't want to kick it with Stacy, he was just downright exhausted for real.

"That's good, 'cause I was hoping to see you tonight. Plus, I have on something extremely sexy right now!

"Ahhh yeah. And, what's that?"

"Nothing," she replied sensually.

"That's my favorite outfit," Sean declared, feeling his manhood rising for the occasion.

"Well, hurry up then!" she demanded right before hanging up the phone. A couple seconds later, his phone rang once more. "Did you forget some'n, baby?" Sean questioned.

"Hello." It was J.R.

"My bad, lil' homie. I thought you was this broad calling back. I see you made it home safe."

"Yeah, I'm at the spot. I'ma let you do yo thang, I'll hit you in the A.M."

"A'ight, lil homie. Get at ya boy."

# Chapter Eighteen

When Sean pulled up to Stacy's parking garage, he phoned her. A few minutes later she came sashaying down the ramp towards the booth.

With Stacy's building being an upscale, highly secured place, the only way Sean would be able to reach her condo was by an elevator that required a seven digit code or an entry card that was similar to the booth card she used. Being that she didn't know him that well, she opted to come down and retrieve him instead of giving him her elevator code. After parking his car, Sean walked over to greet Stacy, who was now standing by the elevator looking sexy as hell. "What's good, sexy?" he said as he embraced her.

"You and me!"

"Okay. Well, that's what's up then. Hey, as much money as these condos cost, how come there's no guard down here? Nigga could get jacked waiting on yo ass down here," he replied jokingly.

"Boy, ain't nobody gone fuck with you! Especially at

my spot! Now, come on before one of my neighbors catch me looking a hot mess," she spoke, entering her code into the elevator's key pad. The minute they stepped inside it, it was on and poppin'! They began to tear into each other like savage beast. Sean had her pinned against the elevator's wall, attempting to take her right there. The fight she put up was so minute, Sean could tell that she wanted it to happen. The boy shorts that she had on were wrapped around her ankles. Lifting up her tee-shirt, Sean began to suck and fondle her firm, meaty breasts. The heat between the two of them was so boiling; it caused the temperature in the once cooled elevator to rise at least forty degrees more.

His tongue wasted no time going to work on her clitoris. He then took her right leg and lifted it up on his left shoulder. Her love nest was wide open. The first climax came for Stacy in record breaking time. She came so hard that her juices overflowed out of her pussy, leaving a trail down the inside of her thick thigh. Seeing her body shake and shiver only motivated Sean to go in harder. Right as she was about to bust a second time, the elevator door opened up. When she looked down at Sean, they both laughed in unison.

Once the two finally reached Stacy's domain, it was nothing for them to pick up where they left off. Their steamy love making session lasted deep into the wee hours of the morning. When Sean opened his eyes the next morning, Stacy was nowhere in sight, but she left a note on the nightstand sitting under his cell phone. Picking up his phone to free the note, he noticed that he had five missed calls. Since his curiosity for the note was greater than the missed calls, he picked it up and placed the phone back on the *nightstand.*

*Hey sexy! I had a few runs to make and since you*

*were sleeping peacefully, I let you be. Your phone has been ringing like crazy, boy! If it's your little girlfriend, tell her she can't be cutting into my time. I don't bother you when you're with her, just kidding! If you decide to leave before I get back, give me a call later sexy!*

*Yours truly, Stacy*

Just thinking about the events that took place last night had Sean all warm inside. Once again, he questioned him self wondering was he really ready to settle down with one woman. At that point, he really didn't know. But for the time being, he was enjoying himself and that was all that mattered.

On the way home, Sean was busy returning calls to those who'd phoned earlier. That included Fat Mike, J.R., Maxeen, and a couple other business associates. After his calls were finished, he was technically forty grand ahead of the game. Now, all he had to do is make the drop offs and collect. The first client he planned to serve was a young, rich surgical doctor.

One hour and a long, hot shower later, Sean was back in traffic doing what he did best, hustle! Between Fat Mike, J.R., and others he met up with, he managed to clear forty-five grand instead of forty. The best thing about it all was he still hadn't made it to work yet. The day was looking as if it could potentially turn into a seventy-five thousand dollar day. "Now, this what the fuck I'm talking about!" Sean stated out loud to himself. Swooping back to the crib, he decided to bring two and a half bricks to work with him. He was almost positive that he'd go home drug free with a whole lotta cash. The drought was still in effect so he knew he'd have no problem moving the product.

\* \* \* \* \*

Over the next three weeks, business began to boom for Sean. He was moving close to six keys a week. It seemed no matter how much dope he left the house with, by the time he returned home it was all gone. Linking up with J.R. turned out to be a wise business decision. He even was starting to grow fond of the youngster. To Sean, J.R. was the little brother that he always wanted but never had.

Being that he was young and wild as fuck, Sean had to constantly stay on top of him, making sure he stayed focused and on the right track. But, keeping him on the right track turned out to be a bigger task than Sean anticipated. It was so big that he himself was starting to lose focus. Every time he would catch himself doing something out of character, he'd quickly correct it. Business was going so well that he finally agreed to take the seventy-five kilos Stacy was practically forcing on him. Why not? The shit was going to sell, anyway.

"I'm telling you, J.R.," Sean preached for the umpteenth time, "you have to think before you act out on some dumb shit! Mafuckas don't be forgetting shit like that nowadays!" he retorted as the two walked toward Sean's brand new pearl white XL Denali getting ready to leave the mall. Just minutes earlier, J.R. had managed to get into a confrontation that could have easily been avoided with three guys at Sabarro's Restaurant.

When one of the guys accidentally bumped into J.R., he clicked, not even giving the guy a chance to apologize. The louder J.R. got, the louder the guy and his two friends became. As Sean stepped in the middle of J.R. and the guy he was arguing with, J.R. swung over him and knocked the kid out cold with one punch. The manager immediately began shouting, saying that the police were on their way. That was all Sean needed to hear. He and J.R. left in a hurry, hoping to avoid the law.

"Man, that fool bumped into me on purpose! That shit was totally disrespectful, Sean!" J.R. Said, defending his actions.

Sean was so pissed that he didn't even reply. He was having second thoughts about whether or not J.R. was worth the trouble. Right as the two were about to enter the truck, two masked gunmen snuck up on both sides of the truck with their weapons drawn. "Nigga, you know what the fuck this is, so don't be no hero!" one gunman stated to Sean. "Yo dirty, bring that bitch ass nigga around here!" he demanded to his partner. As J.R. slowly walked around the truck with his hands high, his mind raced at a hundred miles per second thinking of his next move.

Being that the windows to his truck was heavily tinted, Sean couldn't see what was going on. All he could do was hope and pray that J.R. wouldn't be foolish and try some super hero type shit and put their lives in jeopardy. Of course, he did! Something in J.R.'s naïve little brain told him he could muscle the gunman out of his weapon.

As the two began to tussle, both attempting to gain possession of the gun, POW! it went off. POW! POW! Two more shots followed that sounded like loud thunder as it echoed throughout the parking lot. After the first shot was fired, the mask man that held Sean quickly fled the scene. Next, J.R. came limping from behind the back of the truck with his once crisp white tee soaked in blood. Sean could tell the wound was serious because of the amount of blood J.R. was losing at such a rapid pace. It seemed as if the bullet had struck a main artery.

Sean quickly opened the back door of the driver's side and helped J.R. into the truck, leaving the other gunman's body sprawled out by the back passenger's tire, dead as fuck. All he could think about was getting the fuck out of the area as soon as possible because he knew the cops would soon be arriving.

"Aghhh shit! OG, it hurts! It hurts! Aghhhh!" J.R. announced while laying there in agonizing pain. Sean knew he had to pull over somewhere safe and address the wound if he didn't want J.R. to die on him.

"I know, lil' homie! Just hold on and try not to talk as much. You need your energy! I got you, dirty!" The more Sean glanced into the rearview mirror, the more nervous he became from the sight of all that blood. A few blocks away from where the shooting took place, Sean pulled over at a gas station. He quickly hopped in the back, took off his shirt, and began to tie it around J.R.'s lower torso where the bullet entered. "Yo, J.R., wake up, man! Stay with me!" he yelled after seeing him dozing off. He jumped back up front and started driving again while dialing a number on his cell at the same time. He knew just the person to call.

"A, Bobby! This Sean, man! I need to see you now! It's important, man! Look, we'll talk about that when I get there. Yeah, I'm about ten minutes away from yo spot. Just have the garage door open so I can pull straight in, man!"

Ten minutes later, Sean was pulling into Bobby's garage as if he was Batman entering his Bat cave. Bobby was a client that Sean inherited from Gerald after he got murdered. Ever since Gerald's murder, he'd been faithfully dealing with Sean and no one else. The best thing about Bobby was his profession. He happened to be an ER Surgeon at Alexxian Brothers hospital working the midnight shift. Every night before his shift, he would pay Sean a visit at the job.

## The Hustle

Before their business dealings, Sean was skeptical of a young white boy with a hundred thousand dollar car, a convertible Mercedes CLK. He used to question Gerald about the guy but got nowhere. Gerald would only say that he was being paranoid, that Bobby was cool. That was all the information he was willing to disclose. He didn't want to reveal the fact that Bobby was a walking bank.

The first night of Gerald's death Bobby came to the job looking to score. Since Sean wasn't sure if he wanted to deal with him or not, he simply told Bobby to leave his number and if he found someone who was holding, he'd contact him. The next night after leaving work, he figured what the hell. He gave Bobby a call. Without hesitation, Bobby invited him over to his beautiful, two story brick stucco located in the Soulard area ten minutes from downtown. That night, the two sat and talked for hours getting to know each other. That was when Sean found out that Bobby, whose real name was Dr. Robert Dunn, happened to be an ER Surgeon.

Sean knew somehow when he befriended Bobby, it would later be a good choice on his behalf. Now, as he sat watching Bobby do what he did best, save lives, he developed a newfound respect for doctors and their craft. He thought about how much of a blessing it was for Bobby to be home at that particular time. Sean had no clue as to what he would have done had he not been available. There was no way he could've taken J.R. to a hospital. Too many questions would have been asked and it wouldn't have took the authorities any time to link the freshly dead body that was left in the mall's garage to J.R.'s shooting. It didn't take a rocket scientist to figure out that, more than likely, everything would've been placed on the convicted felon, him!

"Don't worry, Sean, he'll be alright. The main thing he needs now is plenty of rest. He's lost a tremendous amount of blood so when he does come to, he'll be very faint."

"Thanks, Bobby. I really don't know what I would've done without you. I couldn't take him to no hospital," Sean replied.

"Yeah, I know. But, don't worry about it, bud. I told you he'll be okay. Besides, that's what friends are for, right?" he said, smiling showing off his bleach white teeth.

"Fo' sho! Just tell me what the damage is and I got you."

"No, no, no! You don't owe me nothing! This is my job, remember? I do this for a living, just not at my home though, okay?"

"You right. But, I still want you to have this." Sean then handed Bobby an ounce of coke just to show his appreciation. "For your troubles."

"Well, if you insist," the doctor said, grabbing the powder substance out of his hand.

"So, tell me, doc, just how bad was the wound, anyway?"

"Well, actually it wasn't as bad as it looked because the bullet went straight through. He's lucky that no main artery was hit. If the bullet would've struck an inch more to the left, your friend would've probably been paralyzed for life. But, like I said before, he's going to need plenty of rest. Now, this is what I'll do for you. I'll let him go through his recovery process at my house. For the next few days, he'll be so heavily sedated he'll be out of it. By the third day he should be coming out, so it's best that he sees a familiar face."

"No doubt! Matter of fact, I'll stop by everyday

before and after work. That's if it's cool with you?"

"I have no problem with it. I'll be here when you stop by on your way to work, but in case I'm not here when you get off, here's an extra garage door opener. I'll leave the door entrance to the house unlocked, so you shouldn't have a problem getting in."

"Thanks again, Bobby," Sean replied right before walking out of Bobby's house.

Driving home, Sean didn't bother to turn on the radio. He opted for the silence because it helped him think better. Every few seconds his eyes would dart up to the rearview mirror, looking at his blood stained leather seats. He was just thankful that it wasn't the blood of a dead man. When he finally made it home, it was a little after one in the morning. He was extremely tired and in desperate need of a hot bath, but instead, he decided on a shower since he knew it would be much faster. Afterwards, he headed straight to bed. As soon as his head hit the pillow, he was out like a light.

# Chapter Nineteen

A month after the shooting incident, J.R. was back to his usual self again. Getting money and wilding out. One would've thought after facing a near death experience it would have caused J.R. to view things differently, but his case was the total opposite. He felt since he'd cheated death, which was how he referred to it, couldn't nothing or no one stop him.

Sean tried his best to keep his protégé in line, but it soon became evident that his words were going in one ear and out the other. He even went as far as asking Asia to talk to her little brother, but that didn't seem to work, either. The only thing that was left for Sean to do was cut J.R. completely off and hope that he learned a lesson.

Letting J.R. go was very hard to do for Sean because he'd become so attached to the young lad. He was also missing the forty thousand dollar weekly cash flow that came along with him. So, now he was left with no choice but to do what every other good street hustler would do whenever he lost an important client. He hustled harder!

# The Hustle

Not only was his hustle changing, his love life was also taking a turn. He began to see less and less of Maxeen, and more of Stacy.

As far as Meloney, she was still faithfully on his team, but her visits weren't as frequent because of her school situation. In Sean's eyes, she was still his number one draft pick. He told himself after she finished school he wanted to make her his wife. They would often talk about the subject of being married, but Sean hadn't popped the question yet. Even though most of his nights were spent with Stacy, his heart was still with Meloney. He figured that Stacy had an idea his heart was elsewhere by the way she began to act real possessive and jealous. She was much too beautiful to be as insecure as she was acting.

That was a major turn off for Sean. She got so out of control that Sean had no choice but to back away from her. The only time he didn't mind communicating with her was when it came to re-copping. Other than that, he would ignore her calls. But, Stacy wasn't having that! She began to show strong signs of a potential stalker, popping up unannounced and uninvited, catching Sean all off guard. One particular night, she decided to show up at Sean's residence unannounced when Meloney was present.

Unaware of the fact that she was there, Stacy approached the front door with every intention of showing her ass. Peeking through the window, she noticed he wasn't alone. She spotted two silhouettes through the sheer curtains. It was only when the two shadows became emerged that she knew he was in the company of a female. When she saw how they were wrapped in each other's arms, Stacy became furious! Instead of flipping out in public and bringing heat to

211

Sean's home, she jumped back into her Navigator and drove home mad as hell. That was when she knew she had fallen in love with him.

To Sean, their relationship was built around nothing but casual sex and business, but it was much more to Stacy. After she realized she was crying, she wiped her eyes, glanced in her rearview mirror at herself and laughed. She couldn't believe that she was crying over a man once again. Regardless of who he fucked, as long as he was involved in the game he had to come back to her. Especially since he was in her pocket for a half million dollars, he had to see her again... or, die!

\* \* \* \* \*

"Baby, I'm so glad we're spending the weekend together. I needed this sooo bad...Boy, if you only knew," Meloney stated while cuddled up in Sean's arms on the sofa.

"Me too, baby. Me too," he responded, and then softly kissed the top of her forehead. Since he had the weekend off, he wanted nothing more than to spend it making love to his one and only girl. "So, it's just me and you now, right, baby?" she asked, staring into his eyes.

"Of course it is, baby! Why'd you ask that?"

"Because! I love you, baby, and I don't want to have to share you with anyone else," she answered sincerely.

"Don't worry, boo. You ain't gotta share me with no other chick because I'm exclusively all yours," he lied. "Oooh, by the way, I have some'n for you, baby!" he stated, nudging her to raise up so he could retrieve her gift.

"Now, what I tell you about spending money on me, Sean? What I want from you doesn't cost a dime."

"I know. I know," he said, rummaging through his

212

pants that were lying on the carpet. "Just open it, will ya?" he said in a playful tone. He knew Meloney loved when he talked like that.

When she took the velvet ring box out of his hand, she couldn't help but to smile. After a few minutes of staring at the box, Sean said, "So, are you gonna open it or what? Just in case you didn't know, the real gift is inside the box, baby," he joked.

"Duhhh! I know that! Can't a girl take her time opening her present?" she countered.

"You right. My bad, baby. Do you." When she opened the box, a flawless two and a half carat platinum and diamond ring sparkled as soon as it was introduced to light. "Baby, I've been involved in my share of relationships and I've had my share of women. Not that it was really that many," he corrected after she shot him a piercing stare. "Anyway, what I'm trying to say is, none of 'em can compare to you. To make a long story short, I love you, Mel, and I want you to be my wife. So, will you marry me?"

"Yes! Yes, baby! Yes!" she excitedly stated as they embraced. "Wa...wait a minute. Are you positive that this is what you really want, Sean? Are you sure you can remain monogamous, because I promise you I won't be cheated on or fucked over by you nor any other man again!" she snapped. The way she stated it, it was obvious that she'd been hurt really bad before.

In his most calm, convincing tone, he replied, "Yes, baby. I'm sure." Then, he kissed her passionately. "There's some'n else in the box," he stated after they broke for air. Meloney quickly removed the ring. Next, she pulled out the piece that kept it in place to reveal a key.

"Baby, what does this key go to?" she questioned,

looking at the key sideways.

"That's the key to my heart! Naw, just kidding. That's your key to the castle. Now, does that tell you just how serious I really am?

"Mmmm, let me see...I guess," she replied with a smirk on her face. "Okay, okay. I give. Yes, I'll marry you, baby. But, you know it's not going to happen until I finish school, right?"

"Yeah, I figured that much," he said with a hint of disappointment in his voice. Actually that was his plan all along.

"This also means I'm not going to move in with you until I graduate. 'Cause we both know if I'm living here I won't get no work done messing with you." She then kissed him. "See what I mean," she said after reluctantly pulling away from his soft lips.

"Awh, you wrong! You kissed me first, Mel!"

"I know. I have to get all my kisses and things off right now because we both know it'll be awhile before we can do something like this again. At least the weekend thing, anyway. We might, and I stress might, be able to get a quickie in here and there."

"You right. So, shut up and kiss me, you fool!" he said playfully, puckering his lips. That one kiss led to a long night of steamy love making in which the two unknowingly conceived their first child.

After the weekend was over and Meloney had returned back to school, Sean took notice of how the house seemed so lifeless without her presence. Meloney was everything that he'd ever wanted in a woman. He had to force himself to shake off the daze he was in because business was calling. He knew it would be extremely dangerous to run the streets with his head in the clouds and his mind elsewhere. Although he was in love, he knew the game didn't love nobody so in the streets he had to appear heartless. He quickly switched to hustle mentality. That was when he put his game face back on and headed off to work. The streets. Being that he technically didn't have to be at his other job until four, he figured he'd pay his mother a visit.

No one had to tell Ms. Martin that her son was back in the streets because she knew it. Whenever he stopped coming around frequently, the streets were usually the blame. But, regardless of what her son was involved in, whether it was legal or illegal, she still stuck by his side to the end. That was just part of a mother's unconditional love. "Sean, is that you, baby?" she yelled out from the kitchen.

"Ma, how'd you know it's me? I could've been a burglar or anybody!" he replied as he entered the kitchen.

"Now, boy, you know ain't nobody stupid enough to burglarize nothing out here in this neighborhood. Not with all the racist cops running around out here. Anyway, what are you doing over here this time of day? Please, don't tell me you done quit your job for the streets?"

"Naw, momma! What, I can't come and see my mother before I go to work?"

"Sean, don't play with me! And, what did I tell you about answering a question with a question. You better not have lost your job, boy!"

"Naw, ma! You know I'm not going out like that."

"That's good, son. Look, I know you're running them streets again 'cause you haven't been home in God knows when. But, you're a grown man so I'm not going to preach to you about how to live your life. I just want you to be careful and remember what happened to your son, his mother, and Derrick, bless their souls."

"I know, ma. I know. That's why I have been

spending most of my time in the studio when I'm not at work," he lied.

"Good. 'Cause that's what you need to be doing, Sean. Haven't I always told you that you can do anything you put your mind to? Shit! You're just as good as that damn Fifteen Cent and Buff Ditty combined!"

"Who did you just say, momma? You mean Fifty Cent and Puff Daddy?" Sean said, correcting her as he laughed while walking out of the kitchen.

"I don't know what you find so damn funny. Shit! Fifty Cent, Fifteen Cent, that crazy shit all sounds the same to me! And, don't be in there sitting yo behind on my good chair either, Sean!" she yelled from the kitchen.

"Ma, what's so special about this damn chair?" he asked, plopping down in it. He loved to do things out of spite just to get on his mother's nerves.

"I know you just didn't curse in my damn house, boy!" she replied, walking into the living room where he was. "Now, if you must know, besides your grandmother passing it down to my generation, you were conceived in it." Sean jumped up out of the chair as if it was on fire.

"Unhun, that's nasty!" he stated, looking down at the piece of furniture with disgust. Ms. Martin was laughing hysterically. "Boy, ain't nothing wrong with that chair! Ya ass been sneaking and sitting in it all these years. Best believe if something was contagious in that chair, you would've been had it by now!"

Changing the subject, Sean spoke, "Ma, what you in there cooking? It looks like you cooking for more than one person."

"For your info, nosy, I'm expecting company tonight. So, yes, it's for more than one person. Why, are you hungry?"

"Yeah. Why, you about to fix your son something to

eat?"

"Boy, please! I'm not one of your women! You know where the refrigerator is! It's plenty of lunch meat and cheese in there," she said, laughing.

"Damn, ma, that's how it is? You cooking yo boyfriend steaks and shi... I mean stuff. Why can't your only son have a steak?"

"Because my only son didn't call and tell me he was coming over, that's why. Plus, I only took out enough steaks for two people."

"I see how you is," stated Sean, acting like a kid about to throw a tantrum. "That's cool, I have to get ready to go to work, anyway. So, when can I get my momma to cook for me?"

"Whenever you find the time to call your mother up and ask. By the way, have you talked to your sister lately?"

"Naw, why? Is she doing okay? Do she need anything?"

"It seems to me you wouldn't have to ask those questions if you were to just pick up the phone from time to time, huh? Why don't you give her a call while you're here. You might just be able to catch her in her dorm room right now."

"Just write the number down and I'll call her later, momma."

"I just don't understand you kids nowadays, acting like y'all so damn busy all the time! Call yo sister right now, boy! You ain't doing shit else!" Ms. Martin snapped. Sean knew from the tone she'd just used, his mother meant business. Since the last thing he wanted to do is piss her off, he reluctantly agreed to give her a call right then and there.

"Okay. Okay, you win, ma. Calm down, damn... I

mean dang."

"Alright, Sean! I ain't gone tell you no damn more about that mouth of yours. Don't think that you're too grown for me to get in dat ass!" she said, walking back into the kitchen, "Your sister's number is on the refrigerator."

After retrieving his sister's number, he called it. "Hello, may I speak to Rhonda...yeah, okay....What up, lil' sis? I'm good. Is everything okay with you? Yeah...I'm over here now. Naw, she didn't have to make me call, I was gone call you, anyway."

"Quit lying to your sister, Sean!" Ms. Martin yelled in the background loud enough for her daughter to hear.

"I was, ma! Yeah, I'm back. You know she over here getting all jazzed up for a hot date to.. OUCH Ma! Yeah, she just hit me in my arm for telling you about her date. I guess she didn't want me to say nothing," he confessed after escaping to the other side of the room out of her reach. "So, okay lil sis do you need anything? I'll give it to ma so she could send it to you, a'ight? I love you, too, sis! And, you better be using condoms down there...don't give me that! I know what goes on in them damn colleg... Ouch! I'm sorry, ma! Here goes ma before she beat me half to death. I love you, too, baby girl. Peace!"

"Quit crying, boy! You know damn well that didn't hurt! snatching the phone out of his hand. "Heeey, baby! Messing with your crazy brother. Yeah, he giving it to me right now," she said, holding her hand out. Sean reached into his pocket and pulled out a roll of hundred dollar bills, peeled ten from the stack, and handed it to his mother.

"Send Rhonda half and you keep half. I love you and I'll call you later!" He then kissed her on the cheek and ran out the door, leaving his mother sitting on the sofa with a wad of cash in her hand. He knew she would only give her share back to him, so in order for her to keep it, he had to drop it on her unexpectedly, then bail before she could protest. And, catching her on the phone was the perfect opportunity to do just that.

Being that he was running late for work, Sean began to put the pedal to the metal, topping speeds of ninety miles per hour on the long stretch of highway. He'd already been late twice that week, leaving Mrs. Turner to reluctantly cover for him until he decided to show up. So far, she hadn't said a word about his frequent tardiness since the two of them had somewhat become friends. But, regardless of the fact that they were now friends, Sean knew that still didn't guarantee that she wouldn't tell the boss if her job was in jeopardy.

When he finally made it to work, he was only three minutes late. Not even late enough for Mrs. Turner to take notice. Since most of his morning and afternoon was spent with Meloney and his mother, he didn't get a chance to take care of the clients that had been blowing up his phone all morning. That didn't turn out to be a problem because when it came to handling business, he had it all figured out.

After Gerald's untimely death, Sean's boss asked him did he think he could handle the shift by himself or did he need any help. Thinking in a business sense, he declined the offer for assistance. His boss went ahead with that, deciding to give Sean a chance to see if he could actually handle things on his own. He was hoping that it worked out because it gave him a chance to save the company some money. But, on the low, he was still monitoring Sean's performance. After a few weeks, he saw that Sean had his shift under control so he let him be. Instead of riding dirty to work every day risking his freedom, he found a good stash spot in the store to hide his product. In return, it reduced his risk of being caught riding with drugs, down to once, maybe twice a week.

Business had picked up so much that Sean had to keep at least a hundred and fifty ounces at the job weekly, ready for sales. After about a hour into his shift, he began to return all of those unanswered calls that were waiting. As soon as his finger touched the power button on his cell, thundering bass that came from a light grey Cadillac CTS stopped him in his tracks. Curiosity really had the best of Sean. The ride was super clean, plus, it was sitting on some very big chrome wheels. Because of the heavily tinted windows, the driver of the vehicle was not visible. It pulled up to a gas pump and stopped. Sean was practically on the edge of his seat waiting for the driver to exit his vehicle so he could see who he or she was. A slim figure stepped out of the car. Since his back was turned, it was hard for Sean to tell whether or not he knew the individual. Even though his back was turned, there still was something very familiar about the cat. As the figure came closer, Sean then recognized the face that was hidden behind a pair of fancy Cartier frames. It was J.R.

From his appearance J.R. looked as if he was a major player. But behind the car, fancy frames, and expensive clothes, Sean knew the truth.. J.R. wasn't doing as nearly good as he was doing when they were doing business together. But, he had to admit, J.R. looked the part, even if he wasn't really playing the part.

"Hey, What's good?" J.R. greeted, with a half ass smile, as he entered the station..

"What's good, young lad?" Sean replied dryly with no emotion whatsoever from his response, and from the look on his face J.R. could tell that Sean was still somewhat salty at him . And, he had every right to be.

Truth of the matter was, J.R. was in desperate need of a steady connect like he had with Sean. He was willing to do whatever he had to do to get back in his big homie's good grace.

"Don't be that way with me, OG. I realize I fucked up big time. That's why I came to apologize. Shit just ain't been the same since you cut my water off, homie," he confessed. That was all Sean had been wanting to hear. J.R. admitted he was wrong.

"I wasn't trying to tell you how to conduct yo business or life, J.R. I was only trying to save you from going through some of the pain I went through when I was your age. I was only trying to lace you with the same game that older, experienced mafuckas was trying to lace me with, but I didn't listen. You know I got love for you, lil nigga! If I didn't, I would've just let yo lil ass die when you got hit up. It wasn't nothing for me to dump yo narrow ass body off in an alley or some shit!" he said, laughing.

"Ahhh yeah? You right, but check this, if you can find it in your heart to forgive me and give me one more chance to prove myself, I promise, I won't let you down."

J.R. could tell that Sean was seriously thinking over the proposition he'd just threw his way. It took him a minute, but he finally realized the way Sean conducted his business affairs. His method was to handle it as smoothly as possible and try to avoid unnecessary problems at all cost. Unless, shit was just unavoidable. Unfortunately, the wake-up call didn't hit J.R. until after Sean cut him off.

"I tell you what, I'm gone erase that bullshit from my memory bank and start off fresh a..." Sean was forced to put the conversation on hold because a couple of preppy white guys walked in the station. "May I help you?" While he served his customers, J.R. walked to the back of the store where the beverages were located. As he stalled waiting for the white boys to leave, he popped open a Mr. Pure orange juice and devoured the beverage in one swig. It wasn't until after he saw the white boys leaving that he decided to return to the counter. He was extremely happy about being back on the team with Sean, especially since his team was winning. Everybody wanted to be a part of a winning team.

"So, what you been up to, anyway?" Sean questioned.

"Shit, big homie. Just out here trying to get my weight up, you feel me?" He wanted so bad to tell him about the bullshit connect he was forced to deal with, but decided against it. "Other than that, everything has been so-so," he lied.

"You look like you doing real good," Sean replied.

Over the next forty-five minutes, the two talked about events that surrounded each other's lives since their hiatus. When J.R. finally left, he left with the preconception that the misunderstanding he and Sean shared was in the past.

# Chapter Twenty

Every since the first day Detective Jones inherited the double homicide that occurred at the Super 8 Motel, he'd been completely obsessed with solving it. It had nothing to do with Gerald Jackson. Truth of the matter was, he could give a fuck less about him dying. In his eyes, Gerald was a murderous, drug dealing scumbag that got what he had coming to him. What had him so obsessed with the case was the innocent victim that was basically murdered for being in the wrong place at the wrong time, Tonya Hardin.

Never in his twelve years of law enforcement had he really been affected by a victim or their family as he has Tonya's. Especially after meeting her nine year old daughter. He had no choice but to be sympathetic and have empathy for the little girl. Her father was nowhere to be found and her mother had gotten herself killed, all because she chose to associate herself with the wrong crowd. A low life scum bucket like Gerald Jackson. Because of her poor choices, Detective Jones knew, more than likely, the little girl stood less than half a chance at life.

Although there was no solid evidence that pointed in Sean's direction, he had a hunch that he was somehow involved in the murders. As defensive as he was the last time they spoke, it was evident that he was definitely hiding something. All he had to figure out was what. There was entirely too many calls placed to and from the victim for Sean not to know something. From that point on, the detective told himself that he would keep a watchful eye on Sean, maybe tail him from time to time just to see where it led him. Only if the motel's cameras were working like they were supposed to be, he thought as he entered his unmarked vehicle.

\* \* \* \* \*

Three weeks after their reconciliation, things were coming together business wise for both Sean and J.R. It seemed as if money was coming from every which way. The guys were winning majorly, and everyone that dealt with them knew it. When you're doing good in the hood it tends to speak volumes, even if your'e not on flamboyant shit. So far, Sean was successful at keeping away from Stacy as far as being intimate. If only for the sake of the promise he made to Meloney.

Since things were going real well between them, he didn't want to chance it by creeping with Stacy. He didn't want to destroy the trust he'd worked so hard to build between him and Meloney. Besides, he knew he still had a thing for Stacy so it would only make matters worse if he was to keep seeing her intimately. Being that she was his connect, that meant he had to see her. Which was where the problems began.

Down to his last five kilos, Sean dreaded the fact

that it was time to see Stacy again whether he liked it or not. Picking up his cell to call her, he suddenly felt butterflies float around in the pit of the stomach. He hated the fact that his body reacted like that whenever he thought about her. It was like she was some mood altering chemical. "Stacy, what's up, baby?" he asked, trying his best to sound delighted to be talking to her.

"Aahh, so you finally decided to call a bitch, huh? I knew you'd come back to me soon! Every man does when a woman has something he wants."

"It's not like that, baby. I just been going through some thangs, that's all," he lied.

Stacy knew he was full of shit, but she decided to play along. "Oh, I'm sorry, baby. I didn't know. Is everything okay?" she replied, trying her best to sound sincerely sympathetic.

"Yeah, I'm good. But, I got some'n for you, though."

"Ummmm, so you're trying to see me, huh?" she asked, biting her bottom lip.

"Yeah, some'n like that. I mean, if you have time," he replied.

"Do you have to work today?"

"Naw, I'm off today. Why, what's up?"

"Well, since I haven't had lunch yet, why don't you meet me at the old Steakhouse on Grand in about forty five minutes, okay?"

"Yeah, that's cool. I'll see you in forty five." He then hung up and got ready for his meeting with Stacy.

The thing about the dope game was it could quickly capture a person and slowly suck the life out of 'em. Sean was very conscious about the direction he was headed in, but still and all, he continued to participate in a so called game that had no winners. The day he lost track of his original goal was the day he lost track of self.

Everything Sean set out to do, he accomplished. Except, finishing his album and getting out of the game. He stayed true to his word about taking care of Derrick's family, hitting Derrick's mother off with a quarter of a mil. As far as his own bank account, it was looking so lovely that he could've easily walked away from the game right then and he and his future wife would have been well taken care of. But, as you might have guessed, in the dope game greed quickly became the factor which also played an important role in almost every drug peddler's down fall.

When Sean finally reached the Steakhouse, the spot was so crowded he had a hard time finding a place to park. After five minutes of driving around the premises, he was finally able to catch an elderly black woman leaving so he quickly pulled in her spot. As he entered the restaurant, he breathed a sigh of relief once he saw that Stacy was already seated at a table for two. Passing by the long line of patiently waiting customers, he unconsciously estimated that the last couple in line's wait was at least thirty to forty five minutes.

As he reached Stacy's table, she stood and greeted him with a hug and an unexpected quick peck on the lips. The kiss caught Sean by total surprise, leaving him no time to protest or stop her. Being that they were amongst so many strangers and he didn't want to embarrass her, he let it go. But, what he failed to realize was one of the strangers in the restaurant was Meloney's roommate and friend, Rachel, who instantly recognized him as soon he entered the restaurant. What was only a business deal looked more like a romantic rendezvous in the eyes of Rachel.

Although Rachel didn't have a personal relationship with Sean, she felt as if she hated his guts as she sat there watching him betray her friend all out in public. To make matters worse, he was doing it right down the street from Meloney's dorm room. She knew how serious her friend was about Sean and how madly in love with him she was, all because there was no secrets between the two of them.

As she sat nibbling on her lunch with a few friends from school, her eyes were focused on Sean and his love interest's every move. The silent language that their bodies spoke verified that the two were indeed lovers. The way the strange woman seductively reached across the table, constantly touching Sean. How she would giggle and smile looking as if she was holding on to his every word, and the kiss they shared upon entering the restaurant, definitely wasn't a friendly kiss.

After her girlfriends announced that they were leaving, Rachel told them to go ahead, that she would catch up with them later. She knew she had to be one hundred percent sure about the status of Sean and the mysterious lady, so she decided to wait around until they left, just to see if they were heading in the same direction. And, just as she had suspected, they were.

Staring at the two vehicles that were heading in the same direction, Rachel was glad that Meloney decided to change her mind at the last minute about attending lunch with she and the other girls. She definitely didn't want her friend to feel that awkward, embarrassing feeling in front of the other girls, who she constantly bragged about Sean to. As Rachel sat in her car contemplating her thoughts, wondering if she should break the news to her friend, she became totally confused. Being that they were friends, she knew the right thing to do was tell Meloney, although she really didn't want to do it, she knew it had to be done. Picking up her cell, she called Meloney. "Meloney, are you in class yet?" Rachel asked while taking deep breath.

"I was just on my way out the door, why?"

"Stay there, I'm on my way! I got something I need to talk to you about. It's important!"

\* \* \* \* \*

As he drove home in total silence, Sean found himself looking up at his rearview mirror at Stacy. Even though he technically hadn't cheated yet, he was already feeling guilty. He knew he'd crossed the line once again when he agreed to let her come back to his house. Now, the only thing on his mind was giving her exactly what she wanted, a dick thrashing. He couldn't deny the fact that it was something he badly wanted as well.

Sean knew from the jump, when he first agreed to have lunch with her, that it was a bad idea. It was dangerous for him to spend time alone with her, he knew it would only lead to something more. With every touch of her hand, he found himself getting more and more enticed. He could no longer hide behind the wall he 'd built. Stacy knew that he wanted her just as much as she wanted him. All it took was a little reminder. When she revealed to Sean she wasn't wearing any panties, it was a wrap! She had his undivided attention. That, along with the fact that they still had a business transaction to complete, she knew she'd end up in Sean's bed before the day was over with. With a legitimate reason to go back to Sean's pad, there would be no way he could resist her.

After assisting Stacy with the two duffle bags in the trunk of her car that were filled with Columbian cocaine, he carried them into the house. Once he sat them down by the front door, he turned back around and fetched the briefcase he had in the back seat of his truck. In it was five hundred thousand dollars neatly stacked. When he walked back into the house, Stacy greeted him at the door partially nude. His eyes instantly began to take in every part of her body as if they were lungs taking in air. The bronze bra she had on complimented her skin tone very well. She lifted up her mini skirt to reveal a perfectly manicured pussy. She wasn't lying about not having underwear on.

"Why you gotta keep playing hard to get, Sean?" she said, easing closer to him. The closer she got, the faster his heart rate increased. All he could think about was the last time they made love. It seemed like forever. "All this could be yours, Sean. All you have to do is let that little bitch you're fucking with go."

By that time she was all up on him, kissing on his neck. Sean loved the way her lips felt against his skin. He could no longer contain himself.He had to have her! Not only was her body calling him, it was texting and sending out e-mails. As her hands caressed his body, his manhood became erect, begging for attention. Looking down at the bulge in his pants, she smiled. She knew no matter how hard he tried to play he couldn't resist her for long. No man could.

With both of Stacy's ass cheeks cupped in his hands, he planted soft, sensual kisses on her neck. He knew it was Stacy's hot spot. The scent from the perfume she had on only made it that much harder for him to resist her. Every time he tried to catch himself and back up off of her, she reeled him right back in with her kisses and caressing.

"Baby, I can't do this," he said, pushing her off of him for the second time.

"Look at how wet this pussy has got for you, Sean," she replied, and then stuck two fingers in her vagina and pulled them out. Her juices were all over them.

Fighting the feelings and urges he had for her was like fighting a losing battle. The thought of being deep inside her brought a throbbing sensation to his penis. Sean snatched her in his arms and kissed her soft, pouty lips. The two began to hungrily kiss each other. For Stacy to be smaller than Sean, she was easily forcing him back against the door, knocking over the briefcase that he'd dropped the first time he went in. His hands quickly went to work fondling her aching body.

Stacy was busy with the task of trying to undress Sean. It was impossible being that they were entangled in each other's arms. But, it didn't stop her at all. Instead of correctly unbuttoning his shirt, she ripped it open, causing the buttons to disperse onto the carpet. He took it upon himself to remove his pants because he knew there was no way she would get those off. At least, not with him in them.

Once his clothing was at a minimum, they slowly made their way toward the sofa. It was official, the resistance wall Sean had so called built, between he and Stacy, had just come crumbling down. What once started at the front door lead to the sofa, then onto the bedroom, and in the shower. The two were at it for three whole hours. The lovemaking got so intense that it continued back in the bedroom, which was where it ended with the two silently sleeping in each other's arms.

\* \* \* \* \*

For the last eight hours, Detective Jones had been posted on Sean's street surveying residence. He would've been gone long ago, but after seeing Sean and his unknown female friend pull up and go inside carrying two black duffle bags, something told him that the two might just be into something. So, he decided to stick around a bit longer. That was five hours ago.

Nothing really seemed out of the ordinary about the two's behavior, but an eyebrow was raised when he saw Sean come back out of the house a few seconds later and retrieve a black briefcase out of the back seat of his SUV. The paranoid look on his face and the way he nervously scanned the area after retrieving the briefcase instantly sent up red flags to Detective Jones. He's definitely up to something, thought the detective.

Following his gut feeling, the detective decided to sit and wait until Sean or his female friend departed, then would pull the vehicle over just to see if he'd get lucky. That was if he could manage to stay woke long enough. Feeling himself succumbing to sleep, Detective Jones reached over, opened his glove box, and pulled out a bottle of No-doze. He twisted the cap off and popped two pills, chasing it with a lukewarm, flat Dr. Pepper. He hated the bitter taste the pills left in his mouth. He had to make sure he stayed wide awake so that he wouldn't miss the suspects if either of them decided to leave.

As he sat there staring at Sean's residence, the urge to sleep began to get stronger and stronger by the second. What Det. Jones failed to realize was he'd popped No-Doze so regularly that his system had become immune to its effect. He was basically fighting sleep on his own. He was losing the fight by a landslide. His eyelids felt as if they were made of pure lead. There was no way he could keep them open. Detective Jones was out for the count!

\* \* \* \* \*

There was a loud knock at the door "Sean Martin, this is the police! Open up! We have a search warrant!" yelled Detective Jones, making him and his squad's presence known. With assistance from both homicide and narcotics, Jones led the pack of crime fighting dogs. Shortly after announcing their arrival and not receiving an answer, the door came crashing down from the battering ram.

When Sean heard the loud explosive like noise that came from the front of the house, he immediately hopped out of bed. Thinking that it could potentially be a home invasion, he armed himself with a 380. semi automatic handgun that he kept in his night stand drawer right by the bed. After hearing the mass amount of footsteps, heading towards his bedroom, he knew it could only be the police. The first thing that came to mind was the two duffle bags full of coke and how he'd left it laying right by the front door. He knew he was fucked! Next, he thought about the half a million dollars that was still in a briefcase laying right next to the coke by the door.

"Stacy, Stacy! Get up!" he whispered to a hump of pillows that was obviously a makeshift body. Stacy was nowhere to be found. "Where the fuck is this bitch!" Sean asked himself out loud right before the Homicide/Narcotics Task Force came crashing into his bedroom, some ski masked up, with their guns drawn. The first face he seen and recognized was Stacy's. She was wearing a black bulletproof vest that had the letters DEA in big bold white letters written across it. Stacey was the Feds? Sean couldn't believe his eyes....

"He's armed! He's armed!" yelled Detective Jones as he stood right beside Stacy. "Put the gun down now! Get on the floor!" he demanded. Obviously, Sean wasn't moving fast enough because every other officer in the room began to yell that same demand in unison. Being that Sean's body was cocked kind of sideways, it was hard for some of the officers to see his every move. As Sean attempted to turn full view just so everyone could see him lowering his weapon, one itchy trigger finger officer took it as a threat. Fearing that he and the rest of his fellow officers lives were possibly in danger, he fired his weapon. Ultimately, this set off a chain reaction ,causing everyone else to fire their guns .With each bullet that pierced Sean's body, it caused it to jerk and shake until he finally hit the carpet.

"Baby! Baby! Wake up!" Stacy called out, "You're having a bad dream," she said while shaking his body, trying to get him to snap out of the nightmare he was having.

"Huh! What! Oh...damn!" he groggily replied, attempting to collect his thoughts and regain his composure.

"Are you okay, baby? Do you want me to get you a glass of water?" she asked.

"Ye...yeah, please." he said, still somewhat sleep. The dream seemed so real to him. He silently thanked God that was all it was.

Stacy then went into the kitchen to retrieve the much needed drink he asked for. For a second, as she entered the kitchen, she could've sworn she heard footsteps, but brushed it off as being nothing. When she made it back into the bedroom, she decided to tell Sean about the noise she thought she heard, but he wasn't there. He was busy placing his product in his stash spot. He wasn't about to chance getting caught up if his dream was to turn into reality.

"Sean?" Stacy called out, thinking he was in the adjacent bathroom. There was no answer. She looked at the digital clock, which was the only visible light in the room, mumbling it's numbers. "Three fifty in the damn morning," she said to no one in particular. The minute she laid right back on the bed, she was out like a light.

Hearing the toilet flush brought Stacy out of the light nod she was truly enjoying.

\* \* \* \* \*

"Hello," Tu finally answered after six consecutive rings.

"Tu, you woke?" Duke asked.

"I am now," Tu replied sarcastically, in a half sleep tone "What time is it, Duke?" he asked, picking up his Cartier watch off of the night stand.

"It's almost four o'clock," he simply replied as if it was four in the afternoon, not four in the morning.

"Duke, this better be good! Calling my house at four fuckin' o'clock in the morning!" he snapped, looking over at the totally nude female that was sleeping next to him. His dick instantly got hard as he admired her near perfect body.

"It is homie. I found her!" Duke stated excitedly. He just knew Tu would be proud of him for this one.

"You found who? Duke, you better not be smoking that wet shit!"

"Naw, man. You know I don't fuck with that shit no mo'! I found yo wife! I found that bitch!"

"Duke, did you just refer to my wife as a bitch?" Tu questioned as he sat up in an upright position. It didn't matter to him that he hadn't talk to her in almost three years. It didn't matter that she up and left him while he was in prison when he needed her most. Tu was still very much in love with her and wasn't about to let anyone disrespect her. In his eyes, that was still his wife till death do them part.

My bad. But look, don't you remember that time when I told you I could've sworn I seen her in that burgundy Lincoln LS?"

"Yeah, why?" Tu stated dryly.

# The Hustle

"Well, as I was leaving my lil bitch's house on Salisbury, I spotted the same LS I told you about a few weeks back. Like the one I saw your wife riding in!"

"A'ight! A'ight! Calm yo ass down! Give me the address and make sure you stay there until I get there, just in case she decides to leave. I'm getting dressed right now!

\* \* \* \* \*

"Here goes your water, baby." Stacy announced, picking up the glass and handing it to Sean.

"Thank you." Sean took the glass of water and guzzled down the entire liquid substance in one drink. "Damn, that was a fucked up dream I had," he replied, not really wanting to give out details.

"Don't worry, boo, I'm right here," she replied reassuringly as she continued to caress Sean's leg, slowly making her way down to his shaft.

Just the slightest touch of her hand sent chills throughout Sean's body. For a hot second as she began to rub him down, he felt a sense of guilt about being with her. He felt foolish for falling for her scheme. He was usually stronger than that. At that very moment, Sean made up his mind about completely breaking things off between the two of them. Even if it meant finding another connect. He knew as long as he continued to deal with the beautiful woman he'd continue to sleep with her as well.

Once Stacy's soft hand finally reached its destination and she began to stroke his penis, all of the thoughts he'd just had about calling it quits quickly disappeared. Her soft, sensuous touch instantly got blood flowing to his lower region. By that time, he was stretched out on his back enjoying the hand job of a life time. Seconds later, her wet, warm mouth was engulfed over his manhood.

As the wonderful feeling forced a state of relaxation over Sean, he closed his eyes, placed his hand on top of her head, and guided it.

"You dirty mutherfucker, you! Why, Sean? Why?" Meloney yelled as she stood there watching the man she loved dearly enjoy another woman. Since the room was relatively dim, he couldn't see the gun that she'd just taken out of her purse. As soon as he heard her voice, his eyes bucked wide as if they were about to pop out of their sockets. He immediately began reaching for something to put on his naked body.

"Baby! Baby, please, listen. This is not what it seems like," was the only lame excuse he could come up with while he was busy trying to look for his underwear. After finally finding his boxers, when Sean looked back up at Meloney, he was staring right into the barrel of a chrome .380 handgun that she tightly gripped. The gun looked very familiar, only because it was his gun. He had recently given it to her for protection because there had been a stint of rapes occuring on campus.

Sean was suddenly at a loss for words. He wasn't sure if his woman was capable of pulling the trigger or not, so he wasn't trying to say anything else stupid to cause her to get angrier than she already was. Stacy just sat there with the cover wrapped around her naked body, not saying a word. She didn't know the woman personally, so she definitely wasn't trying to piss her off anymore than what she already was. Tears was beginning to fall from Meloney's eyes, but she continued to keep a straight aim at her target. Sean!

"Baby, please. Put the gun down, Meloney," he spoke in a more soothing, mellow voice. He was hoping that the approach would work.

# The Hustle

"I told you in the beginning that I'm not getting played again, Sean! I trusted you! How could you do this to me? I thought you really loved me, Sean!"

"I do, baby! I do! Look at me. I love you, Meloney," he said, easing closer to her.

"You fuckin' liar!" she yelled at the top of her lungs. "You don't love me!" The entire time she was speaking, she emphasized her words through the weapon she had in her hand, jerking it in his direction as she talked, attempting to get her point across.

Stacy was fed up with the bullshit. She knew Meloney wasn't about to use the weapon she had. She knew Sean couldn't have really been in love with her because he wouldn't have given into her as easy as he had. It was the perfect time to get everything out in the open, that way, she'd have Sean all to herself "You don't love her, Sean, so why don't you just fuckin' tell her, goddammit!"

BOOM! BOOM! The sound of the gun firing off brought about a deafening silence in the room as it echoed off the walls. What Meloney failed to realize was the gun that she held in her hand was equipped with a hair pin trigger. BOOM! BOOM! BOOM! Three more shots rang out.

\* \* \* \* \*

The first gun shots Detective Jones heard, he thought he was dreaming. It wasn't until the other three shots were fired that he realized that it wasn't a dream. He knew more than likely that the shots could only be coming from one particular place. Sean Martin's residence. Exiting his car, he quickly made his way to the front door with his standard issued 9mm Beretta cocked and ready to fire. Easing up on the front porch, he noticed the door was ajar. He crept through it as quietly as possible. As soon as he entered the premises, the smell of death and gun powder flooded his nostrils. He was definitely in the right place.

\* \* \* \* \*

As soon as Sean heard the other three shots and saw Meloney fall to the carpet, he knew she was hit. Someone had shot her. But who? He laid there on the carpet playing possum, trying to figure out his next move. He knew it wasn't the police because they would have announced their presence. At least that was what he thought. Suddenly, he heard the gunman walking toward him.

"Oooh nooo! They killed my baby! Stacy! Stacy! It's me, baby. I'm out. I told you I was gone get out," Tu said, cradling Stacy's dead body in his arms "I'm not mad at you, baby. I'm not mad at you for leaving me. I promise," he continued as he rocked her body back and forward.

Listening to Tu make his plea to his dead wife, Sean eased up off the carpet and slowly crept up behind him. Looking at his weapon that was sitting beside him, Sean carefully eased his hand on the side of him and picked it up. Without thinking twice, at point blank range, Sean emptied the remaining bullets in Tu's head. Boom! Boom! Boom! Boom! Click! Click! He continued, squeezing the trigger.

"Police! Drop your weapon now!" Detective Jones yelled as he stared at Sean's back. "I said drop your fuckin'n weapon now!" he yelled louder than before. Sean knew he was a goner.

With three dead bodies, he was looking at a minimum life sentence even though he acted out of self defense. He couldn't do life, let alone another year in prison, so he decided to commit suicide, but not by his own hands. Slowly, he turned to face the officer, pointing the empty weapon in his direction. Boc! Boc! Boc! Boc!

After watching Sean's body fall, Detective Jones eased up on him and kicked his weapon out of arms reach. Next, he checked his suspect to make sure he had the situation secure. Seeing that there was no movement, he bent down and checked his vital signs. He could feel a faint pulse.

"Yes, this is Detective Jones from the homicide division. There's been a 187, I repeat a 187! One suspect's in critical, I need an EMT pronto at 6515 Salsbury Rd.!" he yelled into his radio. When he witnessed Sean point his gun in his direction, the detective knew what he was attempting to do. Since he wasn't man enough to face the judicial system for his crimes, he opted to let Detective Jones do his dirty work. "Stay alive, you cock sucker!" The detective yelled as he tied the bed sheet around his chest to stop the bleeding.

**SIX MONTHS LATER**

"Asia! Asia? Where you at, gurl?" J.R. yelled out as he came through the front door.

"This him now, Blue," Asia replied to her company after hearing J.R. call out her name. "Blue, this my brother, J.R. J.R., this is Blue. Well, now that I've done my part, I'm going to let you guys talk because this is none of my business. Blue, make sure you holla at me before you leave, I'll be in the basement doing laundry," she stated right before she left the living room.

As soon as she was out of ear shot, Blue began to speak. "So, what's good, playa?" he questioned with confidence. Just by the pieces he had around his neck and wrist, J.R. could tell that dude had to be making major moves in the game.

"Shiit, that's what I'm trying to see. Naw, but my sister speaks highly of you. She told me you were good peoples, and that's what I'm looking for. A decent mafucka I can plug you in with that'll keep me straight."

"Oh yeah! So how much you moving a week, dirty?" Blue asked, toothpick dangling from his mouth.

"Shit, me and my crew can shake two, maybe three bricks a week," J.R. proudly replied.

"Okay! Okay! That's what's up!" Blue stated, slapping his palms together and rubbing them. "I tell you what. Give me your number and I'll link up with you tomorrow. Maybe we can further discuss business over lunch." He then looked at his BlackBerry "Do me a favor, holla at yo sister and tell her I said come here for a second."

"Fo' sho!" J.R. got up off the sofa, went into the kitchen where the entrance to the basement stairs were located, and yelled down them. "Asia! Blue wanna holla at you!"

"Tell him here I come!" she yelled back. A few seconds later, she came in the living room with a basket full of clothes.

"Aye, baby, I have some business I need to take care of so I'ma have to get at you later, a'ight?"

"Okay then," she said sadly as she walked him to the door. Before she opened it, she hugged him and gave him a peck on the cheek. As soon as she opened the door, she came face to face with the mailman.

"How are you today, Ms. Combs?" the mailman spoke after he watched her male friend walk away.

"I'm fine, thank you."

# The Hustle

"I have a certified letter for you today. So, if you'd be so kind to sign right here." He handed her a clip board with a postal receipt attached to it. Asia quickly scribbled her name on the receipt card. "Thank you, and have a nice day," the mailman replied, and then walked away.

"What's that, baby girl?" J.R. asked as Asia came back into the house and took a seat right beside him.

"I don't know. I'm about to find out," she said, opening the letter. For the next five minutes, Asia sat there reading the letter, trying her best to understand its contents. She just couldn't understand why she'd be getting a letter like that.

"Damn, Asia, what the hell is it? You just sitting there looking at that paper all crazy and shit like you lost yo damn mind!"

"It's a letter from City Hall," she replied with a baffled look.

"What the fuck do City Hall want with you? You bet not have got no damn tickets on my ride without telling me, Asia!"

"Boy, ain't nobody got no tickets on yo car! I wonder why the City Hall talking 'bout I got ninety days to pay taxes on a property I supposedly own on 6515 Salsbury. I don't own no damn house on Salsbury! They must've made a mistake," she said, looking over the contents of the letter once again.

"Shit, it might just be a house that trick ass Derrick brought you that he didn't get a chance to tell you about. Baby, I got some business to take care of. I'ma be back later, okay?" he said, leaning over and kissing Asia's lips. She welcomed his lips as if they were her salvation.

"Mmmmm, you better be home in time for dinner J.R.!" she demanded after their lips parted.

"I am, baby! I am. And, when I get home we gone

have a long talk about this brother shit! You not gone keep introducing me as your brother. You did that shit with Derrick, then the next thing I knew you moved in with him. You even had the nigga thinking that my daughter was his! Now, you're doing it again with Blue," he snapped. "I'm tired of it, Asia!"

"Now, baby, you know I can't introduce you as my man because niggas of their caliber ain't gone just let you get close to them like that. See, if you was to step yo game up and start saving all that money you be making, we can live the way we want, then I won't have to go out meeting ballers just to keep my man in the game."

"Yeah, whatever. Since you so interested in keeping me in the game, why don't you call and check on that property the city talking about? We might just be able to sell it, or if we lucky, Derrick might've left a million dollars stashed up in that bitch."

# Book Club Questions

1. Why didn't Sean avenge the deaths of his son and Derrick?

2. Do you think he made a mistake, business wise, getting involved with Gerald and J.R.?

3. Out of all the women that he was involved with which one did you think would more than likely become a problem?

4. When he chose to settle down with Meloney, do you think he made the right choice?

5. If you were in the same predicament as Sean, in possession of nine kilos of cocaine, and you were an ex-hustler that just got done    serving a ten year stretch, what would you have done with the drugs?

# Coming Soon

DC BOOKDIVA PRESENTS

?

DUTCH

# Coming Soon

DC BOOKDIVA PUBLICATIONS

SECRETS

Love, Betrayal, and Revenge

NEVER DIE

EYONE WILLIAMS

National Best Selling Author of Lorton Legends

# Order Form

DC Bookdiva Publications
#245 4401-A Connecticut Avenue, NW
Washington, DC 20008
dcbookdiva.com

**Name:** _____ __
**Inmate ID** _____
**Address:** _____
**City/State:** _____**Zip:** _____

| QUANTITY | TITLES | PRICE | TOTAL |
|---|---|---|---|
| | Up The Way, Ben | 15.00 | |
| | Dynasty By Dutch | 15.00 | |
| | Dynasty 2 By Dutch | 15.00 | |
| | Trina, Darrell Debrew | 15.00 | |
| | A Killer'z Ambition, Nathan Welch | 15.00 | |
| | Lorton Legends, Eyone Williams | 15.00 | |
| | A Beautiful Satan, RJ Champ | 15.00 | |
| | The Hustle, Frazier Boy | 15.00 | |
| | **Coming Soon** | | |
| | Q, Dutch | 15.00 | |
| | Secrets Never Die, Eyone Williams | 15.00 | |
| | Dynasty 3, Dutch | 15.00 | |

**Sub-Total  $**_____

Shipping/Handling (Via US Media Mail) $3.95 1-2 Books, $7.95 1-3 Books, 4 or more titles-Free Shipping

**Shipping  $** _____
**Total Enclosed  $** _____

Certified or government issued checks and money orders, all mail in orders take 5-7 Business days to be delivered. Books can also be purchased on our website at dcbookdiva.com and by credit card at 1866-928-9990. Incarcerated readers receive 25% discount. Please pay $11.25 per book and apply the same shipping terms as stated above.